Heart of a Wolf

Viking Wolves Book 1

CJ Ravenna

CONTENT WARNINGS

Depictions of slavery typical for the period

Mentions of a main character being cheating on in a previous relationship

Hunting of prey animals

Graphic violence (including fights between wolves)

PTSD and anxiety attacks

Discussions of parental death

If you have any questions about potential triggering content not listed here, send me an email at cj@cjravenna.com. I'm happy to help!

CHAPTER 1
KIERAN

Museums.

Another thing to add to the exceptionally long list of Things That Make Kieran Grove Irrationally Anxious.

I've got nothing against museums. They're neat. I went to the Museum of Natural History in NYC all the time when I was a kid. I loved those big bones—dinosaur bones, that is. But that's the thing—people go to see maybe one or two exhibits, not the entire museum in one go!

I need to tell that to my friend Amanda. She's been buzzing around Iceland's Viking World Museum like a bee drunk on pollen for the last hour and shows no signs of slowing down. I don't know how many times I can nod along and say, "Cool!" when we've stopped for the eighth time in a minute to look at something that caught her eye. I'll admit, though, the authentic longship was cool.

It's only fair I let her have her fun. She panted along after me on our guided hike to Mt. Esja yesterday. I thought it was great, especially since the guide incorporated yoga and mindfulness into the trek, something I desperately need with all the chaos going on in my life lately. But I could tell it wasn't a highlight of the trip for Amanda.

Why is it that hiking up the side of a mountain doesn't get me nervous but wandering around a crowded museum makes me feel like my skin's too tight?

I'm looking forward to our whale watching excursion later today. Some sea air will lift my spirits... or give me pneumonia. It's cold in Reykjavik, even in early October.

"Kieran, check this out!"

A toddler nearly trips me as I make my way over to Amanda. "What is it?" I peer over her shoulder into the display case, but I'm not sure what I'm looking at. It looks like some kind of metal contraption.

Amanda explains, "Shackles for thralls. That's what the ancient Norse called their slaves. They were the lowest caste of people in Scandinavian society."

"Awful." I fight back a yawn. The jet lag is seriously kicking my ass. I'm still on New York time.

With a snort, she elbows me. "Could you be more bored?"

"No! I'm having so much fun."

"We'll wrap it up soon. I just want to see some of their paintings and then we'll go."

Figures. Amanda and I have always shared a love of the arts, hers for painting and mine for music, though it's been a while since I've had the motivation to play. I follow Amanda's blonde bob through the crowds to a hall full of paintings. When we arrive in the hall, I immediately understand why she's so excited to see this exhibit. The artwork is so beautiful and vivid, oil-on-canvas masterpieces. Digital art is just as valid as any painting, but there's something special about seeing paint on a canvas.

Amanda studies a painting of a battle on a beach with armored warriors clashing with swords and shields raised. "Gnarly," she says. "This shit's gorgeous."

I wander a little ways from her, admiring the paintings but not stopping to stare. We've been here so long, my brain is overloaded and overwhelmed. I'm itching for a change of scenery, especially when a little kid screams into my ear as her dad carries her past. I'm about to tell Amanda I'll wait outside when something catches my eye.

It's a painting of a warrior. One of many, but something about this one demands my attention. It's a full-body portrait and if it's life-sized, then this guy had five inches on me. I crane my neck to look up at him and can't fight a shiver when those painted gray eyes bore into me. His muscular body is clad in armor made of leather and fur, and snow dusts the black fur of a wolf draped over his shoulders. I bet he hunted and skinned the wolf himself.

The closer I look, the more disturbed I am by the little details. His teeth, bared in a snarl, are too sharp. His fingernails are so long they are practically claws. Beads of blood dangle from the tips of his fingers and stain the snow crimson.

"Fucking sick!" Amanda exclaims, coming to stand beside me. She leans down, adjusting her glasses before they slip off her button of a nose. "His name was Wulfric Wolf-Heart."

"He was *real?*" I gawk up at the picture.

"Apparently. It says here that based on his remains and the offerings buried with him, he was nobility, revered by his people. He was a jarl. That was the highest rank, secondary to only a king back then."

Jarl Wulfric cuts a powerful, brutal figure in a hall full of fearless warriors.

I wonder what kind of life he lived.

We grab lunch before we head to the boat. The restaurant serves whale meat as a novelty dish but I don't want to try it. Whaling's legal here in Iceland. It sucks, but it's their way of life. Still, if I can do my part by not supporting the whaling industry, I'll do it. I'd much rather see them in their natural habitat than on my plate.

As Amanda drives our rental car over to the harbor, my phone buzzes for the second time since lunch. I ignore it, even though I'm itching to pick it up and check. We're only here until the end of the week. I should be enjoying the scenery, not glued to my phone.

But what if it's him? Anxiety churns in my gut, ruining the pleasant memory of lunch. I need to know. Maybe he's calling to apologize and grovel to get me back. Maybe—

"Kieran, no!" Amanda groans when I pull out my phone.

"I just need to check something." Heart racing, I look at my messages. "Oh shit."

"What?" she asks, arching a pierced brow. "Don't listen to a word he says."

> Mark: How's Iceland? I miss you. Kisses.

That's it? No bribes? No begging for me to hear him out? "He just wants to know about the trip." I swallow hard. "He misses me."

She rolls her eyes skyward, and my face flushes with embarrassment. "Maybe he should have thought about that before he cheated. The asswipe."

She's right. Shit. I'm being so stupid.

"Do I say something?"

"No!" she snaps. "Leave him hanging. You don't owe him jack shit."

Fuck, she's right. Amanda's always right. Just like she was right from the very beginning when she said she didn't trust Mark after first meeting him. I'd been annoyed at her for not giving him a chance and told her he was just shy and he'd clammed up.

We met because Amanda is friends with his sister, and she'd taken me to see a musical he'd written. I'd been so awestruck by him, this creative guy who'd written and produced an amazing musical all by himself. Mark was everything I'd wanted to be, instead of a loser who wrote songs for a tiny audience on YouTube. I'd crushed on him the moment we'd locked eyes over dinner after the show.

We'd started dating shortly after we met. We were a team. He wrote plays, and while I was no playwright, he and I created music for his shows. Our relationship was perfect, and he helped me blossom into the musician I'd always wanted to be.

My YouTube channel took off after we broadcast our relationship to the world and started writing and singing songs together. When we released an indie album, I began to dream that I could finally quit my day jobs and make a living off my music.

But best of all, his family welcomed me with open arms into their home and gave me a seat at their table. A few years ago, my own parents wanted nothing to do with me after they found out I was dating a guy from school, so having the support of a loving family meant the world to me.

When I came home last weekend and found Mark in bed with one of the actors in the show he was directing, everything fell apart. As I'd yelled at him, he told me repeatedly that he didn't want to lose me. That we could have an open relationship. I said no, and he… he changed before my eyes. Face red, he screamed at me, "You'll be nothing without me! I'm the only reason anyone gives a shit about that crap you write!"

Crazy how a few words could completely shatter my self-esteem down to nothing.

Because he's right. Mark was already an established playwright and musician. I'd just ridden on his coattails. There was nothing special about me or my music.

When I called Amanda, sobbing, she'd given me her couch for the night and a container of cookie dough ice cream. I'd been staying with her for the past week, trying to figure out how to move forward. Honestly, where would I be without her? It was her idea to come to Iceland. Me, I'd never thought twice about traveling outside the USA. If she hadn't invited me, I'd be too nervous to go alone. It's good to get away to somewhere new, especially with my best friend.

Amanda stops the car at our destination. I turn my phone off and get out. I'm keeping it off for the rest of the day. It's not every day I'm surrounded by rugged mountains and gorgeous geothermal scenery.

As the sea air blows bitter cold off the harbor, I manage to smile.

Mark's not ruining this for me.

My friend and I walk the pier in search of the whale cruise ship, and it makes me remember that time we went to Alcatraz Island together. I'm about to reminisce on the past with her when a woman's voice cries out. "You there!" A woman, her blonde hair threaded with silver, stands in front of a table covered with a cloth. She wears what look like real wolf furs over a plain green dress. "How would you like a woodcarving made just for you?"

Something is different about her accent. It sounds similar to the Icelandic accents we've been hearing, yet the differences are notable.

"What accent is that?" Amanda wonders, echoing my own thoughts.

"Not sure." I venture closer to the lady's table. She has a knife and several pieces of wood. From the wood, she has carved beautiful, highly detailed miniature figures from whales to bears to puffins. "Wow! These are so amazing. You make these yourself?"

"The art of woodcarving has been in my family for generations." She smiles. "Is this your first time in Iceland?"

"Yeah. We're loving it so far."

"How wonderful!" She picks up her whittling knife and a chunk of wood. "Let me craft you something, dear. A gift."

Her kindness surprises me. "Oh, no, that's okay. We're actually in a hurry."

Amanda says, "It's okay, Kier. We have time until the boat starts boarding."

Enough time for her to carve something as detailed as her other sculptures? I guess we could always collect it on our way back to the car. "Sure."

The old woman gets to work, and my jaw falls open at how quickly she moves. She works the wood with her knife like it's made of butter. Shavings form a tiny pile on the tablecloth, and I gasp when she finishes the carving in only seconds. It is a wolf, carved with an attention to detail that floors me. On the base of the sculpture, she carves a strange symbol.

"This is stunning! What does that symbol mean?" I ask. I don't even want to touch the sculpture in case I drop it.

The old woman smiles, eyes shining with pride. "It's a rune, lad. My ancestors, the Vikings, used them to write."

"Really? What does it say?"

"This rune," she says, tracing one that resembles the letter R, "is the symbol for travel. And this"—she traces another that looks like an incomplete hexagon—"is the symbol for home." She presses the wooden wolf into my hand, her touch warm and gentle. "Trust that when all seems lost, you will find your way. In travel we find ourselves, and home is not always a place. The Allfather Odin will guide you to where you are meant to be."

I wasn't expecting such a profound encounter. "Thank you." I fish around in my pocket for money.

"I wish not for payment, dear," she says. "Go with Odin's blessing to where you are meant to be."

She's odd but sweet. "Thank you so much." Feeling like I had the rug yanked out from under me, I walk away. What a strange and unexpected encounter. "She was so nice."

Amanda smiles. "That's such a sweet souvenir, too."

I squeeze the wooden wolf. I can't explain why, but it feels precious to me.

Just as we prepare to board the boat, Amanda's face turns an unpleasant green. She clutches at her stomach. "Actually, maybe I should sit this one out."

"Are you okay?"

"Must have been something I ate."

"Let's go back to the hostel."

She shakes her head. "No, no. Go ahead. I'll just wait in the car."

"Are you sure?"

"Go get your ass on the boat and see those whales! You were looking forward to this all day. I'll be fine." With a smile to reassure me, she turns and heads back to the car.

After handing over the ticket, I board the boat with a few other passengers. It rocks side to side beneath my feet, the waves slapping loudly against the sides. The sea air blows cold, so I tug my beanie lower over my forehead and make sure my hat covers my ears. It's in the forties today, but the windchill makes it feel colder, especially on the boat. With gloved hands tucked deep in my coat pockets, I find a seat on the deck.

I look back over my shoulder to see if I can spot Amanda in the car, but she's out of view. Guilt niggles at me. Should I have stayed with her? I hope her stomach won't bother her too much. I pull out my phone to call her and check.

What if something happens and she gets really ill? *Whoa, hold up there.* It could just be food poisoning.

Or it could be appendicitis. What if her appendix ruptures? What would we do if there's a medical emergency?

Anxiety squeezes my chest, and I want to bolt from the boat and run back to her.

"Oh my god, Kier, I'm fine!" she says when she answers my call.

"Are you sure? I can come back."

"Don't you dare. Just take lots of pictures and if you see any seals, holla at me!"

She hangs up before I can protest.

I don't feel right about this. I'm going to get off the boat.

Just as I rise, the guide welcomes us on board. It would be awkward if I left during his talk. Stomach churning, I make myself sit and stew in all my uncertainty. Before I make up my mind, we're off to see some whales. The harbor disappears behind us and I blow out a heavy sigh, hoping Amanda will be okay.

A frustrated growl escapes me.

I can't even take a boat ride without being anxious. Stupid fucking generalized anxiety disorder. What happened to me? I was doing so great on Zoloft. I was really nervous about trying medication, but it makes me feel like a totally different person. I'm able to ignore my intrusive thoughts, my obsessive ruminating is completely gone, and I actually have good days now. For the first time in years, my head is finally quiet.

Or it was. Suddenly, my intrusive thoughts are back, although I'm able to shake them off rather than obsessing over them for hours. Ever since Mark and I broke up, it's like I've regressed back to stupid, anxious Kieran.

Lifting my head, I try and smile but can't quite manage it. No, I haven't entirely regressed. Pre-Zoloft Kieran would have been too anxious and depressed to come to Iceland. I think the breakup just jostled me. In time, maybe I'll feel normal again.

As gloomy inside as the overcast skies on the outside, I watch the scenery fly by. Eventually, though, the dread and uncertainty blow away in the sea breeze. I snap a few pictures of the view while the sea spray dampens my jacket. I feel a bit like a Viking, out to raid and pillage on the high seas.

At least until we go through some rough water and I almost lose my lunch.

People cry in awe and delight as a whale's giant tail breaks the surface a couple miles from us. And my stupid brain immediately supplies, *I sure hope they don't wreck our boat.*

I shove the thought down and try and ignore it rather than spiral into what I'd actually do if our boat wrecked. *Stupid anxiety. You're not ruining this for me.*

Rain spatters my jacket. The clouds overhead have gotten darker. Angrier.

The guide advises us to head inside and apologizes for having to take us back earlier than he'd like. "I really don't like the look of those clouds," he says in his charming Icelandic accent. "A storm wasn't in the forecast today."

I head inside with the other passengers. Torrents of rain cascade against the windows, warping the view outside. The boat lurches left and right so violently, we're told to sit down for our own safety. Fear clutches at my gut. Shit. This doesn't feel right.

We head back toward the harbor, but the going is rough. Waves beat at the boat. As we lurch over one of the waves, people scream in alarm as they're thrown from their seats. Crying out in shock, I grab onto a pole to steady myself so I don't fall. My heart's racing out of control now. Something is definitely wrong.

Fog shrouds us and rain hammers the boat. Are we even going the right way? We should have returned to the harbor by now. Everything's fine, I tell myself. We're going to be okay. Right?

Something vibrates against my thigh. I reach into my pocket, but it's not my phone. No, it's the wolf carving. It's vibrating like it's about to break into pieces. *What the heck is this thing doing?* I gasp as the runes carved onto the base of the figure glow with golden light. "What the—"

A flash of light, bright as a crack of lightning, bursts through the fog ahead of us. Screams split the air, my own voice joining the other passengers as a huge iceberg seemingly materializes from nowhere through the bright light I just saw. The only icebergs I noticed before were miles away. Where did this one come from?

The guide bellows, "Everyone, stay calm and follow my orders! We're going to hit that iceberg, so I need all of you off this boat *now*. Get to the life rafts!" He tries to hold the doors open against the roaring wind and other passengers rush to help him. Out on the deck, the crew has inflated the life rafts. I almost expect to hear someone scream, *Women and children first*!

Somehow, I've found myself playing Rose in this bad rip-off of *Titanic*.

Damn it! Where's my Jack when I need him? Oh, right, he cheated. Jack from the movie would *never*.

The passengers rush to the rafts, carrying children or helping their elderly relatives. "Move, man!" someone yells behind me. The wind is knocked out of me as a passenger bowls me over onto the deck. I hit the ground hard, too terrified to curse the asshole out.

The boat tips upward as a wave rolls beneath us. Water gushes over the side of the boat, salty and ice cold. Shouting in terror, I slide on the wet floor, scrambling for something to grab onto. My feet disappear over the side as I slip beneath the railing. I have enough time to grab the rail so I don't fall overboard.

Freezing waves lap hungrily at my feet. I try to hold on, but the railing is too slick. A scream for help barely escapes my lips before I'm falling, plunging into the frigid darkness of the sea. Above my head, the boat hits the iceberg with a muffled crash.

Water floods my ears and stifles all sound, and my limbs lock up as ice seeps into my bones. I have to move or I'll die, but the shock has me frozen worse than the cold. The water pulls me under, the surface disappearing from view. Everything disappears. The boat. The life rafts. The distant screams. I'm alone. All alone in the darkness.

It would be easy to give up. Easy to surrender to the cold and the dark. To let the water fill my lungs. Mark won't miss me. I was always secondary to him. My bosses will replace me by the end of the week. My parents will mourn me, though, and Amanda will be devastated. She'll blame herself for not being there.

I can't do that to her. Not to my best friend. She deserves better than that.

The wooden wolf I'm still clutching in my fist vibrates violently, glowing so brightly it casts away the dark. I kick.

I claw. Pressure builds in my lungs. My head throbs. My whole body screams for air, for life.

I break the surface, gasping, shaking so violently it's a wonder I don't break apart. Water stings my eyes, blinds me. My teeth chatter in my skull.

I open my eyes and... everything's gone. The distant harbor. The town. The boat. There aren't even pieces of it. No life rafts bearing terrified passengers to safety. The damn iceberg that caused all this is gone, too. I swear to God, I'm never getting back on another boat again.

Ahead of me there's nothing but a vast, sprawling ocean.

Terror.

Isolation.

Despair.

I'd scream if I could.

Something's behind me. It's raw animal instinct telling me something is coming. I can't flee. I can't fight. So I freeze like a baby monkey waiting to be scooped into the arms of its mother.

And something does grab me, burrowing under my arms, hoisting me up.

In my shock, I drop the wooden carving of the wolf into the ocean.

A scream tears from me as I fly up from the water, the wind in my ears. I land on a solid wood floor, cracking my skull and seeing stars. There's a familiar rocking beneath me. Another ship. I'm safe. Relief brings tears to my eyes.

Wiping the tears and water away, I say, "Thank you, thank you so m—"

There's a sword at my throat, razor-sharp against my skin. The words die on my tongue.

A crew of the most terrifying men I've ever seen surround me. They wear their hair long and their beards even longer, accented with beads. Every single one of them is armed to the teeth with axes, swords, and shields. Black paint streaks their faces. They wear furs and wool and chain mail, their well-worn boots caked with dirt. No horned helmets, which wouldn't be historically accurate anyway, but they don't need them for me to know exactly who they are.

Vikings.

Somehow, I've been rescued by a crew of men cosplaying as Vikings. Even their boat is as authentic as can be, as if they took it straight out of the museum I saw. Their swords look real, too. It's a bit dangerous for their weapons to be this sharp, though, isn't it? What if they hurt each other? And the stink of them... my god, the noxious combination of wet leather and furs, unwashed hair and skin, sweaty wool... it's enough to make my throat prickle.

These men are truly dedicated to their role-play.

"Thank you for rescuing me," I say, hoping they know English. Most of the locals Amanda and I talked to did. "My boat crashed. If you could take me to Reykjavik, I'd be really grateful." My teeth chatter so hard, I can barely get the words out.

The man doesn't take his sword away from my throat. Instead, he turns and barks something in a guttural language I've never heard before at one of his cosplay buddies. If I had to take a guess, it's ancient Norse? Maybe?

The unfamiliar words somehow morph into English mid-sentence. "—like a drowned rat, doesn't he, lads?" He laughs, the sound cruel and mocking, and his friends join in. "Look at how he shivers! Mayhap these will warm him up." With a rattle, he yanks a pair of iron cuffs from his belt.

My stomach turns inside out.

"N-no. Wait. What are you doing?" I try to stand, and the man presses the sword harder into my throat. The skin tears and beads of blood squeeze from my skin.

Shit. This isn't cosplay. This is... *real*. These people aren't my saviors. They're my captors. I don't understand. Are they pirates? Who *are* they?

The cuffs snap around my wrists, and with a jerk, the guy with the sword hauls me to my feet. He tugs me across the slick deck toward a hatch in the floor. "W-Wait," I stammer. "Stop, don't do this!" His friends laugh at me. The hatch flies open and with a yelp I fall into the dark. The landing winds me, and the stink makes me gag. The smell of unwashed bodies is even more pungent down here, mixed with the stench of rotting hay, urine, and feces.

Frightened, dirty faces stare at me from the darkness. There are others down here. Men and women, arms and legs in chains. Their clothes are bloody and torn but unlike anything I've ever seen before, because they aren't modern by any means.

Growls rumble in the thick, stinking air. Eyes glow and fangs flash. A scream gets trapped in my throat as two huge wolves materialize from the dark and prowl among the prisoners, growling at them, snapping at them. Guarding us like cattle.

Shaking, I curl into a ball, close my eyes, and pray that I can find a way to return to Reykjavik.

I don't know how long I've been down here in the dark. My stomach cramps with hunger, and my clothes are damp and cold. The ship rocks me side to side and the exhaustion drags me under for a shallow sleep.

Sometime later the hatch creaks open, and my heart lurches out of my chest. I'm on my feet, and the other prisoners rise, whimpering and talking among themselves in hushed, frightened voices.

Our captors haul us from the hold and onto the deck. The sunlight blinds me, and the wind draws a shudder from me.

We've arrived in a harbor. There's a town... but it looks nothing like Reykjavik. It looks nothing like any city or town I've ever seen before. There are no roads, only muddy paths where people have tread. Smoke rises from the chimney stacks of houses made of wood and stone.

There are no streetlamps, no cars. Armored warriors ride horses through the streets, and farmers clad in wool lead dirty sheep through the mud to a bustling marketplace. I'm frozen in place, my mind grasping for any way to make sense of this situation. This must be some backwards, isolated village. That's the only logical thing I can think of.

One of my captors bellows behind me, "Move, human scum!"

Searing pain cracks across my back before I can even register his bizarre insult, tearing a yelp from my lungs. I've gotten the message. I follow the miserable men and women in front of me toward the market. We pass traders selling everything from vegetables to fresh-caught fish. Children run past, spraying mud and snow behind them as they chase each other through the streets. Horses snort and stamp their hooves, watching us as impassively as their intimidating riders.

There's a scaffolding in the town square. Our captors lead us to it, then force us up onto the stage one after the other and make us form a line. A crowd gathers, watching us like we're performers. A guard paces the stage, glancing among us before grabbing me. He makes me turn in a circle before the crowd.

With a sickening twist in my gut, I know what this is.

This is an auction. We're being sold like livestock.

The guard says, "Human. Young and able-bodied. Suitable for farm work."

For *what* now? And why do they keep calling me "human" like they aren't?

"N-no, I'm not! I kill all my houseplants. You really don't want me!"

A man with a smile I do *not* like raises his hand and steps up onto the stage. He comes toward me and reaches out, grabbing my hair. He tugs me in close, and I smell his putrid breath. Leering, he turns me this way and that, his eyes combing over my body in a way that makes me squirm.

Terror claws at my chest. I'm going to be bought and paid for like an object. Subjected to who knows what. His big cold hands grope at me, feeling between my legs, grabbing me. I lurch away from him. "Don't touch me!"

A sneer curls his lip and he grabs my shirt and hauls me closer, growling, "Resist me, human, and I will make you squeal like a pig!"

Shaky gasps spill from my throat. Oh God. I want to go home. I want to—

A deep, gruff voice thunders over the crowd. "Not that one!" Heads turn. The crowd parts, murmuring in voices filled with awe and fear. When I see him, all the air gets trapped in my lungs.

He looks just like his painting as he towers over the crowd, his body bulky with muscle and clad in wolf fur. A mane of blond hair billows in the wind, and beads clack in his beard with every step he takes. Axes sway from his belt and a shield rattles on his back. Piercing silver eyes lock on mine and a shiver rattles down my spine.

Everything turns upside down.

Oh shit. I'm not in the twenty-first century anymore.

Somehow, I've gone back in time to the age of the Vikings.

Jarl Wulfric Wolf-Heart marches onto the stage and says in a deep, low voice, "That one is *not* for sale."

Wide-eyed, the slave trader turns to the man who groped me. "My apologies, sir. You'll have to choose another."

"I'm paying for him. He's mine!" The man grabs at my wrists and yanks, making me yelp as the chains cut into my skin.

The jarl rounds on the man, looks at where he's touching me, and snaps, "Unhand him. *Now.*"

"Piss off!" The man sneers.

The axe flies from the jarl's belt and the man screams. He stumbles back, blood spurting from where his arm used to be. His severed arm still grips my chains but only for a second before the dismembered limb falls to the floor.

My vision swims, my knees going weak. I almost hit the floor, but big hands steady me. When I look up into those stormy eyes, it's hard to breathe. Beneath his mustache, he presses his lips into a firm, scowling line. If I'd seen him in my timeline, I'd have thought he was attractive. Gorgeous, even. But he's also the most frightening man I've ever seen.

He says something. It sounds like a question, but my ears are ringing. I just stare, too freaked out to manage speaking.

Then he says in a voice softer than I expect, "What is your name?"

For a moment, I don't even remember. "I... Kieran. Kieran Grove."

Those eyes never leave mine as he draws in a slow breath, nostrils flaring like he can smell my fear. When he speaks, he says the words I know will change my life forever.

"You are mine now, Kieran Grove."

CHAPTER 2
WULFRIC

Isle of Ulfheim, Off the Coast of Iceland, Year 831

On Fenna's snow-white back, I ride from town. Kieran snores in the saddle behind me, slumped against my back. I gave him my furs to keep warm, but he still shivers against me. I don't understand why he's cold. I've never been cold, not even in my human form. My blood runs hot, and when I'm in my furs, the snow can't penetrate my dense coat to chill my bones.

Following along behind us are my men, their shields and weapons rattling as the horse hooves kick up snow.

"We found him in the sea," my brother Lyall says, riding up beside me. He was on a separate ship during the trip back from our raid. "There was no sign of another ship. We've no idea where he came from."

Some bastard hurled my mate into the sea and left him for dead. That's bad enough. Knowing my men locked him in the stinking bowels of the ship like a common thrall makes my blood boil. By the Father Wolf, if I knew the fool who'd done it, I'd have them thrashed to within an inch of their life.

Taking in a deep breath, I let it out. It isn't my pack's fault. They didn't know who he is to me. It's no matter. As soon as we're home, I'll have him wrapped in blankets heated by fire-warmed pans and fed a feast worthy of an alpha.

Kieran *will* be treated like royalty once we're mated. As my mate, he is equal in every way. I wonder what his wolf looks like. Is his fur black like mine? He must wake and soon. I need to know all the ways in which he's meant for me.

I'm twenty-five, and I'd given up on finding my mate. Until I caught his scent. Mountain flowers. Pine trees. The smell of home.

At once, I knew he was mine.

Everyone else in the crowd ceased to exist the moment those eyes, as blue as the sky, found mine.

He smelled like a human, too, beneath all the sweetness, but I suppose that's to be expected. My men tell me he wore no furs when they pulled him aboard. Whoever left him to drown in the sea must have stripped him of his furs to ensure he died as swiftly as possible.

"What's got you looking so moonstruck, brother?" Lyall asks, a teasing grin on his face.

I'm sure I look a fool. It's been so long since I last smiled. "Later." I want to keep savoring this joy before I share it with my pack.

Hooves thunder and my brother Anders rides up beside me, nose wrinkled. Where Lyall is golden-haired and good-natured, his twin Anders's hair is dark as night, much like his temper on the best of days. "The stink of that thing! Throw it off your saddle before I do it for you."

A growl rumbles up from my chest. "Try it, brother. I'll decorate the road with your entrails."

Lyall huffs a laugh. "Calm yourself, Anders."

"Don't we have enough thralls stinking up the village?" Anders grumbles. "He's human. Weak."

Jerking the reins, I force Fenna to halt and turn her toward Anders. "What did you say?"

Anders sneers. "You truly can't tell? Why did Father name you alpha when your senses are so dulled?"

Lyall looks worriedly between us. "Anders, stop."

"He's *not* a human," I snarl. "He has only lost his furs!"

"He is so. He reeks of one. Look at how he shivers! Pitiful."

I swing, and my claws catch him across the face. Fenna startles beneath me with a snort and Anders's horse shies away in alarm. "Talk that way about him again, and it will be the last thing you do," I growl.

Anders's green eyes flash, wound closing on its own. "Since when are you so concerned over a human of all things? They're the enemy!"

Lyall sighs like he's exhausted. "The pair of you... Father wouldn't want this. He told you both to get along better."

Anders growls but lowers his head and defers to his twin like always. Since birth, their bond has been the strongest. Lyall's light heart tempers Anders's fiery one. Scowling, Anders leads his horse farther up the trail.

Kieran shivers against my back, his teeth chattering in his sleep. Is it possible Anders is right? Is Kieran human? But that would make no sense. Why would the Norns curse me with a human mate? Weavers of fate, the Norns know all too well that the humans are our greatest threat, second only to other ulfhednar. Anders is wrong. Kieran only needs to wear some furs, and I will be graced with the beautiful beast that is his wolf.

If we rest now and wake at sunrise, we will be home by midday. "Wake up," I say to Kieran. I climb from the saddle as he blinks his eyes open.

"Wh-where are we going?"

"To my home." I'm about to tell him where, but my instincts tell me to shut up. If Anders is right and he's human, gods forbid, then he might be a spy. We haven't had trouble with humans in many years, but I haven't forgotten their crimes against us. They see us as nothing but savage beasts for them to civilize. They'd have us give up our ways and bend the knee to their authority and religion, change our entire way of life. A growl rumbles through me at the thought.

Kieran cannot be one of them. He doesn't even sound like they do or dress like them. He doesn't dress like anyone I know, not a warrior or even a farmer. I've never seen a coat like his, or those skintight blue breeches.

"We'll make camp for the night," I declare, my voice echoing for the others to hear. Then I turn back to Kieran and say, "Stay put while I get the tent ready."

Kieran nods, blinking slowly. He's had a rough day.

I prepare my tent. *Our* tent. Kieran isn't leaving my side. Around me, my men gather wood and get a few fires going. I glance back to check on my mate. A few mistrustful looks are shot in Kieran's direction but a growl from me sends my people scurrying along. The meat we bought in town gets skewered and turned over the fire. The smell of roasting rabbit makes my mouth water. "Will you eat?"

Kieran bobs his head, then looks uncertainly over the side of the horse. "How do I, um..."

"Have you never ridden a horse before?" I can't keep the skepticism out of my voice. Where is he even from? I can't place his accent.

"No. I think I rode a pony once when I was a kid." He laughs nervously.

This bewilders me. How has he gotten from place to place without one? Before he can fall out of the saddle, I rush to his side and say, "Hands on my shoulders." I grip his hips. His eyes widen, color rising in his cheeks, but he sets his wrists on my shoulders, his hands still cuffed. I hoist him from the saddle and he gasps. Once he's safely on his feet, I lead him toward the tent.

"Go wait in my tent," I say, motioning toward the largest one in the camp. "I will bring you food."

He eyes me warily. "Why yours?"

"Because you'll be safe there."

He goes without argument. From the slouch of his shoulders to the way he drags his feet, it's clear he's exhausted. Once the rabbit has finished roasting, I tear off a few strips of meat, cursing when I burn my fingers, and bring some in on a plate for Kieran.

Gods above. That bronze hair and icy eyes, his angular jawline and pert nose. He's beautiful and strong all at once—and he's *mine*. I never thought I'd find him. I thought those who believed I was too young and inexperienced to lead my pack were right all along. I feared I had disappointed the gods and so they had cursed me to be alone forever.

"Do you know how long I've waited for you?" I ask, my voice soft and low, the tone one I've only ever reserved for prayer to my gods. "Each night, I prayed to every god I know to send you to me. And they did. At last, they did."

His eyes are impossibly wide. "Okay. Sure. Whatever you say, man."

Not exactly the confession of love I wanted to hear, but mayhap he's only shy. Still, his voice is lovely. I don't like the way he looks at me, though, like he thinks I'm going to hurt him. As if I could ever lay a hand on someone fated for me. Doesn't he feel the same pull I feel toward him? Can't he hear the song between our wolves, telling us our hearts are finally one? Even if he lost his furs and can't shift, he should still be able to feel that connection. I will hunt a wolf for him, skin it, and drape the furs over his shoulders myself if that's what he needs to understand our bond.

Clearing my throat as if to purge the doubts from my body, I say, "I brought you some meat." My wolf rumbles in my chest, pleased we could provide. It's not the same as hunting for him myself, but a proper courtship can wait until we're back in the village. I set the plate at his feet. "It's not much, I know. But I promise you when we return to the village, I will hunt the biggest, most powerful of beasts and lay it at your feet."

Kieran looks from the plate to me, mistrust turning those blue eyes to shards of ice. "What do you want from me?"

So many things. To have him on his back beneath me, taking my cock. To hear him gasp and moan as he bares his throat to me and begs me for my bite. To taste his blood as I bite down, our bond wrapping around my heart like golden threads. I run my knuckles down his freckled cheek. "Share my furs tonight, and you will know all the ways in which I want you."

His breath catches. Arousal spikes in his scent, and it takes everything I have not to hurl myself on him, tear his clothes from his body, and take him until we're both spent. I can't wait until the mating ceremony. Tradition be damned. I must have him.

Curling my fingers gently in his hair, I pull him close.

Then Kieran yanks out of my touch. "Touch me again, and I'll bite your fucking balls off."

All the heat drains from my body.

I'm not sure what this "fucking" word means, but his body language and the anger heating his scent make it damn clear my words haven't had the effect I wanted.

My mate just rejected me. But why?

The anger in his words stokes my own fury, though not at him. At myself, for being so inadequate I can't even court my mate the way he deserves. "Don't pretend you don't feel it. The pull between us."

He shakes his head. "What the hell are you *talking* about? You're fucking crazy!"

I kneel before him so suddenly he jumps. "Don't lie to me." The words are practically a snarl.

His heart is racing out of control. I've frightened him. "Get the fuck away from me." He draws his knees up to his chest, huddling in on himself.

He must not be able to feel our bond, that's it. If he lost his furs, that would explain it. My furs won't be able to help him. They must be furs from a wolf he hunted, blessed just for him by Fenrir.

"Where did you lose your furs?" If I know, mayhap I can help him find them.

"What furs?"

"Furs like the ones you're wearing!" When he continues to look at me like I've grown a third head, I swallow hard. "Have you... never even worn wolf furs?"

He looks bewildered. "No. Just yours."

Sickness churns in my stomach. "You've never even shifted, have you?"

Kieran just stares at me like I've told him where pups come from. "Nope." Kieran chucks my furs onto the floor. "But you're gonna see a real shift in my patience if you don't stop acting like a freak."

"Never? Not once in your life have you assumed a wolf form?"

"No!" Kieran's voice erupts from him as he throws his hands in the air. "I can't turn into a wolf, a poodle, a giraffe, whatever the hell you want me to turn into!"

"That you know of!" This can't be true. It can't be. "Are you sure your ancestors weren't capable of shifting forms?"

He throws up his arms in frustration. "Yes! I'm just a normal human. There. Happy?"

My heart sinks into the depths of my stomach. No. Gods be damned, no! My mate is a *human*. Every wolf's natural enemy. The Norns cursed me by tying me to a man with an inborn hatred and fear of our kind, who can never understand our customs and ways—who can't even feel a mated pair's connection.

"No..." I say, my voice a choked gasp. A furious roar tears from my throat, and I lash out, splitting open the side of the tent. Kieran flinches away from my wrath as I let loose, gouging holes into the tent walls with my claws, knocking over what little furniture can fit in this small space. I smash a table, splinter a chair. The rage builds inside me, and I can feel my control dangling by a thread. One wrong word, and the berserker will come out and I may not be able to stop him.

The despair breaks my heart. I have waited so long to find the love my mother and father had. The one meant for me. It's bad enough my brother is constantly questioning my every move and inspiring doubt among my pack. Do the gods truly see me as so inferior to my father, as such a terrible alpha, that they would curse me with such a poor match?

What wrongs have I done to be deserving of this?

Living when you should have died, the berserker within snarls.

Eyeing the claw marks I tore into my tent, Kieran asks, "W-what the hell are you?" His face is ashen, his sweaty hair stuck to his forehead.

When I scent his fear, shame fills me. I take in slow, deep breaths until the rage has lost its grip on me.

When I'm sure I can speak without snarling, I say, "I'm ulfhednar." How has he never heard of our kind?

"Right. That makes total sense."

"Oh. Good."

"No, it doesn't!" he bellows, making me jump. "How am I supposed to know what that is? None of this shit makes any sense!" He paces up and down, the chains around his wrists rattling. "I get into a boat wreck and next thing I know, there are Vikings everywhere, I'm being sold into fucking slavery, and some werewolf alphahole motherfucker is trying to get into my pants!" He's panting, eyes wild and wet, his scent laced with panic.

"Werewolf?" I ask, unsure what that word means. Or alphahole. Or half the things he said. "I'm ulfhednar. Not a werewolf. Fenrir, Father of Wolves, blesses the furs of the wolves we hunt and allows us to assume their shape. My clan has always cared for and respected wolves, so he rewards our worship with power. It's a ritual my kin have done for centuries."

He rolls his eyes. "So, basically, a fucking werewolf."

I suppose that is his word for ulfhednar. "Call it whatever you wish."

Turning away, he mutters, "This can't be real. This is so fucked. Oh my god…"

"Interesting." I fold my arms now that my fingernails are blunt.

"What?" he grumbles.

"Most who learn of my kind see us as unnatural savages to be hunted and killed."

"You are a savage. Not because you're different—because you're an asshole."

Again, I'm unsure what he means, but I can understand his meaning. He's a good person. Much better than I will ever be. Even if he were ulfhednar, I would be undeserving of him. Of any mate.

Regardless of how I feel, Kieran is in danger. No humans have ever entered our village and lived. Not even our thralls are human; they die too quickly, get hurt too easily, and aren't strong enough for most labor we require. Our thralls are wolves from other packs who thought they could invade and take what doesn't belong to them.

No one will trust him. Not unless I make it clear no one is to touch him by accepting our… bond, if I can even call it that.

"Please. Just let me go," Kieran croaks.

"I can't."

"Why? You can't ransom me."

"Because I need you to survive," I say. I laugh bitterly. As dangerous as I am, he's still safer with me than anywhere else. For now. "And you'll die out there without me. My pack doesn't trust humans. If you leave my side, I can't protect you."

"Why the hell do you care about what happens to me?" Kieran hisses, voice low and pleading. "Let me go!"

"No." He recoils from the fury in my voice. "You are not to leave this tent. If you do so, you forfeit your own life. Am I clear?" No matter how powerful I am, there are some things even I can't protect him from. And if my pack decides he cannot be trusted, their voices will overrule my own. I could lose him, and a part of me would go with him.

Throwing on the furs he cruelly discarded, I yank open the tent flap and call for Lyall. He comes running, a tilt to his head and a curious smile on his face.

"Aye?"

"Guard my tent. After moonrise, have someone take second watch."

He frowns. "I will. Is it about the human? What's so special about him?"

With a snarl, I raise my arm to claw those words back into his throat. "He's not—" But the words die on my tongue. When fear widens Lyall's eyes, shame nearly doubles me over. "I... Forgive me, brother. I don't know what's come over me."

"You are not yourself." Concern furrows Lyall's brow. "It's the berserker, isn't it? It's pulling at your mind."

My mouth runs dry. I nod, too ashamed to speak aloud all the worries and doubts trying to claw their way out of me. An alpha is always strong. He does not force his burdens upon the pack. Without a mate to soothe the natural bestial rage every wolf from an alpha bloodline has, it grows more and more unchecked. A rage that threatens to rob me of all reason and humanity.

"Is he..." Lyall looks over my shoulder into the tent.

My beast doesn't like another wolf's eyes on my vulnerable mate. Growling, I move in front of him and conceal the tent's entrance.

Lyall sighs softly. "He is. Isn't he? He's your mate, and that makes this all the more complicated."

I stare him down. "Not a word to the others about what he is to me. As far as they know, he's my prisoner and nothing else. If anyone tries to enter this tent while I'm gone, make them regret it."

I need to get away. Need to shed my human skin and run on all fours. In my furs, everything is simpler. Without another word, I sweep past my brother and make for the trees. Snowfall dusts my shoulders before I'm within the dark shade of the forest.

Dropping to all fours, I let the shift claim me as the black furs I wear come to life and overtake my body, crawling down my arms and turning my hands to clawed paws. On four legs, my troubles disappear. All that matters is the hunt.

I run, making the earth quake beneath my paws. The scent of a rabbit makes my mouth water, but it's not food I want. It's blood. The need to rip, tear, and kill roars through me like a storm. Wolves don't kill for pleasure but berserkers do. We revel in the spilling of blood. The blood of our enemies, our prey... and eventually, our own brethren.

All wolves descended from alphas are stronger than other wolves and risk going berserk unless we find our mate. Even if a wolf is not an alpha, like my brothers, the risk is still there. It can take years before the rage takes over, but it will happen eventually. Any mate will do, chosen or fated, but I never wanted to settle for anyone but the one fated for me by the Norns.

The rage begins with rising tempers and escalates to bloodlust. Then the blackouts begin. Lapses in memory, filled in by blood and the mangled corpses of friend and foe alike. Eventually, we forget we were ever human as the beast takes hold. Every pack handles berserkers differently. Some are exiled. Others are locked away. Many are killed for the safety of the pack. Stripping an ulfhednar of their furs will not cure the rage. Without our furs, we cannot shift and the wolf lies dormant, but the berserker within is powerful enough to take over even without the furs.

Ahead of me, a rabbit streaks from behind a bush and disappears into the shadows. Prey. I will catch it. Crunch the little bones. Lap up every drop of blood until my belly is bloated with it. But first I will let it run. Let it believe it can outrun fate.

Run, my little rabbit.

I will find you.

I will catch you.

I will tear you with my teeth.

When I open my eyes, I'm human again.

Blood covers my hands, the taste like iron in my mouth, like I've bitten down on a blade. The rabbit hasn't been eaten; it's been mangled. Entrails decorate the snow. Blood spatters the trees. Bile rises in my throat, and I swallow it down.

I'm half-awake when I stumble back to my tent. Another packmate has taken over Lyall's shift at the tent. The candle that was burning inside has been extinguished but my eyes adjust and allow me to see Kieran curled into a ball in the corner, his back to me. He shivers pitifully. So fragile, like all humans are. Dread grips my heart. How could the Norns give me a mate that could be so easily taken from me?

I grab one of the furs from my bed. Bear fur, by the smell. Kneeling beside Kieran, I drape the fur over him so it covers him from foot to shoulder. I stay at his side until his shivering ceases, until I know he won't freeze in the night and leave me.

So fragile, yet so strong and defiant.

"My little rabbit," I murmur, dragging my blood-streaked knuckles over his cheek.

Human or not, the Norns made their choice and gave me a mate. I must claim him, and soon. Before I lose myself to my inner berserker, and I'm lost forever to my beast.

Chapter 3
Kieran

A noise pulls me from my shallow sleep, and all I can make out is a wall of pitch black. The lanterns that were lit earlier have all died in the night. A thick black fur rolls off me as I sit up. I don't remember falling asleep with a fur over me. Could the asshole who captured me have done that? I can't make sense of that guy. One second he's bringing me food, the next he's trying to flirt with me.

Assholes like him have no right to be so damn attractive. And he is extremely attractive. I'm not too proud to admit that by any means. But can I blame my body for reacting that way?

I haven't had sex in months. At first, Mark and I had a great sex life. The first few times we'd done it were great. The passion was there. But he started insisting that I top, even though topping makes me uncomfortable. Bottoming has always been my preference, but I wanted to make him happy, so I tried it. As time went on, I started feeling like I was showing up for him while he couldn't be bothered showing up for me. When I tried to tell him how I felt, he blew up at me and made me feel like shit.

Eventually, I lost interest in initiating sex, which he gave me grief over. As our dry spell got worse, he would openly check out other guys or comment on how hot the guys in the movies we watched together were.

I'd never felt insecure about my body before we started dating. All the guys he was into were big and buff while I was average height with a body that lacked any kind of definition, thin but not fit, soft in the middle but not plump. I shouldn't have been so surprised when he cheated.

My boyfriend of three years couldn't be bothered to have sex with me, but a complete stranger from a whole other time period was about to devour me piece by piece. Maybe even literally.

Blowing out a breath, I blink up at the tent ceiling.

Time travel is real.

Werewolves, or ulf-whatever he called them, are real, too.

The guided tours sure didn't prepare me for this shit. I've got to get out of here and back to my timeline. Amanda must be so worried about me. I wish I could call her, but I lost my phone and... and Amanda wouldn't even exist in this timeline. Nobody I know exists yet. A wave of loneliness washes over me, bringing tears to my eyes.

I've got to find a way back. Somehow I got sent back in time, so that must mean I can go forward. If I can find a boat and return to the spot where I crashed, maybe I can figure out a way home. Who knows what these barbarians will do to me. The cuffs are already a big enough hint of what's to come: slavery. A shiver runs down my spine.

But first, I need to get out of this tent. Noises outside make me think somebody is standing guard, so sneaking out isn't the answer. I've got to bide my time, make my captors think I've accepted my fate, and make a run for it while they're distracted. Except then where do I go? I wouldn't survive in the wilderness.

What do I do?

Dread rises from my stomach until I taste bile in my throat. I force myself to breathe, willing myself not to have a panic attack. I've got to stay calm. But as doubt after doubt piles on, I'm forced to accept that staying calm isn't a possibility.

Violent thrashing makes me jump out of my fur, chains rattling as I scramble to stand. A sudden rush of dizziness hits me, and I stumble to the side. Flailing in the dark, I grab onto a pole in the middle of the tent. Shit. What was *that?* I haven't had brain zaps like that since I started taking Zoloft.

My eyes have adjusted enough to make out the cot where Wulfric is sleeping. It creaks, the blankets rustling as he kicks and claws at something. Is he... having a nightmare? My curiosity compels me closer until my knees bump into the cot's edge. It's too dark to see his face, but from the pitiful whimpers escaping him, I can imagine the agony twisting his mouth and furrowing his powerful brows, the way his chest would be heaving, tremors racking his enormous frame.

Shaky little gasps and whimpers fall from his lips. Wulfric's a big man and a damn werewolf at that. Who, or *what*, could make a Viking jarl whimper in fear?

Should I wake him? No, then I'd have to deal with him and it's way too late at night for that. I turn to tiptoe back to my fur when Wulfric suddenly bolts upright and lunges for something. The telltale screech of metal makes my heart sink. He just grabbed his axes.

"It's me!" I huddle over, shielding my face in case he swings.

His thundering footsteps freeze. In the quiet, his ragged breaths are loud, misting in the chill air. Wulfric's axes clatter to the floor. The cot creaks as he sits back down. "What are you doing up? Trying to sneak off?" He'd sound more threatening if he weren't breathing so harshly.

"Oh yeah. Just thought I'd take a nice little walk in the pitch-black forest and freeze my ass off." Maybe I should be nicer to my Viking werewolf kidnapper but I'm all out of manners.

A growl rumbles in the dark. "You say these things, yet I don't believe you actually mean them."

"It's called sarcasm. It's very popular where I'm from."

There's a rasping sound like he's running his thick fingers through his long beard. It's a nice beard, not unkempt or dirty by any means. He's surprisingly well-groomed for a man who roughs it in the wilds. I guess he makes time for proper grooming between all the raiding, killing, and pillaging.

"And where is it you're from?" he asks.

I snort. *Wait till he gets a load of this.* The Viking werewolf and the American time traveler. What a pair we make.

I blow out a breath. "It's called America where I'm from in the future."

He's quiet a long moment. "You... are a seer?"

"What? No. I'm a time traveler." Not that *that* sounds any better. "And before you call me crazy, just remember you're a fucking werewolf."

"Ulfhednar."

"Can you turn into a wolf?"

"Aye."

"Then same fucking difference!" I huff.

Finally, he says, "It makes sense. The way you speak is unlike anything I've heard before. The way you dress as well... There have been others like you. People I have met in my travels from other times."

My breath hitches. "Really?"

"Aye. Some have got here by boat."

"Like a boat wreck? That's how I got here!" I'm relieved that I'm not the only one. "Have they been able to go back to their time?"

"Many who traveled here did so intentionally. You clearly did not."

I pace, chains rattling between my wrists. "How is this even possible? Why don't more people know about time travel?"

"The Travelers Council, a coven of witches, help keep our secrets safe."

A coven of *what* now?

The cot creaks and I can picture Wulfric lying back on it, maybe draping an arm behind his mane of hair. "For you to have arrived here... you must have possessed a branch of Yggdrasil."

"A branch of huh?"

"Yggdrasil. It connects our world of Midgard to Asgard, the realm of the gods themselves, as well as the other realms, supposedly. The roots of the tree spread deep into the earth, and the branches reach far across the sky. Through these roots and branches, we can travel to other worlds. Perhaps that is how you were able to make the journey."

I squint at where I think he's sitting. "Are you talking about a tree?"

"Yggdrasil is no ordinary tree. Not one we can see with our own eyes. Only the gods are worthy of seeing it."

I'm really wishing I'd studied Norse mythology more so I could have an actual conversation with him about this. It sounds fascinating. "So it's because of this magical tree that people are able to travel between worlds?"

He sighs like I'm exhausting. "Aye."

I can't tell if that aye means *yes* or *kill me now.*

"Wait, so you need a piece of this magic tree to travel? But I didn't have a branch on me. I—" My brain just about breaks. "Holy shit! That woman! It was *her*!"

Wulfric groans. "Must you be so noisy?"

I can't believe it. I *thought* that woman at the pier was off somehow. Almost otherworldly, with an accent I couldn't place. And the furs she wore! The damn furs! She was an ulf-whatever, just like Wulfric! For some reason, she gave me that wooden wolf so I could travel to this realm. Why would she do that to me? "She fucking tricked me!" I'm against abusing the elderly, of course, but I'm so pissed right now I'd at the very least like to steal her dentures or something. I mean, I'd give them back, but—

"What woman do you speak of?" Wulfric sounds exhausted.

"There was a woman! She gave me a wolf! No, not a real one, but like, a wooden one. She tricked me into coming here!"

Wulfric is quiet a moment, and then he chuckles. "Oh. I see."

"What?" I snap, not liking that he apparently knows something I don't.

"It seems we were both tricked." And then as if he isn't the most enigmatic asshole in the world, he says, "Go back to sleep." The furs rustle as he moves around, probably rolling on his side away from me.

"Wait a moment! What do you know?" But the dickwad says nothing. "Fine. Keep your secrets. I'll go back to sleep as long as you don't wake me up again."

He growls. "Quiet. Do not speak of that to anyone."

Carefully, I navigate back to my fur and lie down on the cold ground, pulling it over me. "What were you dreaming about?"

"Not your concern."

I tuck my arm beneath my head like a makeshift pillow. "Fine." What would a Viking werewolf have to fear in his dreams? "We're not in any danger, are we?" I'm not familiar with the events from this time period. I really wish I'd paid more attention to that Viking museum.

"Always." He's quiet after that.

His admission doesn't make going to sleep any easier.

The fur is ripped off me. With a yelp, I sit up and find Wulfric scowling down at me. "Get up and eat. Then we're leaving." He tugs on my chains and forces me to my feet. The icy wind pulls a shudder from me as I step outside, my boots crunching in a thick layer of frost. Wulfric's men are gathered around fires, preparing food or eating whatever is left over from last night.

My bladder is ready to burst. Ugh. The last thing I want is to tell Wulfric I need to take a leak. "Um."

Narrow silver eyes glare at me. "Hmm?"

A man of many words, my captor. "I've got to go."

With a growl, he says, "You're not going anywhere."

"I know that!" I snap back, shaking my chains for emphasis. "I mean I've got to use the bathroom."

He furrows his brows incredulously.

Oh great. "I've, uh... got to go to the loo? Toilet?" Damn it, they don't even have toilets here. What's the medieval word for bathroom? I rack my brains, thinking of all the fantasy shows I've watched where a character might have used some archaic euphemism that stood out to me. "Relieve myself! You know!"

His glower tells me that no, he fucking *doesn't* know.

"I need to... make water?"

That seems to register. Tugging me along behind him, he leads me into the trees and, with the air of a man with exactly zero patience, flops his arm toward a tree. "There you go."

Heat crawls up my neck. "Could I have some privacy?"

If he'd just leave me alone, I could make a break for it. Maybe I could grab a branch and sling it at his head, then run—but who I am kidding? I'm still cuffed, and he's a werewolf, so he's probably got super speed or something. He'd catch me in no time, and then I'd have a pissed-off Viking werewolf to deal with.

Wulfric says, "No."

I sigh. Of course not. "Could you at least turn around so you don't get an eyeful of my dick!"

"Your... dick?" It should not be so sexy hearing the word dick fall from his lips in that gruff Norse accent, like he's trying the word out. "You mean that?" He stares pointedly at my crotch. I adjust my cuffed hands to obscure myself. "Why so shy? Got something down there I haven't seen before?" I want to punch the smirk off his stupid face. "Go now or don't go at all. It's a long ride to my village."

"Fine," I huff. Turning away, I unzip my jeans and wriggle down my warm leggings just enough to get my business done. I feel unexpectedly vulnerable with my back to him and my cock in my hand, especially when the heat of his gaze lingers on my back. Gritting my teeth, I look over my shoulder and hold his gaze. He stares right back unabashedly. I guess I'd give zero fucks if I looked like him, too.

"Done?" he asks.

"I am, Your Highness."

Scowling, he yanks my arm and leads me back toward the encampment to a fire outside his tent. He splashes what looks like soup into a bowl and shoves it at me.

"Thank you," I say out of habit, then cringe. "Have you got any coffee?"

He shoots me a confused, irritated look and I remember coffee probably hasn't been invented yet. How in the hell did people survive without the conveniences of modern living?

Sitting on the cold, hard ground beside him, I accept the spoon he hands me. The soup looks edible enough. There are chunks of meat and vegetables that I think are potatoes and carrots, some green stuff that looks like cabbage. Blowing away steam, I take a bite. It's comforting and hot, spreading heat throughout my belly with each swallow.

"Time to go." Wulfric stands and yanks the bowl out of my hands before I've eaten it all.

"I wasn't finished."

"Took too long," he says, leading me toward his white horse.

Cursing him out under my breath, I reluctantly follow. There wasn't a chance for escape last night or this morning, so I need to keep my eyes open and wait for an opportunity. If they think I've accepted my fate, maybe they'll let their guard down. I put my foot in the stirrup and try to boost myself up, but with my arms cuffed, I can't grab onto anything. I stumble backward and collide with his chest.

Big hands grip my shoulders, steadying me. Heart racing, I look up and find him glaring stubbornly ahead. When I step up into the stirrup again, he gives me a shove and enough momentum to get my leg over.

I don't know why he doesn't stick me in one of the many wagons loaded up with supplies. There's enough room for me to squeeze in there. Why does he want to be saddled, quite literally, with me? Probably to make sure I don't escape.

With a grunt, Wulfric hoists himself onto the horse's back behind me so I'm settled against his chest. His body is big and warm, and his chest would make the perfect pillow if we were in any other situation. If I weren't in cuffs, it might almost feel like an embrace, especially when his arms bracket me on either side, his hands gripping the horse's reins.

I grimace when my cock takes an interest in our position. God, I should have gotten laid while I could. Then I wouldn't be lusting after my captor. The smell of him is all damp fur, leather, and pine trees. Rugged, natural, and wild.

Clicking his tongue, Wulfric urges the horse forward and we ride toward my uncertain future in this strange world that's both ancient and new.

The sun climbs higher as we travel. The riders stop numerous times to feed and water the horses or fix a loose wagon wheel. I have to say the views are incredible. The ocean is on one side with gray waves reaching toward an equally gray sky and ice bobbing on the water's surface.

To my other side are rolling mountains and vast forests yet to be tainted by deforestation or pollution. The world is yet to be ruined by humanity. There's beauty in that and also sadness in knowing how badly we'll fuck everything up in the future.

There's no opportunity for escape. Wulfric keeps me pinned to him the entire ride. Even if I could get away, my ass is so sore from riding this damned animal that I wouldn't make it far. With my hands cuffed, I'd be far too vulnerable anyway. In the distance, ribbons of smoke climb into the sky.

"That's it," Wulfric rumbles. "We're almost home."

His home and my prison. A wave of dread rises in me. What will become of me? Will I ever know life outside of these chains again?

As we ride, the village comes into view. First, we pass by farmhouses with sheep, pigs, goats, and cows roaming the fields. The houses get more concentrated the closer we get, the distance between each home shrinking until we finally arrive in the heart of Wulfric's village.

There's a harbor with boats rocking on the water and canoes beached on the rocky shore. A bustling market full of livestock and produce with everything from vegetables, butchered meats, freshly churned butter, and cheeses. Smoke billows from a forge where a smith hammers away.

It seems like a normal village until Wulfric cups his hands to his mouth and howls. From the trees, a chorus of howls echoes back to us. My mouth goes slack as dozens of wolves burst from the trees and gallop to greet their pack members. They are all the colors from gray to black to white, some big and others small pups. I instinctively freeze as they sniff around the horse, but she must be accustomed to wolves because she only snorts and flicks her tail.

The villagers gather around us, greeting us. My skin prickles when their eyes land on me. Some sniff the air and growl, even those in human form, and their gazes become decidedly colder. I avert my gaze, trying to ignore them. Their voices get louder, more accusatory, less friendly. Something smacks into my chest and splatters all over me. Rotten fruit.

"Get the human out of here!"

"He'll destroy us all!"

A snarl rumbles from Wulfric's chest and the crowd backs away. "Do not touch him!" he says, his voice full of authority, which has the crowd dispersing. Clicking his tongue, Wulfric urges his horse onward toward a house bigger than all the others—a longhouse with smoke climbing from the chimneys. He dismounts, and I stagger clumsily from the horse. He leads her into the stables adjacent to the house, then urges me toward the front door.

Before we've reached it, the door swings open. A woman with blonde hair threaded with silver and wrinkles around her eyes smiles.

My mouth falls open. "You!"

It's her! The woman who sold me the damn woodcarving!

"It's all right. There's nothing to fear from him," Wulfric says, but she just laughs.

"Oh, I know, dear. He's a very nice lad."

I won't be so nice in a minute. Before I can give her a piece of my mind, she rushes out the door and straight up to Wulfric. He towers over her, but she reaches out and tenderly pats his cheek, her smile bright and joyful like she isn't aware of what a huge asshole he is. "I'm relieved you're home safe."

"It is good to be back."

Wulfric gives me a shove inside before I can interrogate the woman. The home is spacious and warm from the heat of a huge fire blazing in the center of the room. The high ceilings in this place make the New Yorker in me jealous, even with all the animal skulls nailed to the wooden beams that crisscross the ceiling.

It's nice, overall. Very barbarian-chic.

Wulfric marches me toward a door that leads into a bedroom. Furs are piled on the bed, and another fire crackles in the hearth. The pelts of skinned animals hang on the walls. While I'm busy gawking, Wulfric gives me a shove in the back and I stumble into the bedroom.

"Stay," he barks at me like I'm a dog, then slams the door.

I'm left alone in the bedroom. Shuffling over to the fire, I stretch out my cold hands and let the heat warm them. I wonder what he does to pass the time. I don't see any books anywhere. He doesn't look like the reading type, more like he drinks the blood of his enemies from a goat's horn for fun.

Sinking to the floor, I lean back against the wall and close my eyes. In the quiet, the distant bleating of sheep and the noises from the market carry on the wind. Am I going to spend the rest of my time here locked in his bedroom?

Resting my cheek on my knee, I try and catch up on the sleep I missed out on last night.

The door rattles and my heart lurches into my throat. The blonde woman shuffles into the room. In her hands is a tray stacked with bread, a chunk of cheese, and a mug of something. "You must be hungry, dear. Won't you eat?"

"Will the food send me into another time period?" I grumble.

"Of course not." She sets the tray on the floor.

"What does he want from me?" I ask before she turns away.

"It's not my place to say, lad."

So she knows and won't tell me. Meaning he does have plans for me.

"Can you take these off?" I rattle the cuffs.

"I'm afraid I cannot. Not until Wulfric gives the order to do so."

I swallow the uneasy lump in my throat. "What's your name?"

"I'm Wulfric's aunt. Call me Helga."

I sigh and she turns to go, then stops and looks back at me. She offers a tiny smile that warms the cold lines of her face. "You will not come to harm, lad. I would not have sent you here if I knew no good would come from your arrival."

"Why would you do that?" I snap, jumping to my feet as fury erupts from me. "Did you get a kick out of it? Send me home, now!"

Helga smiles sympathetically. "I cannot, dear. Your place is here."

"The hell it is! I have a job back in my time. I have friends! A life!"

"But you were unhappy."

I choke on my anger. "I... Yeah. Sure. But that doesn't mean you had the right to just uproot me from my life like that!"

"Mayhap not. I understand that you are frightened and angry. I'm only going to ask that you trust you are here for a reason."

"No. Fuck that shit. Take me home now, before I'm made into a thrall or—"

"If Wulfric meant you harm, you would not be here. I assume the lad's told you what we are."

"Yeah. Were—uh, ulfhednar."

She dusts off her apron. "Aye, and you're someone very important to him."

That bewilders me. "What? No, I'm not. I'm his prisoner."

"It will not be that way for long, dear. He needs to know that you won't run. Gain his trust and melt that icy heart of his, and he'll warm to you in no time."

I scoff. "The guy doesn't have a heart."

She laughs softly. It's a charming sound, full of warmth this cold, harsh land hasn't stolen from her. She's kind. Too trusting. I could use that to my advantage. Oh God, what is *wrong* with me? Besides, she's a werewolf, *ulfhednar*, too. She may look soft but she could probably bench-press me.

"Oh, I assure you, he has a heart. But it's guarded. Once you earn his trust, there is no one kinder in all the world."

I barely contain my laugh.

"As long as you stay near Wulfric, you are safe, lad. Safer than anywhere else. That is all I can say."

I should be relieved but I'm not. I wish I could trust in her small smile and reassurances. "I want to go home." My voice cracks and to my dismay, tears prick my eyes.

"Oh, lad," she says. "This is your home now. Your place is here, with your mate."

"I—my *what*?"

She sighs in great exasperation. "That foolish pup hasn't told you?"

I scoff. "No. He's not much of a talker."

"Aye, true enough." Straightening her apron, she takes a seat at a chair by a small dining table in the corner. "You are human. There's much you do not know of our ways. You should really hear this from him, but you ought to know something. Can't have you being too surprised when things get... intimate."

I choke. "Things are not getting anything!"

Mouth dry, I join her at the table, the mug of mystery liquid in hand. How can what she says possibly be more surprising than time travel and werewolf Vikings? I'm afraid to find out.

As I gaze into the mug, realization hits me. Shoot. I haven't taken my Zoloft since I got transported to this place. That can't be good. I left it back in my world. I have no idea what will happen if I just quit my meds cold turkey without the guidance of my psychiatrist. Hopefully, my brain won't break before I can get out of here and back on my meds.

"When we ulfhednar come of age and undertake the ritual to change us from human to beast, we are told that the Norns, goddesses of fate and destiny, will bless us with a mate. Our other half who completes us, who helps us remember our humanity in times of crisis. We will know them at first glance and by their scent."

"So... soulmates are a thing for your people." I shouldn't be surprised, not after everything else I've learned since coming to this strange new world. A shiver runs through me as I remember the intensity in Wulfric's eyes as he forced his way through the crowds at the auction. Like I was the only person in that moment who existed for him.

"Being ulfhednar comes with many great boons. We are fierce warriors and natural hunters. But those from alpha bloodlines risk losing themselves to their wolves and becoming berserkers unless they can find a mate who can soothe their animal rage simply with their presence."

Shit. I don't like where this is going. "And going berserk is bad, right?"

She nods gravely. "We could fell whole armies if we lose ourselves to our rage. Wulfric has been without a mate for so long, we feared we would eventually lose him. Until..."

My heart sinks. "Until... me?"

"Aye, lad. We all worried when he wouldn't choose a mate. He insisted on finding the one fated for him. So I prayed to the gods and they showed me visions. I looked into the past, the present, and the future, and I found you. Only I knew not where you were or that you were human. Only that someday I would come across you in the future. So I traveled there as often as I could for many years, waiting to meet you. I began to lose hope we would ever meet and I would be forced to watch my beloved nephew lose himself to his beast." She smiles big and bright. "And then there you were. Just as handsome as the gods envisioned. I knew at a glance that despite your differences, you were the perfect mate for Wulfric, and that you had to meet at once."

I'm Wulfric's mate? That doesn't make any sense! "Fuck that! I don't want to be that asshole's anything!" Maybe a one-night stand, sure, but—whoa, whoa, whoa. Nope. *Don't even go there, brain between my legs.*

She laughs softly. "Give him a chance, dear. This is a shock for him, too, but he is a good man, and so long as you are here, he will never let anything hurt you."

She leaves me alone with my mouth hanging open. So, fate and destiny are real. Werewolves are real. And I'm the mate of a Viking werewolf.

What the fuck is even my life at this point?

I take a sip of the stuff in the mug and wince as it burns. It must be alcohol of some kind and it tastes almost like beer. Mead. I had a few glasses of this in modern-day Iceland. I tip the mug back and down the whole cup in a few gulps.

Fuck everything about this.

Time to get drunk.

CHAPTER 4
WULFRIC

ALL I WANT IS to drown myself in a few flagons of mead and fall into my bed for the rest of the day, but my people will expect stories from our travels beyond the island, so I open my home to the villagers.

To celebrate my return and the Althing, a meeting between myself and my people, the thralls have prepared a feast. They load the tables with enough food to feed a small army: loaves of freshly baked bread and dishes of butter waiting to be spread, steaming bowls of cabbage soup, wheels of cheese piled high, Aunt Helga's sweet rolls dripping with glaze, and of course a whole roast boar, the skin browned and cracked, dripping with juices.

It's good to be home, even if I must hold this gathering instead of holing myself up in my room for rest. I glance toward my sleeping quarters. Kieran's scent is faint beyond the door, but it tempts me to follow it into the room. My wolf bristles at the idea of only a few inches of wood separating my mate from a pack of wolves. No one will harm him, though. Any who try will die, be they kin or foe.

"He's a nice lad," Helga says, setting a platter of drinks on the table. "He's scared. Be kind to him, won't you?"

I hum and remain by the door to greet my people when they arrive. "You could have told me my mate was a human, Auntie."

"I must say, I was surprised the Norns chose a human to be your mate, too. Our kind have never gotten along."

Grinding my teeth, I say, "It makes no sense."

She lets out a disapproving huff. "It's fortuitous, if you ask me."

I didn't, but that's never stopped Helga from having an opinion about my love life.

"This is the sign we have been waiting for. The gods are telling us it is time to set aside our differences with humans and come together."

"Our differences," I say through clenched teeth, "stem from humans hunting us like cattle."

"I'm aware," she snaps back. "The times are changing, lad. Tell me you don't plan to reject the match."

I should. My people will not be pleased when they learn my mate is a human. There will be dissent, of that I'm certain. "I can't afford to." I look down at my hand, waiting to see claws sprout from my fingertips.

I don't *want* to, but I keep that to myself.

"I've got to be strong for this pack and to do that, I must take him as my mate. And he must want me to." Fear grips my heart. "How am I to court him when he can't even bear to look at me?"

"I seem to remember your ma and da barely being able to meet each other's gaze. Their mating was an arranged one, but they came to love each other deeply." She blinks fast, pain bright in eyes the same shade of gray as my father's, Gunnar's, and mine.

I never knew Mother but from what my aunt and father told me of her, their love ran so deep.

"Giving him free rein would help," Helga adds, giving me a barbed look as she goes to grab a cauldron of soup.

"Out of the question! He isn't safe, not yet. The village must adjust to his presence. Besides, he'll leave the moment my back's turned, and then..." The berserker will take over, consuming me in bestial madness.

She slams down the cauldron of soup and rounds on me. "Then stop acting like an ass and spend time with him. Find a way to make him fall in love with you."

She makes it sound so easy. "How?" I ask, desperation seeping into my voice. "What do I do? What do I even say?"

"Being kind to him would be a good start. Showing interest in his life. Not treating him like a thrall."

She's right, of course, but I'm terrified that the moment I decide to trust him, he'll be ripped from me. I've faced down foes determined to spill my blood without a second's thought, but put me in front of sky-blue eyes and it's like my heart is going to burst from my chest. I hate feeling weak and uncertain. I hate the way Kieran makes me feel. I want the feeling gone but without it, I'm lost.

"I cannot and will not force him to accept my bite." Even if the survival of my pack depends on me and my mating with Kieran, I'll never force myself upon him. "I must make him trust me."

She sighs. "You can't rush these things. Trust in the Norns, lad. Trust that you are meant to be. He's a good lad, I can tell, and he's perfect for you."

"Oh?" I look up, hopeful.

"Aye! Can you not see it? He's got you as flustered and red-faced as a boy."

I slap my hands over my cheeks, scowling when they're warm. Before I can defend my honor, my people are at the door, clamoring to greet me after my long trip away. Among them is my brother Lyall and, I notice with a sigh, his twin Anders.

When I see there's a woman on each of Anders's arms, I grimace. It seems our brother is determined to avoid finding his mate and would rather bed down with anyone who would have him.

Anders's cocky smile from the women's attention falls off his face. "The human's stink is everywhere! Why can't you keep him outside or with the other thralls?"

"He is no thrall," I growl, rounding on him.

Lyall throws his brother a playful smile. "Perhaps we should put you outside on a leash?"

"Try it," Anders growls. "Get me a drink, wench." He sends one of the women on her way with a smack on her ample bottom that makes her squeal in delight.

Lyall looks disgusted but says nothing, as do I. We've talked to him countless times about taking his duty to find a mate seriously, for his own good as well as ours. He's a fool, but he's also our brother. I'm unsure what else can be done to make him take his duties seriously.

"Is our human friend settling in?" Lyall strides to the table and happily accepts a flagon of mead a thrall hands him, her head bowed and eyes averted. She's a pitiful-looking thing, underfed and clad in torn rags. I'd feel sorry for her, but there can be no pity for wolves as weak as her, especially from enemy packs. It's simply the way of the world.

I shrug. "As best as he can be."

"Human friend..." Anders mutters with disdain. We ignore him.

To keep from smacking Anders's head from his shoulders, I ask, "Is Gunnar coming?" I haven't seen our other brother since before I left for the raid. Last I heard, he was off on one of his many treks into the wilderness in search of game. I've hardly laid eyes on him in months with how frequently he disappears into the wilds. Not that anyone can blame him after all he's been through.

Lyall nods. "He's returned from the hunt. I believe that boar was his doing." He motions to the fat pig on the table. "He's gone to see... them. He told me to tell you not to wait on his behalf."

Sorrow grips my heart. "Of course. I understand." I will have to make time to see him after the Althing.

Anders accepts the cup of mead the woman brings him and takes a bite of a roll the other woman offers him. Thumbing away crumbs from his beard, Anders says, "He's got to quit sulking."

"Sulking? His mate and child were killed!" Lyall's nostrils flare. "Leif wasn't his fated, but he was the one he chose. Do not mock his heartbreak."

"If he doesn't get over himself, he'll go berserk" It's rare to hear Anders concerned over anyone but himself. "I miss little Bjorn as much as anyone else. Of all of you, he was the only one I could stand to be in a room with. But unless Gunnar takes another as his mate, we'll have to put him down ourselves. He wouldn't want the Travelers Council to strip him of his wolf. Death would be preferable to him. Is that what you want?"

Taking a gulp of mead, Anders drops into a seat at the table and puts his muddy boots up. Helga shoots him an exasperated look, one I share with her. How a cretin like Anders came from our father, I will never know. He has none of our father's honor or the kindness I was told Mother possessed, and he's been nothing but insufferable since *I* was chosen as Alpha-heir when I was five and not him, the eldest of us.

"If I were alpha, I'd force our brother to take finding a mate more seriously!" Anders growls.

"But you're not," I snap, silencing him. Heads turn at our display. "And you're one to talk about finding a mate." I motion at the women he brought in.

"I can take care of myself. Besides, I'm not the one snarling like a rabid beast anytime someone speaks poorly of the human." Anders's smile widens, all teeth. "You're no fun at all. Mayhap that human's tight little body will loosen you up a bit."

I reach for my axe. "Do not speak of him like that." Just knowing that he has pictured my mate in such a sexually suggestive scenario has my blood boiling.

"Enough," Lyall growls. "We need to start the meeting."

I take a few breaths to calm myself. To the crowd I say, "Everyone, have a seat." Notable members of the community find their seats around the long table. I know all their faces from the smithy to a few farmers, crafters, and hunters. My heart begins to race as I anticipate the disgust that will twist their faces with what I say next.

"I have finally found my mate." Excited whispers and gasps buzz around the room. "Once we consummate our bond, I will never fear losing control over my berserker rage. We will stand strong against those who would destroy our way of life."

Anders clears his throat. "Ahem. Aren't you forgetting a rather important detail, dear brother? Say, the fact that your mate is *human*?" All whimsy disappears from his voice as his eyes narrow in contempt.

Grinding my teeth together as a gathering storm of whispers rise around us, I say, "Yes. My mate is human. And a man." Not that gender has ever mattered among our pack. I have known some packs where relations between two men are forbidden if one of the men allows himself to take a more... passive role. But among ulfhednar, any mate is a gift from the Norns to be treasured and revered regardless of their gender.

"Yes, a human!" Anders announces, sweeping to his feet, his fur cloak swaying behind him as he stalks the room, eyes bright with anger. "The very same as those Christian missionaries who came to our shores all those years ago. The same who killed your neighbors, your friends and family—our very own alpha!"

Memories claw at me and try to drag me down to the icy depths.

The joy that brightened the faces of my people fades to fear and cold contempt. The whispers spread, and I catch snatches of words I never wanted to hear.

"How could the Norns choose a human as the Alpha-Mate?"

"Must be a mistake…"

"If his father were still alive, this would never have happened!"

Anders slams a fist onto the table. "My brother's choices are not those of an alpha but of a man who would have us throw away our way of life to appease the humans! As your Alpha, I would never—"

"Enough!" The roar tears through me, rattling the plates and goblets, making the ground tremble. The beast tears at my self-control until all I want is to shed this human skin and tear the room apart. The crowd flinches back from me.

"Wulfric, calm yourself, brother. Or you'll lose control." Lyall lays a hand on me, and my brother's touch soothes some of that bestial rage. But it's not enough. I need my mate or else this room will become a bloodbath.

Clearing her throat, Helga rises and says, "Please, help yourselves to the feast."

I pick at my food while the townsfolk discuss their issues. One man wants me to settle a dispute between him and his neighbor, who he believes stole his goat. Another wants me to arrange a duel between himself and a father who refused to pay a debt to their family.

My skull throbs. Red leaches into my vision. Saliva floods my mouth as I imagine their bloody, broken bodies piled at my feet, their blood like wine upon my tongue.

Kill them all, the berserker snarls. *They will come for our mate unless you tear them to pieces.*

They can't take Kieran away from me. I won't let them. I'll kill anyone who so much as looks at him wrong.

Fortunately the room soon empties. Once everyone has left, Helga rounds on Anders. "If your father were here to witness such disrespect toward the man he chose as Alpha, he would box your bloody ears!"

Lyall tugs Anders outside before the two can argue. Helga bolts the door after them. She takes one look at whatever fury is etched on my face and sighs. "Poor dear. Go and see your mate."

Breathing harshly through a mouthful of fangs, I go to my room. My claws tear strips of wood away from the door as I yank it open.

"What the fuck?" Kieran yelps, sitting upright from where he lies on a fur rug by the fire.

His scent blankets the bedroom. I breathe in deep and a wave of calm washes over me as his mountain flower scent tickles my nose. The rage drains from me, leaving only exhaustion. I lean on the wall for support. "Have you eaten?"

He shrugs. "Not hungry."

"I can bring in some food—"

Scowling, he shakes his head. "I don't want anything your thralls have cooked. How can you eat food they were forced to cook? When's the last time they were offered anything from your table?" He spits the words, like he finds the idea disgusting... like *I'm* disgusting to him.

If he's going to be my mate, he needs to understand that things are different from what he may be used to. "I take it you don't keep thralls in your time."

Kieran looks offended at the very thought. "No. Not for a very long time. Slavery is illegal in the modern world. There's no place for it. People are not property."

I cock my head at him, confused. "Thralls are not people."

"Says who!"

I'm too tired for this. I undress, squirming out of my woolen shirt that suddenly feels too hot. "It's the way things are."

Kieran crosses his arms, making the chains connecting him to one of the legs of my bed rattle. "It isn't right."

Pulling my breeches down to my ankles, I kick them off so my legs are bare and I'm dressed only in my tunic. "They are too weak to fight and die with honor. Too poor to be landowners. It's their role in life, and it's a role we depend upon to survive."

Another disgusted noise escapes Kieran. "That's not true. Nobody needs slavery to survive. But I guess it's easier to tell yourself that than to fix the issue."

I'm done with this discussion. What were the Norns thinking, tying me to a man who can't understand our ways? Bunching my shirt into a ball, I chuck it into the corner and turn around only to see Kieran snapping his head in another direction. I'm clad in only my undergarments. I get too hot at night beneath the furs, even when it's freezing out.

My gaze is drawn to him, now pacing by the hearth, chains dragging on the floor. "Makes no sense," I snarl to myself. "Why would the gods tie my soul to a man like you?"

"What are you looking at? Go to bed or something," Kieran gripes, staring at a spot on the wall in the opposite direction of me. His scent has shifted, notes of anger heating into spicy waves of... lust.

My blood, always running hot in his presence, flows to my cock. If he were ulfhednar, I wouldn't even hesitate to wrap him in my arms. I'd ask him to my bed, and our bodies would be one in the way only true fated mates can be. It would be so much more than sex; we'd be bound to each other, heart and soul.

A force greater than anything I've ever felt compels me toward him until we're inches apart. My heart yearns for him, but my mind is in turmoil. He is almost perfect, and yet he is human.

"Your aunt told me about... uh... mates."

If I weren't counting the freckles on his nose, I might have scowled. "Did she?"

"Yeah." He clears his throat, his gaze dropping to the floor. I want those beautiful eyes back on me. "So. I'm your—"

"The gods believe so. I am not convinced."

He snorts. "Wow. Way to make a guy feel wanted."

Guilt gnaws at me. I should be grateful. Happy. Over-joyed. And I was, at first. Until I realized just how complicated his humanity would make things. "I dreamed of meeting my mate." Turning away from him, I drag my feet to the fireplace, resting an arm on the mantle. "Every night, I thought of you. Of what you might look like. Thought of all the ways in which I might find you. I dreamed of running with you as wolves beneath the northern lights and howling with you beneath the stars."

I rub my chest to massage away the ache of disappointment. I will never experience that with him. I will never get to see Kieran's wolf. He's my mate, but he will never understand the most sacred part of me that I love most. He will never understand the ways of my people. Odin's beard, he isn't even of this time and place!

Kieran sighs. "You know, you're not the only one disappointed with the shit hand he's been dealt. I'd rather be anywhere else than on this frozen rock surrounded by shape-shifters."

"And I would rather have anyone for my mate than you," I snap back, and instantly regret twinges in my chest. Trying to explain myself, I add, "Your kind are my pack's greatest enemies. Your people want nothing more than to destroy our way of life."

"If you hate me so much, then just let me go," Kieran demands.

I pace to my bed. "If I could, I would. But I need you if I want to keep my humanity, and like it or not, you need my protection. My pack isn't exactly pleased that a human is my mate. If you leave my side, I can't promise my pack won't make you a target."

Kieran's quiet for once, his hands in fists at his sides. "Guess we're stuck with each other then." He stalks past to the fire and sits on the fur rug in front of the flames, which are burning low, in danger of fading.

I curl onto my side away from him. The room darkens as the fire dies. Something chatters behind me. It's Kieran. He's cold, his teeth chattering. Damn it, what if he freezes in the middle of the night? Humans are so fragile.

I rip a sheepskin blanket from the pile of furs on my bed and toss it by the fire. "There. So you won't freeze in the night."

Not sparing me a glance, he tugs the sheepskin over himself and lies down, his back to me.

I snuff out the candles on my bedside table, covering the room in darkness.

Chapter 5
Kieran

Damn stupid Viking werewolf. Such an asshole has no right to be so hot without his clothes on. As pissed as I am with his shitty personality and this whole soulmate crap, if Wulfric weren't such an ass, I'd have jumped on his dick in a heartbeat.

To make matters worse, I'm starving. I didn't eat the bread or cheese Helga gave me. I don't know if the thralls bake the bread or make the cheese, but I can't eat food prepared by unfree people with a clean conscience.

I've got to get out of here and back to my own time. I can't believe only a few days ago, the worst thing in my life was that my asshole boyfriend had cheated. I'd take that over being stuck in the past where everything is so backwards. Once I'm back in my timeline, things will be different. I'll find a guy worth my time. Someone with Wulfric's looks but a far better personality. I'll start writing music again.

If Wulfric thinks I'm going to tolerate his surly ass, he's got another think coming. He thinks we're soulmates, that

I'm going to settle for him because I need his protection? Fuck him. I settled for the last guy and look how that turned out. Never again.

But I'll play nice a little longer. Make him think I've accepted my role as his mate. Then when I've earned his trust, I'll make a break for it. If I can just get a proper look at my surroundings, and get out of these damn chains, I could figure out where to go.

Once the sun rises, the day begins. Well, for Wulfric and his people. Wulfric gets up, and it's unfair that his hair looks good straight out of bed without any effort on his part. Dickheads like him don't deserve nice hair. Or fantastic asses.

Stretching with a low groan that absolutely doesn't make my cock twitch, he pads over to the fireplace and throws in a few fresh logs. There's a sharp click as he strikes what I assume are two stones together. Behind my closed eyes, firelight blooms and warmth caresses my body.

Yawning, I feign sleep, peeking from beneath my eyelashes until he's out the bedroom door. I pretend I don't notice the way the muscles above his ass ripple with every step he takes. Once he's gone, I sit up, the sheepskin sliding off me. Did he… light the fire for me? That was awfully nice of him. Or maybe he just wanted the room warm while he's gone.

He didn't lock the door. Ugh. But my chains are still attached to the damn bed. Before I can stew in frustration, the door swings open and Helga strides in with a sunny smile. "Good morning, lad!"

"Morning!" I infuse my voice with as much false cheer as I can.

"I hope you're hungry. I had the thralls prepare a meal." Any appetite I did have diminishes just imagining those poor people slaving away in the kitchen for my benefit. Yet when she sets a plate stacked with grilled leeks and salted fish on the table, my stomach moans in longing.

"Thank you." She's the only kind soul among these rugged barbarians. I really should use that, even if it is scummy to take advantage of a nice lady like her. I stand up and make a show of wincing as the cuffs jerk around my wrists. "It's hard to eat with these on."

She looks at my cuffs, then follows the chain to where it links to Wulfric's bed. "He chained you up like a dog?" she asks, eyes wide in horror.

"He wanted to make sure I wouldn't run."

Helga tuts her disapproval. Bustling about the room, she checks every nook and cranny until with a triumphant cry, she produces a key from inside a vase above the mantel. Kneeling, she unlocks the chain from the bed, then crosses over to me. "Let's get those off you."

This is what I wanted, but I hesitate to hold out my arms. "Won't you get in trouble if he finds out?"

She sniffs. "Let him fuss. He's got to learn that he can trust his mate not to stray." She unlocks my cuffs, and I sigh in relief. My wrists are chaffed but being able to stretch out my arms feels so good I hardly notice a thing.

"Do you need any help around the house today?" I ask.

"Oh, don't you worry about that."

"I'd like to help. If I'm going to be..." I nearly gag on the words. "Wulfric's mate, I should get to know the village and the people in it."

"Aye, I suppose there's no harm in that. As it happens, I've got to pick up a few things from the market. I'd be happy with your company. We'll leave as soon as you're done eating."

My stomach gurgles, but I think of the thralls stuck in the bowels of the ship, how dirty and terrified they were. "I'm not feeling very well. Must have been something I ate."

I regret my words when pity softens her face. "Oh, poor dear! I'm sure we'll find something at the market to ease your troubles."

Anything sounds better than being stuck in the longhouse. But first... "Could I have a bath before we head out?" I can't remember the last time I bathed, and my clothes reek.

She smiles. "Certainly, and I'll have some clean clothes prepared as well. Wulfric must have something that will fit you."

Another brain zap hits me when I stand up too fast, making the room spin. Damn it. I need to get back on my Zoloft. I hope my withdrawal symptoms don't get too bad.

"Are you well, lad?"

Drawing in a deep breath, I close my eyes and feel like I'm spiraling down a whirlpool. "Y-yeah. Just a sec."

Once the dizziness passes, Helga leads me from the bedroom and to the outdoors. The grass is stiff with frost, and my breath streams in the air as I follow her toward the back of the house. As we walk, the air warms.

We arrive in a clearing with steaming geothermal pools. Wulfric has a natural hot spring right in his backyard! How he's so grumpy is beyond me.

"Here you are, lad." Helga lays some fresh clothes and a bar of what looks like soap on a rock near the pools. "Come and find me when you're done."

Once she's gone, I look both ways. There's nobody around, only rugged mountains and forest for miles. It's incredible. Shedding my clothes, I step into one of the pools and submerge myself, sighing as heat envelops me from neck to toe. I fumble for the soap I left on the ground behind me. It's hard as a rock, more like stone than a bar of soap, but when I dip it in the water, it softens and becomes sudsy. It doesn't have a fragrance, but historians are always talking about how clean medieval Scandinavians were for their time, so I'll trust in their weird soap.

Standing, I lather myself up quickly so I don't freeze, then sink back into the water. The suds foam and fizzle on the surface. Now would be a good time to make a break for it, but the vast wilderness that surrounds me looks more formidable than even Wulfric. If I got lost, I could freeze or starve. I'll have to think of something else.

The frosty grass crunches behind me. Heart lurching, I whirl around.

"Oh! My apologies." It's one of Wulfric's brothers. And he's naked. Wulfric may be an ass, but his genes? Fucking impeccable. This brother, whoever he is, is just as stunning as Wulfric, though he has ebony hair and bright green eyes. He's also completely confident in his nudity, the kind of confidence that comes with knowing he's hot.

"Did you want to use this?" I rise from the springs, shivering as the cold air nips my damp skin. I cover my crotch with my hands.

A soft laugh escapes him, snide and mocking. "Are all humans so reserved? You've nothing on you I haven't seen before." Those eyes flick up and down my bare skin, his lips pulling up into a predatory smile with too many teeth. "I can see why my brother is so taken with you."

I laugh more nervously than I mean to. "Oh. Um. Thank you?" *Ugh, Kieran, just shut up...* "I can leave if you want. I'm meeting Helga anyway."

"Don't run off on my account. Stay. Enjoy the springs. I know I will." He prowls toward me, muscles rippling, cock bobbing between his thick thighs. I tear my eyes away and look anywhere else until he sinks into the water... beside me.

Great. Just two naked guys sitting in a hot spring. Right next to each other. And one of them's a werewolf Viking. Totally normal.

"You're one of Wulfric's brothers?"

"Aye. Anders," he responds. He runs the soap over the thick black hair on his chest. "There are four of us. My twin Lyall and I are the oldest. Then Gunnar three years later. Then two years later along came the beloved Alpha Wulfric. Don't tell them, but I'm the fun one." From a nearby basket, he produces a bottle and flashes me a grin. "You should have been fated to me. Wulfric can be a boorish brute." After taking a long swig from the bottle, he offers it to me. "Mead. You'll need it if you're going to be stuck with Wulfric."

I gulp down a mouthful. When I go to hand the bottle back, Anders is staring right at me, a curious tilt to his head. Maybe it's knowing that he's a wolf, but I can't unsee the wolfish qualities he possesses. He's more animallike than Wulfric.

"There's something different about you. Everything from the way you speak to the way you dress yourself... You aren't of this time, are you?"

The steam tickles my throat, and I cough trying to reply to him. "Did Wulfric tell you?"

"No. But it isn't hard to guess." He takes the bottle back and has a gulp, swiping his tongue over his lips. "Lyall travels back and forth from this time to the other, and you walk, talk, and act just like you waltzed right out of one of his stories from the future—but don't tell anyone I said that. Wouldn't want him to get in trouble." There's a note of sincerity in his voice. Maybe he and Wulfric don't get along, but he clearly cares for his twin.

My heart skips. "Really?" I lean in before I can stop myself. "How is Lyall able to travel between timelines?"

Anders's smile widens. "Has Wulfric told you about Yggdrasil? The sacred tree that binds the nine realms together?"

I nod and he passes me the bottle.

"Yggdrasil connects our worlds, allowing travel between the realms. It's said that Yggdrasil is an ash tree. There are no trees as special as Yggdrasil, but it's birthed many mighty ash trees. Using the branch of an ash tree, one can travel between realms." Lowering his voice, he leans in close, his breath cool against my ear. "Don't tell anyone, but Lyall still keeps such a branch to travel to the future."

My heart thuds faster. "Would he give me the branch if I asked?" I hand the bottle back.

With a snort, Anders takes a drink then sets the empty bottle aside. "Not likely. It's his only connection to the future. But don't you worry about that. Leave it to me."

"You'll... you'll help me escape? Why?" He'd go behind both his brothers' backs to help a stranger? He could endanger himself by helping me.

Anders runs his soapy hands through his mane of wet hair. "It's quite simple: you belong in your world, not ours. Your kind has caused our people enough trouble. It's better for everyone if you return home safe and sound."

But can I trust this man to get me there? It's not like I have a choice. He's my only hope. "Can't argue with that. But how will I get out of Wulfric's longhouse without being spotted?"

He rolls his eyes. "Do you want me to hold your hand through every step of the process? Figure out where he keeps the cuff keys. Free yourself while he sleeps. While you are making your getaway, I will 'acquire' Lyall's branch. Need I explain further?"

Without waiting for a reply, he rises from the hot spring and gives me an eyeful of his dick. Sweeping his wet hair over his broad shoulder, he walks away from the pools.

"Meet me by the stables. They're the second-biggest building in the village aside from the longhouse." He throws a barbed look over his shoulder at me. "Don't get caught." He disappears into the trees.

Excitement makes my stomach churn.

It's happening. Before sunrise, I could be back in Reykjavik.

I can go home to my time, and this nightmare will finally be over.

My mind is elsewhere, planning my escape, while Helga and I visit the market. I don't know if I trust Anders. Humans and ulfhednar are enemies, but he's willing to help me? Something's up. Unless he just really wants me gone, I should expect him to demand something in return. Unfortunately, I'm not in a position to refuse his help.

What could he want in exchange for helping me? The uncertainty makes my stomach churn as I follow Helga along the pier. She does all the talking to the fishermen and I offer to carry the hefty bags of fish, but she insists on doing it herself. She barely breaks a sweat carrying three whole huge fish around. Must be her supernatural strength. I know I'd be winded hefting around fish half the size of my body.

When we get back to the house, Wulfric still hasn't come back from wherever he went this morning.

"Where did Wulfric go?" I ask Helga.

"Off to hunt."

"Will he be gone long?"

She looks out the window. "He usually returns before sunset, and we can prepare whatever he's caught for supper. It's important that he exercise his wolf. It eases his berserker rage. Make yourself at home."

She pours us some mead and we quench our thirst. Outside the garden windows, people pass back and forth. There are a few pens with livestock out back, and the thralls are tending to the goats, cows, and chickens. A few thralls appear to be plaiting baskets or lugging weighty armfuls of firewood to the house from the woods, chains around their hands and feet rattling as they walk. A scowling man walks among them, armed with a lash. Dirt smears the thralls' faces, their hair disheveled, bags heavy under their eyes, and their clothes hang off their thin frames.

"When's the last time they had a proper meal?" I ask.

She just shrugs. "They eat plenty of whatever is left over."

"So table scraps."

My distaste must show because she frowns at me. "We can't just give them the food from our table. There's only so much to go around. Do you not have thralls where you're from?"

"No," I say, incensed. "It's illegal. But that doesn't stop people from selling and buying humans for sex or forced labor."

"How do you get anything done? Don't you need help tending to your crops or livestock?"

I shake my head. "Things are different in my time. If farmers need help, they hire people and pay them for their hard work."

Her eyes go wide. "Oh, aye? You have the means to pay them?"

"Yes. It's illegal not to." I turn away from the thralls, unable to watch them work. "Where do they come from?"

"Many of them were born into this life, but a few others were prisoners of war who agreed to serve rather than die at the sword."

"And they're all ulfhednar?"

She nods. "Aye, but we took away their furs and without them, they cannot shift."

"Do you go hunting with the men? What about the other women in the village?" I'm not sure how many rights the women of this time have.

Her eyes light up. "Aye, in the days of my youth, I once hunted the biggest bear to ever venture into these parts. He'd slaughtered many of our best hunters, my father among them."

"Oh. I'm sorry."

Folding her wrinkled hands in her lap, she goes on. "I was determined to avenge my father, so I left with the other hunters. We tracked the beast for days until we finally caught it. We shifted and fought the murderous creature for what felt like hours before it was too worn down to fight back. The hunters gave me the honor of being the one to end the creature's life." She bares her teeth in a smile. "So I tore out the bear's throat with my own fangs."

"Whoa. That's awesome." I'd never have guessed this kindly older woman would have ripped out a bear's throat.

"They called me Helga Bear-Slayer. But that was long, long ago. Many of the women in our village go hunting with the men. Those who are capable. Used to be only men were considered worthy of becoming ulfhednar, but Wulfric's great-grandmother decreed that we needed every able-bodied warrior to take up arms and hunt or fight to defend our village. Outsiders are not allowed to share in our gift, not usually, but I'm sure Wulfric will make an exception for you."

I look up, shocked. "I need to become ulfhednar?"

"Of course, lad! It will be expected of you. How do you expect to survive life out here if you can't take the form of a wolf? There will be backlash, of course, but Wulfric will put any dissenters in their place."

I lurch out of my seat. "I won't become some monster."

"You wouldn't be a monster, lad. You'd be a wolf. Mighty and fast. A lethal hunter."

A laugh escapes me. "I'm not any of those things. The only hunting I do is foraging for snacks in my kitchen at three in the morning." And maybe I killed a mouse once that got into my apartment and squashed a few cockroaches under my boot. It's good I'm leaving tonight. I wouldn't last a second in this life.

Leaving the kitchen, I return to Wulfric's room and try to rest. Since he isn't here, I curl up in his bed. The furs smell like him. I'd thought he would smell bad, but he doesn't. His scent is woodsy, crisp mountain air, dirt, and grass. It's... not unpleasant. His clothes are big on me, which I expected. I had to belt the breeches because they sag on me, and the tunic is practically a dress with how far it flows down to my knees. The woolen sweater I wear over everything is so large I'm swimming in it, but it's warm enough until my clothes are clean and dry. Helga told me she was washing them.

Hunger gnaws at me. My limbs are shaky and weak, and I'm exhausted just from the short walk around the village. I can wait a little longer for food. The first thing I'm eating when I return to my timeline's going to be the biggest cheeseburger I can get my hands on, a mountain of fries, and a milkshake from my favorite fast-food place. Fuck the calories. God, I miss modern food not prepared by enslaved people. I miss my home and even my shitty jobs. I miss the familiarity of modern living.

Soon I'll be free.

When I open my eyes, the room is stained red with the light from the setting sun. Something smells good, and my stomach cramps with hunger so intense, I groan in pain. No, I won't eat. I just need to hold out until I can go home.

The door bangs open and I jump out of my skin.

Wulfric crowds the doorway, glowering like always. "Come and eat."

I grind my teeth. "I'm not—"

"Don't tell me you aren't hungry!" he snaps. "I sniffed out the cheese and bread you hid. You haven't eaten in days."

"I'm not eating food your thralls made."

He stomps over to my bed. "You will eat. That's an order from your Alpha."

"You're not my anything," I snap back.

A smirk quirks his mustache. "Oh, but I will be soon and until we are equals in our mating, you will respect my authority."

Folding my arms over my chest, I hold his glare. "What are you going to do, tie me down and make me eat?"

He tilts his head, his smile widening. "Why, would you enjoy that? Being tied up and at my mercy. Unable to do a thing but lie back and let me please you."

My mind says no. My dick says fuck yes.

My brain latches onto his phrasing.

Let me please you.

I would be at his mercy like he said, but he would be pleasing *me,* not himself.

Oh fuck, why does that sound so tempting? Not so much the bondage thing, not really my scene, but giving up control to another person. Mark couldn't understand that giving up control to someone I trust helped so much with my anxiety and self-doubt in the bedroom. My life is so busy, the last thing I want in bed is to be in control. But Mark never respected that and, stupid me, I gave up on asking him to give me what I needed every once in a while.

Planting one boot on the bed, Wulfric leans over me, nostrils flaring.

"No, I wouldn't like that," I insist, looking away.

A raspy chuckle rumbles from him. "You can't hide a thing from me, lad. I can smell how much you love the idea."

Fuck me. Heat flames my cheeks, but I refuse to look away from his narrowed eyes. My trousers are huge, so I don't need to worry about him seeing how hard I am, but knowing he can smell the effect his words have on me makes me vulnerable in a way I'm not used to.

"Aye, I think you'd enjoy that very much, wouldn't you?" His voice is practically a growl. "Perhaps a rag in your mouth, too, so you can shut up and let me give you what you need."

Oh fuck. I all but whimper at the thought.

"And... what do I need?" My voice is dry, my cock twitching in my oversized trousers.

Leaning in until our noses are inches apart, his breath hot on my lips, his beard tickling my skin, he whispers, "Food. Now." And yanks me out of bed.

I yelp indignantly as he tugs me from the bedroom. "I told you I'm not—"

"Yes, you are eating, because my thralls didn't prepare the food. I did."

I stop walking. "You... What?"

Rolling his eyes to the back of his thick head, he growls out, "I. Made. Supper. Now sit down, shut up, and eat." He wrenches out a chair, stomps to the other side of the table, and plops down in his own seat with all the dramatics of an overgrown, beardy teenager and not the adult Viking warrior he is.

Wulfric didn't make supper. He made a whole damn feast. "What is all this?"

Wulfric points from one dish to another. "Bread. Boar stew with turnips. Vegetables from the garden. Now eat."

My mouth salivates at the sight of so much delicious food. "Is... is this what you were away all day doing?"

Sighing through flared nostrils, he nods so hard I'm surprised his head doesn't fall off his shoulders. "What do you think? I hunted the boar for the stew, harvested the grains. The turnips came from the garden."

I'm astounded. I can't even remember the last time someone cooked for me. Mark sure never went to the effort. Maybe early in our relationship, yeah, and for a while after we moved in, but then he started finding excuses not to, all the while being happy to make me cook even if I was dead on my feet after a long shift at work.

There's a suspicious lump in my throat when I say, "Wow. Wulfric, this is incredible."

Wulfric's too busy shoveling food in his mouth to talk. At her seat, Helga hides a smile behind her hands, eyes twinkling when she meets my gaze.

"I can't believe you went to such trouble for me."

He says, "It isn't any trouble. It's a privilege to hunt and provide for you."

That's not what he said during our fight last night. "But you said—"

"I know what I said." Regret is heavy in his voice, and he doesn't meet my eyes. "I was ill-tempered, and I took it out on you. It wasn't right. Human or not, the Norns brought you to me for a reason. I have to respect and trust their judgment." Exhaling, he looks up at me like a big kicked puppy. "It would be an honor to dine with you."

I don't know what to say. He must have done a lot of soul-searching during his hunt. I wouldn't have expected such a hot-headed, proud warrior to admit to a mistake. Wulfric has completely caught me off guard. Maybe there's more to him than meets the eye.

"I will. Thank you." I sit and take my time choosing from the array of dishes before me. Wulfric's eyes are on me but when I look up, he's staring at something on the floor. I take a bite of the boar stew, and flavor bursts across my tongue. It isn't as sophisticated as food from my time, but it's all homemade and just for me.

"Do you like it?" he asks.

I'm too busy stuffing my face to answer right away. "It's fucking delicious."

A smile quirks his mouth. "I'll take that for a yes."

Nodding, I dig in and we eat in a silence that isn't heavy with frustration or dislike.

It's almost... nice.

It's a shame I've got to throw his kindness back in his face by leaving tonight. The thought makes me pause mid-chew. I have to. I've got no choice. I don't belong in this world, and I never will.

After dinner, I head to Wulfric's room while he and Helga clean up. I tried to help, but they sent me to bed. Lying on the furs by the fire, I tuck an arm beneath my head. My heart begins to race. Soon I'll be able to leave and return to my timeline. Once everyone is asleep, I'll go.

The door creaks open and Wulfric comes in. Fabric rustles as he undresses, no doubt stripping down to his underwear like yesterday. I can just imagine the way the firelight would flicker over the ridges of his abs. Desire makes my cock twitch, but I ignore it. First order of business when I'm back in my time? Find a hot Icelander to have a one-night stand with.

"Aren't you going to cuff me?" I ask when he walks by me to the bed.

He pauses. "You had ample opportunity to run today." Then he snuffs out the candles and settles into bed. Looks like he just made things easier for me.

I lie awake unmoving for a long time until he begins to snore. As quietly as I can, I stand and tiptoe to the door. I twist the knob inch by inch and open the door as slowly as I can, praying it doesn't creak. When the door is just wide enough to squeeze through, I slip through the gap.

The house is dark and empty as I tiptoe to the front door. My clothes dried during the day, so I pull on my coat and shuck off my huge trousers in exchange for my jeans. I tug on my boots and tie them, then lift the latch.

The frigid night air draws a shudder from me. There's no one in the village, though candlelight still flickers in the windows of some houses. Distantly, farmyard animals cry in the night. More alarmingly, wolves howl. The sound is both haunting and terrifying, seeming to come from everywhere all at once as the sound travels through the vast wilderness around us.

I need to hurry before those wolves decide to return to the village. I stick close to the trees on the outskirts of the village just in case people might be patrolling the streets. I can make out the stable roof in the dark and even though it's close, it feels far away as I slowly make my way toward it. Any second now, I expect to hear a door open as Wulfric pursues me or for someone to lunge at me from the shadows and drag me back.

Nobody stops me. I make it to the stables and ease open the door. Horses snort in the darkness as I strain my eyes to make out if there's anyone else here. I trip over something and nearly fall on my face.

"All that crashing around must be you, human." Anders sounds amused at my expense. "Fenrir's balls, be louder, why don't you? I don't think the deaf old man in the cottage a mile away heard you."

Scowling, I stomp up to his silhouette where he's reclining against a stall door. "Did you get the branch?"

"Of course I did, and Lyall wasn't any the wiser. Did anyone see you leave?"

"No."

Humming his approval, he opens the stall door and leads out a black horse, the pelt blending perfectly with the shadows. "We need to find a spot where one of Yggdrasil's roots twists beneath the soil."

I step into the stirrup and try to heave myself over the horse's back. "How will we know when we've found it?"

"There's a rune carved into the branch. When it glows, we know we're in the right place. Lyall frequents a spot not far from here. I know the way." Before I can climb into the saddle, he leads the horse toward the door, ignoring my frantic whispers of protest. "Take this." He shoves something wrapped in cloth into my free hand. I unwrap it, revealing a silver dagger. "In case we encounter trouble."

"I can't fight," I hiss, still with one leg over the horse's back and the other caught in the stirrup. "What's out there that I'll need to stab anyway?"

"Whatever you can think of. Creatures that snap and growl." A grin curls his lips, revealing his pointed fangs. "Like this." And he lets loose a rumbling snarl that sends the horse into a panic.

With a squeal of fright, the horse shoots out the doors. I wrap an arm around the horse's neck, fingers clawing at the mane, too shocked to hold back my holler of fright. The horse bucks, and I tumble from the beast's back. The collision knocks the breath from my aching ribs and for a few agonizing seconds, I can't move.

When I find my feet, Anders is marching toward me. Something's wrong with him. His eyes are flashing, fangs sharp, claws ready at his sides. My fight or flight instinct kicks in. I choose flight. I've only run a few steps when he hurls himself on my back, crushing me to the ground. Pinning me down, he howls loud enough to wake whoever wasn't already woken up by my panicked shouting.

The son of a bitch planned this. He's going to get me caught!

"You tricked me," I snarl, struggling to push him off.

Anders laughs, a grin splitting his face. "How naive could you possibly be, human? Letting you walk out would be far too boring. This? This makes a point! When the whole village sees what you've done, they'll realize how foolish Wulfric really is." He grabs me and hauls me to my feet. "Go ahead, try and fight back! Run, and I'll make you regret it."

I point the dagger at him and it shakes in my grip. "S-stay back!"

Anders grins through his fangs, eyes wild and bright. I've never seen a human look so much like a monster before. He doesn't stop. He charges me and all I can do is thrust out the dagger, close my eyes, and look away.

CHAPTER 6
WULFRIC

A DISTANT HOWL WAKES me, but it's the pain that has me bolting upright in bed, agony twisting through the pack bond that ties me to Anders. Something has happened. We're under attack. I must protect Kieran.

I leap from bed, but Kieran's spot by the fire is empty. Kieran is gone. Fear and fury make my fangs descend and turn my claws razor-sharp. I hurl my black wolfskin cloak over my back as I tear from the house and out into the streets.

A crowd has gathered, carrying candles or hoisting torches high. I shove past people and through them. I must find Kieran, kill whoever took him, and save my brother from harm. In my chest, Lyall's bond flares to life, then Gunnar's. They're coming to Anders's aid.

Father Wolf, let that fool be safe... I'll never forgive myself if my last memory of Anders is an argument about who should have been alpha. Like we're both fool pups and not grown men. The iron tang of blood hits my nose. Anders's blood. With a roar, I force myself through the crowd—and completely freeze.

Anders is hunched over, blood dripping from the blade buried in his stomach, and Kieran is with him. Kieran's face is bloodless, eyes wide in horror, hands outstretched in front of him like he's still holding on to something.

There's no one else there with them. The rage drains from me. "What is going on?" I ask, breathing hard from exertion and fear.

Anders rips the blade free with a strangled snarl. Smoke curls from the wound in his gut.

The blade is made of silver. But who in the village would have such a thing? None of us can so much as touch a silver weapon. Unless... No.

Anders grunts. "Damn human. Stole from the stables. I chased him down, cornered him. R-ran me through."

Furious snarls erupt from the crowd.

My head begins to throb.

Kieran stole from our stables? Stabbed my brother with a silver dagger?

"Move!" Lyall bursts through the crowd beside me.

At his side is Gunnar, lips curled in a snarl. "The human did this?" Fury blazes in his eyes. "You dare spill my brother's blood?"

Kieran takes a step back, hands raised. "No. No, I didn't mean to. Listen to me!"

But ever since the death of his chosen mate and child, Gunnar has been overprotective of us. I know just from the look on his face that he won't hesitate to kill Kieran for harming his pack. And I...

I should be at his side, fighting in my brother's defense. I...

I should hurl myself in front of Kieran to keep him from harm. I...

With a roar, Gunnar hurls the hood of his fur cloak over his head. His fur cloak possesses him, changing him from a man to a huge bloodthirsty wolf as big as a horse.

"No!" Lyall shouts. "Wait, something isn't right!"

Kieran turns to run. A big mistake. Gunnar leaps, flying toward my mate.

I don't think. I don't have to. I made my choice the moment I caught Kieran's scent. The shift tears through me but I don't take the form of a regular wolf. No, not for this. To stop Gunnar, I will need more strength than four legs can provide. My body swells with power as I shift to an enormous cross between a wolf and a man; my berserker form. I run, clawed feet slamming the earth, wind tearing through my fur.

Lurching in front of Kieran, I brace and absorb the impact of Gunnar's body. I reach out a huge hand fitted with hooks for claws and lock my fingers around my brother's throat. Gunnar yelps and thrashes as I hoist him off the ground, his paws kicking in midair.

I shove my snout in his face and snarl, "Touch him, brother, and I will rip you apart."

Hurting Gunnar would destroy me, but I would do it in an instant to protect Kieran.

Gunnar shifts, his fur falling away. Grasping at my thick, hairy forearm, he pants, "How can you defend him? He's human!"

"You will not harm him. Am I clear?"

Shock and hurt widen Gunnar's silver eyes. I know how hard this will be for Gunnar to understand after losing his family to humans, but I pray he will try. Grinding his teeth so hard a muscle ticks in his jaw, Gunnar gives a stiff nod. I drop him, and Gunnar gasps for breath at my feet.

"Holy shit," Kieran whispers, sounding both awed and frightened.

He's safe. The rage settles and allows me to shift back to a man. "Are you hurt?" I ask him, voice gruff.

Wide-eyed, he shakes his head.

Still, the beast rumbles in my chest. The crowd around us snaps and snarls, hungry for blood. Kieran isn't safe, not yet, and if my people don't get away from him, I might slaughter them all. "Helga," I snap, fangs sharp in my mouth. "Take him home. Lock the doors."

"Aye!" She rushes to Kieran, takes his arm, and leads him away.

"Anders, we need to get you to a healer. Now." The silver will inhibit his body's natural healing.

Grimacing, Anders allows Lyall to help him walk to the healer's hut just up the road. The crowd follows us, shouting over each other. My head throbs, a growl rolling through my chest.

Kill them, the berserker snarls. *Kill them all.*

Grinding my teeth, I force myself to follow my brothers to the healer. Lyall and Gunnar go inside with Anders. I watch them until they're out of sight, then turn to the furious crowd. "I need to know what you saw."

Everyone starts talking over each other.

"One at a time!" I bellow.

The baker shuffles forward. "I saw the whole thing, Alpha. The filthy human"—he winces when I growl—"tried to steal one of our horses. Anders chased after him and when he got close, the human stabbed him!"

"Humans can't be trusted!" a woman cries.

"He doesn't belong here! He'll bring hunters and war!"

"Kill him, Alpha!"

A snarl from me silences the crowd. "Let me think." This is bad. The crowd is determined to kill Kieran. They're fearful, and Kieran's actions tonight have only made them more distrustful. If the whole village decides they want Kieran dead, I won't be able to protect him, but that won't stop me from trying.

I will flood the village with my own people's blood to keep Kieran safe. No. That can't happen. I must find a way to keep Kieran alive while convincing my people he can be one of us. I have to talk to him now and hear his side of the story before I can decide the next step.

"Return to your homes," I tell my people. "The human will be under close watch. Get your rest and in the morning I will have made my choice."

By the time the crowd has trickled away, Anders emerges from the healer's hut. He's still scowling, but his wound appears to have healed. Gunnar stands beside him, arms crossed as he surveys the area like he's expecting an enemy to emerge and strike at our vulnerable brother. Side by side, he and Anders could have been twins. They both share our mother's dark hair, but Gunnar's eyes are silver like mine while Anders's are green like his twin. Remorse shudders through me as I remember Gunnar's shocked, wounded expression.

Odin's beard, I have failed them so. I'm supposed to be the alpha they deserve. Instead, I'm fighting one brother to protect my mate, and I can't convince the other that I'm even half the leader our father was.

Gripping Gunnar's shoulder, I clear my throat. "Apologies, brother."

Gunnar shakes his head, but I can't tell if he's angry with me or not. "Your mate is a human. Why wasn't I told this?"

"You were away when I returned," I say, careful to avoid the subject of his family's graves.

Despite my efforts, sadness touches his face. "It feels like I'm away too often."

It's true, but I don't say so out loud. He disappears into the wilderness so often, sometimes for weeks at a time.

"Did I hurt you?" I ask.

He rolls his shoulders. "Nothing hurts anymore. Not really."

I wince, understanding what he means. When you've gone through the losses Gunnar has, first with losing our parents, then his whole family, physical injuries don't seem so terrible.

Lyall sighs, raking a hand through his golden hair. "You should go home and rest, Anders."

Gunnar frowns thoughtfully. "What *were* you doing out so late?"

Anders scoffs. "What? Are you the only one allowed to walk the streets late at night and brood?"

"I do not brood," Gunnar snaps.

Anders flashes a grin. "You do too."

Sighing, I swing an arm around Anders, gripping Gunnar's sleeve with my fingers, then put my other arm around Lyall. I pull my fool brothers in and hold them close. These men are all I have left in this world, and I keep failing them as their Alpha. "I wish I could be the alpha you deserve. An alpha worthy of Mother and Father's memory."

Lyall butts his head into my shoulder, a wolfish gesture that makes me smile. "You are."

Gunnar cups the back of my neck, gripping hard. "You protected your mate. They would be proud."

Anders says nothing and squirms out of my arms. I ignore how that stings.

"I will make this right," I swear to them. "But I need you all to understand that Kieran is… important to my wolf. He is human. But I have to trust that the Norns chose him to complete me for a reason… or just to drive me to insanity."

They laugh, even Anders.

"I can't lose him." Fear clogs my throat, trying to suffocate me. "But if I try to keep him for myself, my people will only doubt me even more."

Gunnar wriggles free and says, "Then Kieran will have to prove he is worthy of being your mate, human or not."

"How—" The answer comes to me, freezing my insides. "The Hunter's Moon trial? No. No, he would never survive!"

Lyall's face lights up. "Yes! That's it. That's the answer!"

Anders shoves me hard, sending me stumbling. "He ran me through with a silver dagger, no doubt acquired from our enemies! And you want to give him another chance? Are you mad?"

"Why are you being so dramatic?" Lyall rolls his eyes. "Hunters haven't troubled us in years."

"Doesn't mean they won't start now! That human tried to kill me."

"It was just a little cut. I bit the tip of your ear off when we were pups."

Anders snaps his teeth at him. "You were playing, not trying to kill me! If he can make an attempt on my life, he can do the same to any of us!"

My pulse races. I need to broach the idea to Kieran. Lyall is right, the trial may be my only hope of keeping Kieran alive. My people must trust him and for that, he must be worthy.

By the Father Wolf, I only hope he is willing to hear me out.

Clenching my teeth, I push open the door to my bedroom. Kieran is pacing so furiously across the floor it's a wonder he hasn't burned a hole through it. When the door closes behind me, he jumps, spinning toward me. He opens his mouth, then seems to think better of whatever he was about to say and snaps it shut with a scowl.

My mate tried to run away from me. After how coldly I've treated him, it's no wonder, but it only makes me realize what a poor match I am for him. I thought that making him supper would begin a truce between us. Nothing I do is ever the right thing.

Fury at my own incompetence thickens my voice when I growl, "Hold out your arms."

Eyes wide, he complies. I grab the iron cuffs I'd hoped not to use again and snap them back on his arms. This time, I brought some chains for his feet.

"Seriously?" he grumbles.

I yank on his leg and make him step into them, then lock them around his ankles. "I thought I could trust you. I will not make that mistake again." Rising, I glare down at him. He meets my glare head-on, like I couldn't rip him in half with my bare hands. Not that I want to. "Are you mad?" I growl at him. "Leaving my home, fighting with my brother?"

"Oh gee, can you fucking blame me?" he snaps. "You haven't exactly been a gracious, welcoming host! Whyever would I want to leave?"

"You could have been killed!" My roar fills all corners of the room. Finally, he shows some gods-damned fear. I was beginning to think there was no sense in that beautiful red head of his. "Do you understand that, fucking?"

He gapes at me. "That's... not how you use that word."

"Is it not an insult?"

"It is, but—damn it, never mind!"

"Why did you have a silver dagger? The only ones who carry them are hunters." Pain twists through my heart, sudden and savage. Gods. Could the Norns have truly fated me to not just a human, but my pack's enemy?

A muscle twitches in his jaw. "Fuck it. Even if I tell you, why would you take my word for it?"

"I asked because I want to know."

"You wouldn't believe me!" He stomps as best he can in those shackles, so much like the angry waddle of a furious puffin, over to the fire and drops down onto his ass.

Desperation claws at me. He can't push me away, not now. Not when it's imperative that we come together. Before my own pack rips him from me.

"My pack will want a better answer than that!" Kneeling, I grip his jaw and force him to look at me. His glare could melt iron. "Your life is in danger, do you understand that? You attacked a member of our pack with a weapon only our greatest enemies carry, Kieran. They will want blood for blood."

Kieran's throat bobs, his blue eyes softening. Fear clouds his scent. "They'll kill me?"

I wish I could say no. I wish none of this were happening at all. This was never what I imagined happening when I finally found my mate. "Unless you can prove your loyalty to me and this pack, prove that you are worthy of being mine, then they will never trust you. I can protect you from my brothers but not from my whole pack. Their voices will overrule mine, and you will die if that's what they want."

His breathing turns harsh. "F-fuck..." Panting, he draws his knees to his chest and hides his face from me. "Want to go home. I just want to go home. Oh god..."

Pity and terror squeeze my chest. I can't lose him. Without him, I'm lost. Unless we complete the bond. "Listen to me," I say, trying to make my voice softer. I'm not sure if it works. "There is a way we can both get what we want. Among my people, there is an ancient rite. It's called the Hunter's Moon trial. All ulfhednar undertake the trial when they come of age. If you want to earn the pack's respect and trust, you must prove you are a strong, worthy hunter, capable of providing. You must hunt a beast and win."

"Please tell me that by beast you mean a cute little bunny or squirrel..."

"A fellow wolf. You must slay it, don the furs, and become one of us."

Kieran looks up, eyes wide, chest rising and falling as he sucks in oxygen. "I... I can't. I'd never pass."

"I would teach you how. We have a week before the hunter's moon rises. If you are truly dedicated to learning, that's more than enough time to become a novice archer. Once you pass, the pack should be more comfortable having you around the village."

"And how do you benefit from all this?" Kieran asks, cuffed hands shaking.

I wet my lips, considering if I should tell him my condition. "I get you."

His little intake of breath is loud in the quiet.

"You would have to become my mate before I can let you go, Kieran. If I let you go before then, the berserker's rage will consume me, and I will be lost."

Releasing a sigh, Kieran says, "And why should I give a damn what happens to you?"

"Because I'm your only hope of leaving this place alive and returning to your time."

"Fuck." Closing his eyes, Kieran sits in silence for several seconds. "And by 'get me,' you mean..."

Heat flares in my cheeks. I hate that he's making me say it out loud. "After you are made one of us, you must come to my bed. You will lie with me, and I will claim you as mine."

Color rises in his freckled cheeks. "And if I don't want to?"

"You will." I'm sure of it. The gods wouldn't have given me a mate who didn't want me. And he does. No matter how we bicker, I can smell the desire on him every time we fight. He wants me, and I would kill for one night with him. "When the full moon rises, neither of us will be able to resist the urge."

"That sounds horrible."

"Far from it. A mating between two chosen by the Norns is said to be the most intensely pleasurable experience in the world. You can refuse. But why would you want to?"

Rising, Kieran hobbles a few steps, running a hand down the bronze stubble on his jaw. "That's it? Have sex with you, and you'll let me go?" He barks a laugh. "How considerate of you. Meanwhile, I have to do some life-or-death *Hunger Games* bullshit just so your pack doesn't make kibble out of me. Cry some more about how your life sucks."

Gnashing my teeth until it feels like they're breaking, I pace away from him. "If the gods had chosen wisely, you would have already been one of us. Ulfhednar, like me. You would not have to prove a damn thing, or fight for your survival."

Kieran taps his chin thoughtfully. "You know, maybe being killed by a wolf won't be so bad after all. That's more than I can say about being stuck with your moody ass for the rest of my life."

Balling my hands into fists, I whirl around and snap, "Then go ahead and run into the wolf's jaws! You're the very last man on this earth I'd ever choose as my mate!"

Immediately, I want to take the words back. Just because he is being cruel to me does not mean I need to return his barbed remarks. But it's too late. Our bitter words heat the air between us.

Gripping his chains, I urge him toward me. The breathless sound he makes when our bodies come together has my cock thickening. "Despite what you may think of me,

I am not a monster. You will want my bite. I will make certain of it."

Kieran swallows audibly, eyes wide and fearful. "How can I trust you?"

Gripping his jaw, I angle his head and bring my lips to his neck. I breathe in his mountain flower scent, rubbing the bridge of my nose over his skin. "On my hands and knees, I will devote myself to your pleasure."

Closing my teeth around his earlobe, I apply just enough pressure for him to gasp, his lithe body arching against me. "Tell me what you need, and I will worship you, heedless of my own wants and desires. I will only have you when you beg me to. And you will beg. I will not take you until you do."

Curling my fingers in his hair, I pull him in closer, rocking my aching cock against his own arousal. "And I will not give you my seed until you've spilled yours first. Between our bodies. In my mouth. Between my fingers. As many times as I can make you. Even if I have to keep you in my bed until sunrise. By the time I'm through with you, you will be begging for my bite."

I've seen the sun rise over the snow-capped mountains, watched the northern lights dance across the sky, and thought those were the most beautiful sights I'd see in this lifetime. Until him. Everything from his eyes, blue as the ocean, to his freckled cheeks flushed pink when our eyes meet, to hair as bright as the fires of Muspelheim, captivates me so. Even for a human, he is beautiful.

Our arousal makes the room smell like a damned whorehouse. Kieran's panting against my neck, his cock as stiff as iron between us. I'm no better, barely holding back my claws and teeth. I want him beneath me, against a wall, anywhere I can have him—it doesn't matter. Not as long as I *have* him, speared on my cock, howling with pleasure as I claim him. I have to shove him away from me before my berserker takes over.

"Let me know in the morning if you've made your decision." I turn away.

"W-where are you going?" His voice is rough, like he's already been screaming my name for hours.

"I don't trust myself to be in the same room as you. Not smelling like I've already had you beneath me all night." I have to squeeze the doorknob to anchor me, damn near crushing it between my fingers. "Make your choice."

I throw open the door and leave my mate in the bedroom, smelling like every temptation known to man.

It is the single hardest thing I've ever done, but I am certain the anguish will be worth it when I finally get him beneath me.

When I finally make him mine.

Chapter 7
Kieran

The door has barely closed after Wulfric before something in me breaks. As best I can with my wrists cuffed, I wrestle my pants down just low enough to tug my cock free from my underwear. A single stroke has my toes curling, abs clenching, as I fuck my fist.

I hate Wulfric Wolf-Heart. I hate every contradiction he stirs in me. I hate what he's doing to me, asking of me. But more than that, I hate everything he *isn't* doing to me, everything I want him to give me that he keeps refusing me.

I want his mouth on my skin, the scratch of his beard chafing me. I want his body against mine, his cock hard and thick in my hand, my mouth, filling me up.

Every time we're alone together, I want to slap him senseless then throw myself at him. I want to tell him to fuck off, then demand him, beg him, to fuck *me*.

Damn it.

Wulfric is right.

I would beg him to give me what I need, and then I'd beg for more. On my hands and knees, on my back beneath him. I'd let him do whatever the fuck he wants to me and love every second of it. It's disgusting. It's shameful. And I don't care.

Back arching, toes curling, I come so hard I have to clench my teeth to keep from groaning out loud. My release spatters the floor and, face burning, I kneel and clean it up with one of the furs piled on the floor by the fire. Once I've tucked my soft cock away, I stumble to Wulfric's bed and collapse into the furs.

I want to pretend I struggle with the choice presented to me.

That I stay awake for hours, wondering what I should do.

Maybe even plan another escape.

But I don't. I know what my choice is.

And I fucking hate Wulfric for it.

Wulfric made breakfast again, but he isn't at the table. Helga is finishing up her meal and she uncuffs me so I can eat. "Wulfric said you can keep them off the rest of the day. It will make training easier," she says.

I stretch out my arms. "Where's His Royal Alpha-ness?"

She laughs softly. "Out training in the yard with some of the village pups."

Joining her at the table, I take a bite of food. It's delicious, damn it. I hate that I enjoy his cooking. Or feel any of the non-negative things I feel about him. His way of life goes against everything I stand for, all the raiding and pillaging, murdering and enslaving. And it's not like he's got a stellar personality to make up for all of it.

"Where's he training?" I ask. The sooner I speak to Wulfric, the better.

"Behind the house," she answers.

Pulling on a wool sweater over my tunic, I head outside. Wulfric's fairly easy to find; I just follow the shouting of children behind the house. Honestly, I expect to see Wulfric terrorizing the little kids. What I actually find... well, it makes me stop in my tracks and blink twice.

The murderous, pillaging Scandinavian equivalent of a pirate is lying flat on his back in the dirt while a bunch of little kids scream and beat him with sticks. Wulfric's making a strange sound, which I realize is laughter. Wulfric is *laughing.* It's a deep, rich sound that rumbles up from his chest and escapes in a warm, raspy chuckle.

He leaps to his feet so fast it makes me jump and sends the kids scattering, screaming with delight. Snapping his teeth like a wolf, Wulfric pounces on one of the kids, a little girl, and scoops her into the air. He spins her in a circle and she shrieks with laughter while the other kids shout, "Me, me! Do me next!"

Wulfric stumbles to a halt, blond locks flying around his face. Chest heaving, he sets the girl on her feet, tossing back his head so his hair flies out of his eyes. A big toothy grin lights up his face, so radiant it's like the sun breaking through gloomy storm clouds.

My stomach flutters at the sight.

It's a shame he's such a prick. He has the most beautiful smile I've ever seen. Fuck. Why does he almost look... cute right now?

Wulfric sees me, and the smile falls right off his face and—there it is. The storm clouds are back. Good. I wasn't sure what I'd do with a smiling, happy Wulfric.

I slap an obnoxious grin on my face and wave. "Hey! Good morning."

Wulfric grumbles something, not sure what. Could be good morning or go fuck yourself—his scowl doesn't leave a whole lot of room for interpretation.

"Having fun?" I ask, my boots crunching over snow as I go to meet him.

"Just training the pups." He kicks at one of the sticks. "Was the food to your liking?"

I glare at him. "Terrible. There's such a thing as too much salt, you know."

He smirks, and I want to throw something at him. "I'll remember that next time, little rabbit."

That stupid smirk shouldn't set my blood on fire for all the wrong reasons, but it does. My dick likes having his eyes on me, knowing I've made him smirk or scowl. And it *really* likes Wulfric covered in mud, his hair long and loose, and the way he's loosened the strings tying his tunic so his furry chest is exposed.

My face reddens and I try and avoid remembering how furiously I jerked off thinking about him last night. Infuriatingly, his face splits into a wolfish grin, sharp with too many teeth. Fuck. I keep forgetting that he can smell my stupid raging lust. No matter how hard I glower at him, he knows that as much as I want to punch him, I also want to roll around in the mud with him. Pin him down beneath me and tug off his breeches.

Grabbing a sword from where it's propped against a tree, Wulfric approaches a training dummy and takes a swing. The sword sings as it flies through the air, slicing a gash across the dummy's midsection. If that were a real person, they'd be disemboweled, I realize with a shudder.

"Did you come to a decision?"

My food becomes a lump in my stomach. "I did." Bunching my hands into fists, I force the words out. "I'll do your trial. And if I pass the trial, then I'll become your mate."

With a final swing, Wulfric thrusts the sword into the mud. He turns slowly to face me. "You will."

"Yes. And you'll help me return to my time after we're... you know. You won't go all Hulk, or berserk, or whatever, right?"

He nods. "I'll be fine. Mates, chosen or fated, who have bonded can be separated without the alpha going berserk. Unless the mate is killed, of course. Such trauma has pushed many an alpha into losing themselves."

"Okay. Well. I'll try not to get killed after we do the deed. But otherwise, I'll be good to go?"

Wulfric meets my gaze solemnly. "I will let you go. You have my word."

The tightness in my chest disappears. "Really?"

"Aye. My wolf will be settled after our mating. You won't be of any use to me." Yanking the sword from the ground, he spins and swings viciously at the dummy, slicing it nearly in half.

I feel like I hurt him somehow, but maybe that's just guilt. Or Stockholm syndrome or whatever they call it. I'm going to need a shit ton of therapy after this...

Suddenly looking back at me, Wulfric says, "But first, you have to survive the trial."

Right. There's that. My heart sinks into my stomach. "You said you'd train me."

"Of course. Who better to teach you to kill a wolf than a wolf himself?"

"Bet you'll love kicking my ass, huh?"

With a jerk of his head, he motions for me to follow him back to the house. "What weapons are you familiar with?" He opens the door and motions to a rack of weapons in the entryway. I see his axes, a shield mounted on the wall, and a bow with a quiver full of arrows.

"Uh... I have to use a kitchen knife sometimes. You know. For cooking." When he sighs, I snap, "Look at me! You honestly expect me to have any idea how to use a weapon?"

Shaking his head, Wulfric grabs the bow and quiver of arrows. "How do your people survive in your timeline?"

"Things are different." I jog to keep pace as he marches from the house. "Regular citizens don't have to fight for our lives every single day. At least, not physically. Not everyone in your village fights, right?"

"No, but at least one member of the household should know how to wield a blade so he or she can defend their family." Wulfric shoves the bow at me. "A human like you in close quarters with a wolf can only end in disaster. You're better off trying to hunt your prey from a distance and only engage up close if absolutely necessary."

"Okay..." The bow is surprisingly heavy for something so slender. "Show me."

The weight of his stare glides up and down my body as he circles me. My mouth runs dry, my heart rate escalating. Under his piercing eyes, I feel like the prey to his predator. "First, use this to protect your fingers when you draw a bow." He hands me a thick strip of leather that I can tie around my fingers. "Feet shoulder-width apart. Knees bent."

This is a really bad time for my dick to decide I like being ordered around.

"Like this?" For reasons I don't want to admit, I only sort of follow his instructions, spreading my feet just a tad.

A dissatisfied grunt escapes him. "Try... this." And his hands run down the outside of my thighs. "Open your legs."

Swallowing hard, I spread my legs to where he wants them.

"Good." His voice is a low rumble in my ear.

Oh, fuck me.

"Your torso's position can impact the accuracy of your shots. You should turn... this way." I'm like clay in his hands as he shapes me, molding me into the proper position. The breath gets stuck in my throat as he drags his hands down my body, angling me.

"And your head should be at an angle." He's taller than me but leans over to speak low in my ear, his breath heating my skin, his beard ticklish against my cheek. "Like so." One of his big calloused hands comes up to my face. His finger pads are rough as they scrape over my skin, drawing a shudder from me, but certainly not one of revulsion. Gripping my jaw, he angles my head so my chin is level with the ground, my face forward. I swear his thumb glides along my jawline before he drops his hand.

"Keep your arrows in reach at all times." Wulfric slips the quiver across my back. Ripping an arrow from the quiver, he holds it out to me. "Draw the bow. I need to see your posture."

I try and draw back the string and immediately drop the arrow. Heat flares in my cheeks as I brace for Wulfric to mock me. Mark loved to make it clear when I fucked up.

"Here. Try this." The warmth of Wulfric's body presses in close behind me. I know he's strong but damn, it's like a wall of muscle against my back. The heat radiating from him makes the chilly day feel several degrees warmer. Gripping my hand in his, he positions my arm. I'll be feeling his rough skin against mine for hours. "Find your anchor point."

"An anchor point?"

"It's the place you'll return to time and again after every shot. For me, it's under my chin, but it's different for every hunter. Draw the bow."

I draw, fighting the bow's resistance. "Can't," I huff as my arm starts to burn.

"You *can*," Wulfric insists.

"How?" Desperation bleeds into my voice.

"Keep going. Breathe with me, Kieran."

I think that's the first time he's said my name.

Patience is not something I've come to expect from him. He thinks I can do this, and I don't want to disappoint him.

Wulfric's chest expands against me, and I follow his breath in and draw. There's no frustration or sarcastic remarks to disrupt the silence of the woods.

"Find your target," he whispers in my ear.

My hand shakes as I take aim at the training dummy. The arrow whooshes from between my fingers and soars way clear of its intended path, disappearing somewhere in the woods. I exhale around a curse. Damn it! It would have been so cool if I nailed it first try. Wulfric would have been so—

So... what? Impressed? So what if he's impressed? I shouldn't care. I don't. Survival is all that should matter.

An arrow appears under my nose. Wulfric says, "Again."

I'll hear that damn word until the end of time because for the next hour, it's all I hear as I fuck up shot after shot. Drawing the bow gets easier and I become familiar with the posture, but my shots are all crap. How am I going to learn this in six days?

At the end of the day, I go to bed frustrated, arm aching from drawing the bow.

I dream of Wulfric's hands on my skin, his breath hot against the back of my neck.

Wulfric seems to be dedicated to my survival, I'll give him that.

Every day he wakes me up early and takes me out to the woods to practice my archery. By the end of the second day of training, my arm is killing me, but I'm a better shot. My fingers develop calluses as the week nears its end, which makes releasing the arrow less painful even through the leather strip.

Wulfric's patience with me takes me by surprise. He's relentless, and he pushes me to my limits, but no matter how frustrated I get, he never snaps at me or criticizes me when I fuck up a shot. He's not afraid to dole out critiques and I wish he'd praise me more, but I'm learning fast under his guidance.

When I finally manage to hit a training dummy dead center, I turn to him with a huge grin. "Yes! Did you see that?"

Frowning, Wulfric walks around me and approaches the dummy. He runs two fingers along the arrow's shaft until they touch the point of impact. An impressed noise escapes him. He turns to me, a smile softening his rugged features. "An excellent shot."

My chest glows warm with pride. "Thank you."

I did it! I impressed Wulfric.

Wait. Why do I care? All that matters is I hit my target where I needed to.

Clearing his throat, Wulfric rubs his face like he's physically wiping away his smile. There's a patch of pink in his cheeks. It's adorable, even if it's from the cold.

"Since you're taking well to the training, how about we try something different tomorrow?" Wulfric asks as he comes back toward me.

"Sure. I can handle anything."

A low, raspy chuckle rumbles from him. "Cocky, aren't you? We'll see how you fare. Meet me here tomorrow at dawn." He passes by me, then lifts a hand and squeezes the nape of my neck. "Well done," he murmurs, breath warm against my ear, and then he walks away before I can catch my breath.

The next day, I wake by the fire and roll out my shoulders. Rolling over toward the bed, I find it empty. Once I'm dressed, I head outside. The cold nips at me, grass stiff with a light fall of snow crunching beneath my feet. The training yard is empty when I get there except for the training dummies, their straw-filled bodies dusted with snow.

"Wulfric?" I call, my voice echoing for miles.

The hair on the nape of my neck stands up. Something's watching me, but scanning the trees, I see nothing. Until I turn around and every bone in my body freezes.

A wolf the size of a horse strides from the trees, muscles rippling beneath a dense black coat speckled with snow. The wolf's jaws are the length of my forearm, its teeth like thick spikes in its mouth. Razor-sharp claws flatten the grass beneath it. If I weren't so terrified, I'd think this creature is the most beautiful, magnificent beast I've ever seen. All my instincts scream to run and before I can stop myself, I turn tail and bolt. I can climb a tree. If I can just get off the ground, then—

The wind is knocked out of me as the beast collides with me, bowling me over. A cold nose presses against my ear, hot breath hitting my neck in harsh pants. The beast's powerful body rumbles with a growl that makes my heart sink to the pit of my stomach. The wolf's body shudders above me and then a voice says, "Didn't anyone ever tell you not to run from wolves, little rabbit?"

That son of a bitch! I roll onto my back and find not a wolf but Wulfric leaning over me, hands planted in the snow on either side of my shoulders. He's wearing his wolfskin cloak along with his usual tunic and breeches. I'm almost disappointed he's not naked like how werewolves usually are in the movies after a shift. The cloak's hood is a wolf's head minus the lower jaw, as if he's peering at me from within the maw of a wolf itself.

"You... you asshole!" I snap, punching his shoulder. "I thought you were gonna eat me for sure!"

"I ate before you arrived."

"As a wolf?"

A smirk curls his plush lips. "Ate a little lost rabbit whole. Bones and all."

I should *not* be turned on by that. This asshole has messed with my brain. "Is this your idea of flirting? Telling me you'd like to eat me whole? Because if so, it needs serious work. I can't believe I'm saying this, but just a 'did it hurt when you fell out of heaven, baby' would be better than that."

"Did it not arouse you? Do not lie to me. I can smell how much you want me." He cocks his head like he's still a wolf, and some of him still is. His fangs are sharp and there's a wild gleam to his eyes.

"You're smelling me? God, you're creepy. Get off me, you prick." I shove at him until he's up on his feet.

He offers me a hand. I blink at it like this is the first time I've seen it. Before I can reach out, he snatches it away and averts his eyes with an awkward cough. Oh. Did he think I hesitated because I was insulted?

"Why'd you sneak up on me like that anyway?" I ask, dusting snow out of my clothes.

"You'll be hunting a wolf tomorrow night. The time is right for you to practice on one."

I grin. "You mean I get to pepper you with arrows?"

He huffs, glowering at a tree. "Could be less excited about it..."

"And once I'm... *if* I'm successful, I'll become one of you?"

A nod. "Aye." And he walks off into the trees without another word.

"You know, we need to start working on your conversation skills!" I call as I follow him, struggling to keep pace with his long-legged stride. "How are you able to shape-shift like that anyway?"

"There are many stories of how we came to be as we are. They have changed throughout the generations. My father told me that during an especially harsh winter, my kinsmen prayed not to Odin the Allfather but to the great wolf Fenrir. We prayed to hunt as wolves do to provide for our families, and so the Father Wolf sent a mighty beast into the woods for us to hunt. The beast put up a fight. Many warriors died by his fangs and claws before the mighty wolf was finally felled. My great-grandfather drank his blood and consumed his heart, skinned his pelt, and wore it as we do now. He inherited the wolf's strength and became a mighty hunter, and we never had to fear starvation or cold again."

I can certainly see the perks of being able to transform into a fearsome predator at will. "But you're dependent on a mate or else you risk turning into that thing forever." The memory of that huge bipedal wolf makes me shiver.

Wulfric dips his head in a solemn nod. "You make it sound like a curse, but a mate is a cherished person who can save us from the worst of our bestial nature. The one who can help us maintain that balance between man and wolf. It is a blessing."

"Too bad you got stuck with me." My ex got stuck with an overly anxious boyfriend nowhere near as talented as he was. Now Wulfric's stuck with a weak human.

He glances at me but doesn't say anything.

"Gee, Kieran, you're not so bad," I say, poorly imitating his Scandinavian accent.

He only grunts.

What a guy, my Viking captor.

"Here's a good spot." Wulfric stops amid a cluster of trees, branches heavy with frost.

For what? What does he have in store for me?

Swallowing my nerves, I say, "What are we doing? Going to lick a tree, see whose tongue sticks first?"

Wulfric makes a face. "Is that what you do in your time for entertainment?"

I roll my eyes. Don't make jokes around Wulfric. Noted.

"I'm going to shift, and you're going to hunt me."

I choke on the frosty air. "What—"

"I will act as real wolves do, and they are often skittish of humans and will avoid a confrontation unless provoked." Striding toward me, Wulfric says, "Don't let me hear you coming. Don't hold back. If the opportunity to shoot presents itself, do not hesitate. But try and avoid my face. I want to be presentable for the ceremony."

"What ceremony?"

He narrows his eyes at me. "Our mating ceremony on the night of the full moon."

The shock of his words falls heavy into the pit of my stomach. Training for the Hunter's Moon trials has preoccupied so much of my head this week that I haven't stopped to think about what awaits me at the end of all this... if I don't die during the hunt. Something else I am trying hard not to think about. Oh god. I could die trying to kill this wolf, and if I live, then... then I will be mated to Wulfric.

"Kieran." Big hands slap down on my shoulders, making me jump. "Stop."

"W-what?"

"Whatever you're doing now. You cannot hesitate. Hesitation is death."

I try to swallow but even the muscles in my throat are paralyzed.

Wulfric shoves my bow against my chest and squeezes my stiff fingers, making them curl around the wood. His steady hands make me envious. How can he be so fearless? "You did this trial, right?"

"To earn my furs, aye. All ulfhednar undertake the Hunter's Moon trial."

"Weren't you freaked out? Scared, I mean."

I expect ridicule for even asking. Surely a great and powerful alpha like Wulfric has never known fear. He probably popped out of the womb, cut his own umbilical cord with an axe, and killed his first enemy by age one.

"Terrified." Wulfric turns away from me and surveys the woods. The trees tower over him, making him appear small. "I forget that I was human once. Vulnerable in ways ulfhednar are not. Many undertake the trial. Many do not survive. I wasn't sure I would live to don my furs as my ancestors did before me. But I did. As will you. The gods would not give you to me only to tear us apart. This I believe, even if I question their choice of mate."

"Not exactly my first choice either," I grumble. At least it will only be temporary. And once I'm back to my timeline, good riddance to him. Although, once past his constant scowls and the fact that he has a giant monster inside him on a hair trigger, Wulfric isn't that bad. He's growing on me. Kind of like a benign tumor.

"Turn away. I will shift, and you will pursue me."

I do as he says, facing a tree and closing my eyes like I'm a kid playing hide-and-go-seek again. Frost crunches under huge paws. I wait a few seconds longer, then open my eyes and turn around. Wulfric is gone, but his huge paws left an easy trail to follow. Still, I'll need to be quiet so he doesn't know I'm following him.

Freeing an arrow from my quiver, I bend my knees and creep into the trees to begin the hunt.

A black wolf the size of a horse seems like it would be easy to track, but Wulfric is surprisingly stealthy. His dark coat blends in with the shadows of the woods and boulders. The only reason I can track him at all is because of the snow. When I glimpse a ripple of movement between the trees, I freeze with my heart in my throat.

I know he's still human, but it's hard to convince the primal instincts screaming *Predator!* at me that the huge wolf prowling through the trees still has a human mind. It doesn't seem like he's heard me coming as he lopes farther into the trees. Am I supposed to... what, shoot at him? What if I hurt him?

Well, he did tell me to hunt him. If I don't, he'll probably bitch and moan at me later. Swallowing hard, I grab an arrow and draw back the bow, inhaling deep. The muscles in my arm begin to burn as I aim, and my fingers shake. And... now! I release the arrow, heart racing. It bounces off a tree next to Wulfric. The big wolf gives me the bitchiest look I've ever seen on an animal, then takes off into the trees.

"Damn it!" I mutter and give chase.

For almost an hour, Wulfric makes me track him through the woods. A few times I make the stupid mistake of being upwind, which blows my scent toward him, or snapping a twig under my boot, or tripping and stumbling through the brush. But I get an idea. I decide to wait him out. Wulfric is expecting me, after all. If he thinks I got lost and lets his guard down, that could work to my advantage.

So I park my butt behind a tree and wait. Wulfric keeps going on ahead while I get as comfy as I can on the cold, hard ground. Kind of wish I brought some snacks. Some time passes. I close my eyes as I take in deep, refreshing breaths of the forest air. The woods are nice and quiet. It's almost relaxing. I never had time to just chill like this back in my time.

After an indefinite amount of time, the unmistakable snapping of twigs and rustling of leaves gets louder and louder. Yawning quietly, I grab my bow and peer around the tree. The big black wolf sniffs the ground, then looks both ways. A confused whine is tugged from his chest. Aww. He almost sounds like a dog missing his family.

I draw the bow as he turns in the other direction, looking west. With the perfect shot all lined up, I fire—only for Wulfric to move a few inches to the left. A pained yelp makes me gasp. Wulfric lifts his back leg, snapping at the arrow embedded in his flank but unable to pull it out.

Oh fuck! I would have just shot the ground near his paw. I didn't want to *hit* him!

"Wulfric!" I throw down my bow and dash around the tree as the big wolf collapses onto his side. Shit! How bad is it? What if I nicked a super important artery or something and he's about to bleed out?

Kneeling in the mud, I hover my hand over the arrow protruding from his leg. The dark fur around the injury is already glistening with blood. "I am so sorry! I didn't mean to hit you!" Fuck, what do I do? I grab the arrow shaft and wince when Wulfric whines, clawing at the ground. "I know, I know! I'm sorry!" His pained whines are killing me. He kicks at me, trying to crawl away.

"No, don't move!" I grab handfuls of his fur and tug him back down. His silver eyes are so wide, the whites are visible, and a snarl curls his lip. A quiver racks his body. Is he... scared? Shit. He'd mentioned how much trouble humans have caused. Could being injured and vulnerable bring back some bad memories?

"Wulfric." Carefully, against every instinct I have, I touch his side and begin to rub. His fur is coarse and thick, matted with leaves and a bit dirty but still surprisingly pleasant. "I'm sorry. I'm going to help you, okay? Just... trust me. I have to get it out, okay?"

Wulfric growls.

"I'll do it quickly, and I'll warn you before I do. I promise."

With a resigned groan, Wulfric lays his head back down.

"Just don't bite me, please." I grasp the arrow shaft. "I'm going to pull in one, two... three!"

I yank as hard as I can and Wulfric yelps as I wrench the arrow free. Some blood gushes down his leg but before my eyes, the wound knits itself closed. I continue petting him until the blood has stopped flowing. Exhaling, I pat his ribs. "There. Feeling better?"

His body ripples below me and in seconds he's human and lying in the dirt. His heaving breaths slow and he relaxes against the ground. I can't seem to pull my hand away from his body. His pained whines continue to play on repeat in my head.

"I'm so sorry. I wanted to hit the ground, not your leg. You moved at the last second."

Wulfric just shakes his head. "That was a good shot. If you do that tomorrow, it should slow the beast down."

"Are you okay? It doesn't hurt?"

"I've had worse." Wulfric shrugs. It's not reassuring. I don't like the idea of him being hurt like that.

"Wulfric. Come on. Be honest."

Silver eyes find mine. "The wound healed cleanly. I'm fine."

Blowing out a breath, I glance at the hole in his trousers where the arrow entered him in his wolf form. "Seriously, if you need me to get you something—"

"Kieran." Wulfric grabs my hand, making my heart leap. His gaze leaves mine, lingering on where our hands meet. The sensation of his warm, calloused skin on mine feels good. Really good. Wulfric wets his lips and looks away. "Thank you."

"For shooting you in the ass?"

He snorts. "For..." While he finds his words, his thumb traces circles into my skin. "For helping me."

Something that feels suspiciously like affection warms my chest when I notice his blush. "No problem. And hey, your wolf form is adorable."

He glares at me. "A predator is *not* adorable, Kieran."

"Have you seen your big ears and fluffy tail? They're precious!"

Scowling, Wulfric shoves to his feet. I follow him back to the village, teasing him all the way.

For some reason he lets me, and I don't realize that I've stopped trailing behind him until I find myself suddenly by his side. Our hands knock together as we walk. He doesn't push me away, doesn't demand I walk behind him in some show of superiority. It feels like we're on equal footing or closer to it than before.

But what scares me is that I don't hate it.

Not even a little.

Chapter 8
Wulfric

THE DAY OF KIERAN'S trial arrives. Dismissing the thralls from the kitchen, I gather a hunk of boar's meat from the morning's hunt and boil it in a pot until it is falling off the bone. I melt a hunk of butter in a pan and stir in some chopped leeks and greens and a handful of mustard seeds. I boil some wheat with the stock from the boar meat, then throw it all together and stir. There we have it, a hearty feast for a hunter of wolves.

"Is he awake yet?" Helga asks.

Grabbing three bowls, I fill them with the boar stew. "Bathing."

She sighs softly as I hand her the bowl. "I hope the lad will be well. He's only just learned how to use that bow."

I squeeze my wooden bowl so hard I hear it crack. "I taught him well. His aim will be true." It must be.

Helga tastes a mouthful of the stew and hums her satisfaction. "Are you not worried for him?"

"No." My heart trips in my chest and a low chuckle escapes Helga.

"Oh, lad. You're fond of him, aren't you?"

"Hardly." I shovel down a mouthful of stew. Kieran should hurry up with his bath. His food will get cold. "He's still human. If he can't prove his worth as a hunter and as my mate to our pack, then I have no use for him." Harsh, mayhap, but true. In this life, if you're not strong enough to fight or provide for your loved ones, then this world will eat you alive. Death would be kinder. And yet... the image of a wolf's jaws around Kieran's throat fills me with icy dread.

Kieran gets lost in his thoughts and freezes up rather than making a decision. That cannot happen, not today. He must not hesitate or he will die and I... I can't lose him. For my own sake. Not because I care for him in any capacity.

Grinding my molars, I say, "If he's so weak he can't kill one wolf, then what good is he?" I stab my spoon into my bowl and shove the food down my throat.

Helga smiles and reaches out, her fingers settling on the back of my hand. "Mayhap you could convince your brothers with that tone of yours, but not me. You need not worry for the lad. The gods would not bring you together just to tear you apart."

"Not worried," I say around a mouthful of food.

The sauna room door adjacent to the kitchen creaks and Kieran comes in, skin dewy from steam, red hair sleek and flat from moisture. From what I heard, Kieran insisted on lugging water from the hot springs himself rather than make the thralls get off their hides and do it for him.

"Come eat." I motion at his steaming bowl.

"Smells good," he remarks, sliding into the seat opposite me and tucking in. He moans softly, and pride flares in my chest like it always does. My wolf and I delight in providing for him, pleasing him.

Kieran asks, "When does the trial begin?"

"Around midday," I answer. "Wolves are most active at night, so they will be sluggish during the day."

"An easier target," Kieran guesses.

"No." I slam my spoon down and glare at him. "Nothing about this will be easy! Get that thought from your head, or you won't survive this trial."

He's unfazed by my short temper. If anything, a smile hooks the corner of his soft lips. "Worried about me?"

Why is he the second person to think I'm worried?

"No, but you should be." My jaw's so tight I can hardly get the words out. He could die, and he's sitting here making jests.

"I'm the one who has to kill a fucking wolf," Kieran snaps. "I am worried. I think. It hasn't really set in yet." He chews his lower lip.

"You'll do well, lad," Helga says. "Just focus on keeping your distance, and make sure your aim is true."

And don't die. You can't die.

I keep those fears locked away in my heart and finish my meal.

A light snow falls as my brothers and I lead Kieran to the woods. The villagers watch as we pass, forming a line in the streets to wait for Kieran's return. Excited whispers carry through the air. They want to know if they'll have a new Alpha-Mate when the moon rises, or if I will return from the woods alone.

Gunnar was hunting in the woods yesterday when he caught a wolf's trail, and he leads us now through the trees toward where he last scented the beast.

The quiver of arrows across Kieran's back rattles with every step he takes. His face is stony, devoid of any humor. The reality of what awaits him in these woods must have set in. He knows he'll either be walking out of these woods victorious or he'll meet his end.

No matter what happens, I can't interfere. This is Kieran's trial, and he must earn this victory.

"My brothers and I will accompany you to observe the fight," I tell him.

"But you won't be able to help me if—"

"No." I force out the word, squeezing my fists together. "Use every technique you learned in practice. Hunting a wolf is the ultimate challenge, but it is not impossible."

Kieran breathes in frantic puffs that cloud in the cold air.

At my side, my fingers twitch in an aborted attempt to reach out and comfort him. But what good would words or gestures do? They will not help keep him alive.

Ahead of me, Lyall scents the air. "I smell a wolf."

Gunnar narrows his eyes. "Just one?"

A wrinkle creases Lyall's nose. "Aye. A loner. Smells sick."

"And look, prints." Gunnar points at the snow. "This looks like the place where I scented him yesterday." He tips his head back and sniffs. "Trail's stale. But his tracks lead west toward where the reindeer herd is."

Behind us, Anders snorts. "You really think the human can handle one wolf, even a sick one? He's as good as meat."

Grinding my teeth so I don't lash out at him, I forge ahead.

"I don't know," Lyall says, a wry smile curling his lips. "He got you pretty good, didn't he?"

Kieran gives him an appreciative smile.

Right. Lyall has a point. Human or not, Kieran still has a fire in him. Mayhap he stands a chance against the beast after all.

A growl rumbles from Anders. "Of course *you'd* defend the human."

A curious arch to his brow, Kieran turns to Lyall. "What does that mean?"

"Odin's balls, all of you shut up!" Gunnar snaps, his teeth flashing white beneath his bushy black beard. "The wolf will hear you coming for miles, and we'll be stuck out here all bloody day. Human, take the lead. You're the one supposed to be following the wolf's trail."

"R-right." Hurrying ahead, Kieran follows the wolf's tracks. He's not the best tracker and occasionally loses the trail in places where the snow is too thin to leave a trace behind, but Gunnar sets him back on the right track.

Distant bleating makes me cock my head in the direction of the noise. "There's a herd to the southwest. That's where our wolf will be."

Kieran swallows visibly. "A lone wolf's going to take on a whole herd?"

Gunnar makes a disapproving noise in the back of his throat. "Not bloody likely. But he'll pick off the sick or the young." Suddenly, Gunnar kneels, brows furrowing as he reaches out and touches the earth. "Something's disturbed them. They're on the move. Heading north. Must have spotted our wolf."

"No. It's more than that." Lyall sniffs the air.

Kieran looks from one brother to the next. "What?"

"Blood," Lyall says. "Our wolf's or a reindeer's."

We pick up the pace, moving in the direction of the herd. As we break free from the trees, a herd of reindeer runs up the hill from the field below. The wind carries the scent of freshly spilled blood to my nose. Saliva floods my mouth. It's not wolf's blood I smell.

Kieran gasps. "Look!" He points.

A reindeer calf lies twisted on the ground, and gorging itself upon the carcass is a white wolf with blood-matted fur. The wolf is young but full grown and holds its left back leg close to its body. From the smell of the wound, it's been infected for some time. "Do not underestimate it," I say to Kieran. "That beast is sick but still a worthy opponent if it could take down a calf of that size." Kneeling beside Kieran, I say, "Take aim and strike while it is distracted."

"O-okay." Kieran's voice wobbles. Adjusting his stance just like we practiced, Kieran takes in a breath and draws the bow back. I follow his line of sight and with a sinking feeling in my gut realize his shot will be off seconds before he lets the arrow fly.

The arrow soars, landing with a *thwack!* beside the wolf. The beast startles from his meal and runs, limping away into the trees before Kieran can shoot again.

I sigh, and Lyall groans in sympathy. Anders tosses back his head and laughs. "Seems to me the human must have spent practice doing something else. On his back, mayhap, with you, brother?"

A growl rumbles up from my chest as I stare Anders down.

Kieran's nostrils flare as he glares at Anders, but he doesn't bother with a retort. Before I can stop him, he shoots off down the hill and pursues the wolf into the trees.

"Kieran!" I call, my heart stopping at the idea that he might come face to face with an injured, desperate animal.

Ignoring Anders's snide remarks, I follow Kieran down the hill and back into the cover of the woods. I can't interfere, so this need to have him in my sights makes no sense. If anything, watching him fight while unable to intervene will drive me mad. But I have to see him, to know that he's okay.

Kieran has covered ground fast in his pursuit. As I run, the ground slopes up, growing steeper. "Kieran, wait up!" The trees grow thick around me and conceal him from sight. His scent is tangled up with the smells of the forest. Panic claws at me. Where is he?

Where is my—

A furious snarl echoes through the trees to my left. The beast inside me roars, and I don't know if I'll be able to hold back if Kieran's been hurt. A flash of white through the forest has me running faster. The trees thin, revealing a narrow cliffside with a steep drop into the forest below. When Kieran and the wolf come into view, I have to drive my claws into a tree trunk to keep from sprinting in and ripping the wolf to pieces for threatening what's mine.

Kieran doesn't smell hurt, not yet, but his heartbeat thunders in my ears.

The wolf bristles with fury. The beast has trapped itself against a boulder, favoring its injured leg. But a cornered animal is the most dangerous kind.

Drawing the bow taut, Kieran prepares to strike.

But so does the wolf. The muscles coil, its body pressing low as it gathers all its strength for one final blow.

I know what's coming. I've seen hunters lose their lives just like this time and again. Kieran thinks he's won. In the time it takes to line up his shot and fire, the beast will have already struck. If Kieran misses, he's a dead man. If I run fast, I can get to him. I can stop this. I—

The wolf pounces just as Kieran shoots. The arrow misses the wolf by inches. Then its jaws are around Kieran's throat, and he's crushed beneath the wolf's body. His bow tumbles out of reach.

"No!" I rip my axe from my belt.

"Don't!" Lyall slams into me and pins me against the tree. "You can't interfere, brother. If you do, Kieran dies at the fangs and claws of our pack."

"Let me go!" I roar, fangs sharp in my mouth.

Lyall flinches but shoves back against me, his arm trapping my neck against the tree. "Have faith in him! The Norns wouldn't be so cruel."

Snarling, I grind my teeth, driving my claws into the bark until sap sticks to my fingertips. From here, I can only watch as Kieran and the wolf struggle. Kieran's strangled shouts tear at me. I can't bear to watch, but I can't look away as the pair thrash around.

With a shout, Kieran tugs an arrow from his quiver and stabs at the wolf. Yelping, the wolf stumbles off, snapping at the arrow lodged in its shoulder. Kieran rips a dagger from his belt and shouts, urging the wolf toward the steep edge of the cliff and effectively cornering it. The wolf lunges, its front legs grappling around Kieran's shoulders, jaws snapping toward his face. They struggle, and Kieran's back ends up facing the cliffside. Drawing back his arm, dagger in his grasp, Kieran plunges the blade toward the wolf's neck.

This is it. He's done it. He won. He—

The wolf snares Kieran's shoulder between its teeth, and both man and wolf plummet from the cliff's edge and disappear from view.

"Kieran!" I roar, charging toward the edge. Gunnar and Lyall both grab my arms as if they knew I'd go leaping down after him if there was a chance I could save him.

The first thing I see is blood, a pool of it beneath Kieran and the wolf. Kieran lies atop the wolf, motionless. Bile rises in my throat and regret claws at me, dragging me down until I fear I will drown in it. He was just a human. He didn't belong in this world. If I had never laid eyes on him, if I had just stayed away...

Gods. I should have been better to him. I should have appreciated the one and only mate the Norns gifted me instead of yearning for another.

Closing my eyes, I sink into despair.

"Brother, look!" Lyall says, his voice full of hope.

Kieran lies still. So still that my heart stops and I fear the worst.

Then his chest swells around a great inhale, and he bolts upright. Leaves are tangled in his red locks, and dirt streaks his freckled cheeks. Lyall stumbles away from me, wide-eyed and mouth gaping. Slowly, Kieran pushes himself up, and the sun frames him in golden light. He yanks on the dagger he stabbed into the wolf's eye seconds before the fall and holds it up triumphantly to the sunlight as his face breaks into a radiant smile.

The breath catches in my throat.

I'm in awe of him, this little human whose heart beats with the strength and bravery of a wolf.

How could I have thought for one moment that this man wasn't worthy of being my mate?

I see now it is I who was not worthy. I let myself be distracted by all that he isn't instead of trying to see all that he is. His kind heart and smart mouth, his compassion for even the lowest castes of society, the strength of his spirit for thriving in this world so unlike his own.

Gods, forgive me for being so foolish. I only hope he will allow me to make it up to him by proving myself a mate deserving of him.

"A thrilling hunt, Kieran!" Lyall and Gunnar carefully climb down to meet him.

Leaning on a rock, Kieran exhales shakily. "Thought I was a goner there for a second."

Gunnar nudges the corpse with his boot. "A good kill. You should be proud."

Kieran meets my eyes. Before I can go to him, Anders bursts through the trees behind me. Shoving past me, he looks from the wolf to Kieran, unharmed, and rounds on me. "This is a trick! You interfered, didn't you, Wulfric?"

I chuckle, unfettered by his rage. "Not at all! The glory goes to Kieran."

Kieran stands up straighter and sticks out his chest. "Yup. I did that."

A burst of laughter escapes Anders, and he howls until he's doubled over. His humor fades as he looks among us like he's waiting for someone to tell him who really killed the wolf. "You... you're serious? No. No, it can't be." His reaction doesn't sit well with me. As Anders's heart races out of control, I realize my brother's not just angry; he's terrified. "He's going to be one of us? An outsider?"

Folding my arms, I meet his gaze head-on. "Aye. He will." Kieran has proved himself worthy of being one of us. He should never have needed to prove his worth to me, though. I should have trusted the Norns.

Turning away from his outraged face, I rush to Kieran's side.

My relief and worry wage war inside me. I'm shaking from how close I came to losing him. "You could have been killed."

Kieran's smile falls off his face. I didn't mean for my words to come out so harsh. "I know. I forgot a lot of my training."

I fold my arms so I don't reach out to him. "You did. It could have cost you your life. By all rights, you shouldn't have survived. You're human. Soft and weak."

"Brother," Lyall begins sharply.

I push on, ignoring him. "That's what I believed. No matter how hard I trained you, you could never be one of us. The events of today have shamed me."

Kieran winces. "Wulfric—"

I take one step, then another, and yank him into my arms, holding him to my chest. "Never in my life have I been more wrong about another as I was about you, my mate. I am so sorry that I ever doubted you."

Kieran goes still in my arms with a soft, shaky gasp.

I hide my face in his hair, my lips brushing against his ear when I say, "You fight with the bravery and cunning of any wolf, little rabbit. Never let anyone tell you otherwise."

Slowly, Kieran lifts his arms and wraps them around my shoulders. It's a stiff, awkward embrace at first, until he leans into me with a quiet sigh, squeezing me tight. My wolf preens, loving how near he is, the way his scent wraps around me like a blanket.

"So, I did it?" Kieran asks, looking up at me with wide eyes. "I passed the trial, right?"

My mouth twitches into a smile I quickly stifle. He's cute when he's nervous. "There was another part of the trial I neglected to mention. You must kill three other animals. A raven. A salmon. A bear. Only then—"

"Are you kidding me?"

I can't help it and burst into laughter at his shocked face. "I'm only teasing you. Aye. You passed. Once you don the furs tonight, you will officially be one of our pack."

And worthy of being my mate, but I don't say that part aloud. He knows.

He exhales, shoulders sagging in relief. "You asshole. Don't joke like that." He shoves my shoulder, practically pouting. "Your face is so damn serious all the time it's hard to tell when you're joking or not."

"Apologies." Reaching out, I wipe a smear of blood from his freckled cheek. "Are you hurt?"

"N-no. Not badly." He touches his neck. A shiver runs down my spine. I almost lost him. Never again will I know fear like that. From this moment on, Kieran will have the protection of my pack's name and my body. I will throw myself in front of a whole pack of ravenous wolves if it means keeping him safe.

"Let's get you home and prepared for the feast."

Draping my furs around his shoulders, I lead him back to the village.

As the sun bleeds the sky red, I skin the wolf Kieran hunted. I work with sure, steady hands but inside, my heart won't stop racing. When I realized Kieran was human, it was like my heart had been torn from my chest. I thought I would miss out on so many experiences ulfhednar couples share, such as shifting and running together. My heart quivers knowing that tonight I will get to see my mate experience the thrills of the shift for the first time.

Once the pelt has been skinned carefully and expertly, if I say so myself, I tuck it under my arms and step out into the darkening village. The sun has gone down, and the moon is bright in the night sky, almost completely full. Come Frigga's Day tomorrow, it will be a full moon, and Kieran and I will mate.

Excitement flutters through my stomach as I make my way through the village and into the woods where we hold the rituals. A crowd has gathered around a rune stone painstakingly chiseled from a boulder. It is stained with wolf's blood and decorated with the bones of prey animals and wolves. A shrine to Fenrir.

There's the beat of drums, sounding like thunder on the horizon. When the crowd parts and my eyes land on Kieran, it's like a hook pulls in my chest, urging me to go to him. He looks small beneath the shrine, his face streaked with wolf's blood and ashes from the burned body. Blood smears his mouth from the wolf's heart he would have consumed prior to joining us. I almost chuckle imagining his reaction. Pride courses through me. How could I have been so wrong about him?

He has been baptized. The time is now.

Holding out the fur, I say words I have spoken many times before but tonight they have new meaning. "You are one of us now. Blood of our blood and flesh of our flesh. We are your pack. I am your Alpha. You will never hunt or howl alone in this life."

A shaky sigh escapes him, and his eyes are wide. With trembling hands he clasps the fur and pulls it over his shoulders. As soon as the wolf's white fur falls over his head, the change begins. Kieran drops to all fours and gasps, limbs jerking as fur spreads down his body.

Reaching out, I grab his hand as it becomes a white paw and hold on tight. "I am with you," I promise him. "I am here. Don't fight this. Embrace who you were meant to be."

Wide blue eyes find mine beneath the hood as he pants through a mouthful of fangs. "W-Wulfric..."

"You can do this." I cup his face in my hands. "Let go."

A strangled snarl escapes him and his face shifts from man to wolf. In seconds, where a man once knelt is a beautiful wolf with fur so bright and white it makes the moon look dull by comparison.

The wolf's glorious blue eyes find mine and a little whine escapes him, full of confusion and awe. I take his face between my hands and whisper, "You are more beautiful than the moon itself."

His tail wags and he bumps his head into my nose. *Ouch.* Laughing, I tug my hood on and let the change take me as well.

The pack howls their greeting around us, having shifted while Kieran was undergoing his transformation. On all fours, I approach Kieran as a wolf. His mountain flower scent coaxes a pleased rumble from my chest and makes my tail wag. Reaching out, I touch his forehead with the tip of my nose, then rub my body along his, greeting him as any mate would.

To my surprise, he leans his long, lanky body into me and almost falls when I wander out of his reach. Before I can walk away, Kieran chases after me, sniffing me everywhere, tail wagging furiously. Then he drops into a play bow, wagging tail high in the air.

Joy surges through me, and I tackle him. We wrestle then break apart, and he runs off into the woods, commanding me to give chase. Just like I've always dreamed of, I run beside my mate beneath the glowing northern lights.

Chapter 9
Kieran

The wedding... mating ceremony, whatever they call it, happens on Frigga's Day, the day after my trial. All weddings are held on Frigga's Day, the day dedicated to the goddess of marriage and fertility. No one in the village seems to care that two guys are getting mated. To me, it's pretty cool. Wulfric's union to a man is being celebrated over a thousand years before same-sex couples were allowed to get married.

It's a fact I try and distract myself with to keep from acknowledging that today I'm getting married—mated—to a man I barely know who took me captive. A man who barely more than a week ago said he would never see me as his mate.

Except somehow I don't think that's still how he feels. After I killed that wolf, the way he looked at me was... different. Like he saw me in a new light. The awe in his eyes as he knelt before me, holding out the wolf's pelt, still makes me shiver when I recall it.

When I shifted for the first time, I saw the whole world differently. Like someone had flicked a switch in my brain. My vision was sharper. Every scent commanded my attention. I was faster than I'd ever been on two legs and all the anxious noise in my head finally shut up. All that mattered was smelling all the smells, chasing whatever moved, and then... then I smelled him.

As Wulfric's huge black wolf came toward my smaller white one, he eclipsed everything and everyone else. His scent was familiar and yet so different, like the world I'd found myself in. The crisp mountain air and pine tree aroma that always clung to him was even more pronounced. Wulfric smelled like my past and my present all rolled into one.

He smelled... like *mine*.

As I think back on that moment while lying on my furs by the hearth, I shake my head. I don't know how else to describe the primal urge that came over me in that moment. A rush of possessiveness and need I'd never felt for anyone before.

Good thing my wolf seems to like him. I just wish I was surer of how I feel toward him. I mean, he's not a complete asshole. He's cooked meals for me so I don't go hungry, trained me, and I owe my survival to him. Without Wulfric, I could never have passed that trial.

Now it's time for me to keep my end of our bargain... and mate with him.

Groaning, I yank the furs up to my face and hide in them.

It's not like having sex with him will be a hardship at all. I can imagine it all too easily. It's the whole marriage part. At least, I assume mating with a werewolf is the wolfy equivalent of a human marriage.

Oh god. *Is it?*

I still don't know shit about ulfhednar.

The door swings open and Helga practically skips inside. "Wake up, lad! It's your big day!"

"Don't remind me," I grumble into the furs.

"Get out of bed, break your fast, and then meet Lyall in the woods."

Rubbing my eyes, I sit up. "Where specifically? Am I looking for a special tree stump or something?"

She laughs. "You're ulfhednar now, lad. You'll find them by their scent."

I sit at the table and she plops a bowl in front of me. It's some kind of porridge. Closing my eyes, I sniff and recoil.

Helga's eyes twinkle with amusement. "I still remember my first shift."

"It's like I was living in black and white and someone went and switched on the Technicolor."

She cocks her head, clearly confused.

"Nothing." I sniff the bowl again, parsing through the ingredients. "Leeks. Barley. Some kind of fish? And something else. Something herby."

"Aye, that would be the angelica you're smelling."

"And the fish?" I lift a spoonful and blow away steam.

"That would be stockfish."

Never heard of it, but it tastes pretty good. My mind wanders to memories of my shift last night.

"How does it feel being one of us, lad?" she asks.

I stare at my hand, expecting to sprout claws. I've seen Wulfric do it seemingly on command. "Well, the trial sucked. It was a horrible experience. Then you had me eat that disgusting heart." My gag reflex prickles just remembering. "I didn't think anything could be worth that, except my life, obviously. But then I shifted and... it felt amazing."

She grins. Her teeth are stained and she's missing a few. I wish I could find a way to bring my knowledge of modern dental hygiene here. People could really benefit from the advancements in the future. "Doesn't it?" She sighs wistfully.

"I can't wait to do it again. It was so... freeing! My head is such a noisy place."

"Oh?" Concern knits her brows.

"Yeah. I second-guess everything. I worry all the time. But as a wolf, all of that nonsense just went away. Everything got so quiet." It's crazy that I had to become a werewolf to feel the way normal people without anxiety must feel. "I wish I could feel that way all the time."

She hums thoughtfully and stirs her stew. "Wulfric feels that way at times."

I can't stop the snort I make. "Yeah, right. Like that guy ever worries about anything."

"Oh, he does. Being Alpha is very hard. He must make decisions that impact our community every single day."

When she says it like that, I feel like an asshole. So many of my own anxieties are about stupid shit that shouldn't even matter but that my brain can't stop picking at. I could never be a leader like Wulfric. "I wouldn't even think that he gets anxious. He's so..."

Wulfric's everything I'm not. A warrior. Confident. Brave and strong. I could never be good enough for him. I shake my head to clear it. Why do I care about being enough for Wulfric? It's not like we're friends or even dating. The mating ceremony is for his sanity's sake and so I won't be targeted by his pack. How he feels about me isn't important.

"Where is Wulfric anyway?" I ask. "Does he have to do some ritual, too?"

"Oh, he'll be off hunting for you, to prove he can provide."

"What about me? Do I need to do any more rituals?"

"Go and meet Lyall. He'll aid you."

Once breakfast is done, I wander outside and look around for Lyall. Right. I'm a wolf now. That's going to take getting used to. Breathing in deep, I wrinkle my nose when an abundance of smells hits me all at once. It takes me a moment to pick apart each scent that clouds the air, but I know I've caught Lyall's trail when I find it.

In the woods beyond the house, I follow Lyall's scent up a hill. There's a big tree that looks like it's been there forever, its branches reaching high enough to overlook the village. Lyall sits at the foot of the trunk, head back and eyes closed. His long golden hair blows loose about his face, a face so like his brother's, just softer where Wulfric's is stony.

"Lyall?"

His bright eyes fly open, and my acute hearing doesn't miss his sharp intake of breath.

"Sorry. Didn't mean to disturb your nap."

"Wasn't sleeping." The sunlight filters through the tree's leaves, shining on his face. Bags hang under his heavy-lidded eyes. It doesn't look like he slept at all last night.

I plop down beside him and yawn. "Last night wore me out."

He hums, closing his eyes. "I can only imagine." His baritone is softer than Wulfric's, who manages to sound like he's growling every word most of the time. "You did well."

What happened after my shift is a blur, but most of what I remember is of Wulfric. Running with him. Hearing him howl. The way he rubbed along my body. "How old were you when you first shifted?"

"Old enough to wield an axe and draw a bow." He runs a hand over his beard, bushy and decorated with a few beads. "It's been a long while since we've had a successful Hunter's Moon ceremony. Only the most worthy survive the trials." Rising to his feet, Lyall says, "Come, brother! Let us hunt."

I don't know what to be more confused about, that he considers me family so easily or that we're going hunting again. "You don't need to call me that, you know. I haven't done anything to earn it."

Lyall looks bewildered. "Of course you have. You're part of our pack now, Kieran. From here on out, we're brothers, you and I."

For some reason, a lump gets stuck in my throat. "Oh. You really feel that way?"

"Of course!" He smiles, bright and warm as the sunshine.

To be accepted by him so simply warms my heart. My own family never accepted me or made me feel like I was good enough, but somehow this pack who I've only known a short while is slowly welcoming me as one of their own. "Thank you." I clear my throat. "So, we're hunting?"

"Aye. It's tradition. Every mating ceremony, the mated pair must present the other with prey they hunted themselves. Proof they can provide."

"That's... cute." And completely archaic.

As if sensing my reluctance, Lyall elbows me, grinning. "Relax. We're only hunting something small."

"Oh. Like a rabbit?"

He guffaws, slapping his thigh. "A rabbit! Mayhap that's suitable, aye, for a farmer's son! But not for an alpha like Wulfric." Grabbing my shoulders, he steers me down the hill. "Come! We're hunting my brother a bear cub!"

My mouth falls slack. "What? No!"

We don't hunt a bear cub, thank fuck. Lyall is much easier to talk out of stupid ideas than Wulfric. We do bring down a reindeer, though. We spend the whole afternoon stalking the beast. Lyall's wolf is huge like his brother's, so I'm able to drape the reindeer calf over his back.

"The herds are getting thinner."

I jump, alarmed when a very Scandinavian voice speaks very close by me. "What was that?" I look every which way but there's nothing around us except wild, rugged wilderness.

With a noise similar to laughter, Lyall bumps his huge head into the small of my back.

"Me, my friend. I can feel you through our bonds ever since you shifted." Lyall's voice rings through my head.

"Bonds?"

"Aye. When we're shifted, every pack has the ability to communicate through the bonds that connect us to each other. When you became ulfhednar, you became pack."

I rub my chest, not feeling any different. "So you can communicate with everyone in your village?"

He sneezes, then gives his big shaggy head a shake. *"No. Can you imagine how loud it would get up here?"* His face breaks into a wolfy grin. *"It's only with our immediate family or those we have a very close bond to."*

A memory of Anders's snarling face makes me shiver. "I won't be able to hear Anders's thoughts, will I?"

"No. He barely communicates with us as is." Lyall's lips curl over his sharp fangs. *"I wish he'd understand that not all humans are bad. Some of them are, aye, but when I was a pup, there was this lad my age. A human. He..."* His tail droops, and his head hangs low. I've never seen an animal look so sad before.

"He what?"

Giving himself a shake, Lyall lopes ahead. *"Nothing."*

I'm curious, but I never want to be the one to make light-hearted Lyall look so sad, so I shove my questions down and follow him back to the village. Lyall shifts back to a man, hefting the calf over one broad shoulder. "Oh, hold on a moment. Helga wanted me to loan you some of my old clothes for the ceremony tonight."

My stomach lurches. "Oh. Yeah. The ceremony."

Kicking open his front door, Lyall dumps the calf across the table, then urges me to follow him into his bedroom. I freeze as I cross the threshold, remembering Anders's broken promise to bring me a branch that could transport me back to my present. Supposedly, Lyall has one.

A realization makes my heart skip. This could be my chance. They trust me. I'm one of them. I could take the branch and go without even becoming Wulfric's mate. My stomach churns uneasily. I know for sure if I try and escape again, I'll break any trust I've worked so hard to build. But what would that matter when I could finally go *home?* I could go back to where everything is familiar. Plumbing! Iced coffee! I could see my family again, my coworkers, Amanda, and be back in my apartment in New York City. All without binding myself to Wulfric.

That would be such a betrayal to Wulfric and somehow, I hate the idea of hurting him like that.

A voice growls in my head, *Wulfric. Mate. Mine. Stay.*

Before I can stop myself, I've bolted across the room, driven toward the door by a force I can't name. I need to see him. I have to go to him. Now. Right now. Bring him the reindeer, show him I'm worthy. Run with him. Hunt with him. Bite him.

Claim him.

"Shit!" I wrench my hand back from the doorknob by sheer force of will. The tips of my hands end in claws.

"Everything all right?" Lyall calls.

"Y-yeah. Fine!" I have to grind my teeth against the growing urge to sprint from the room. Fur sprouts on my arms, white as the pelt I wear. Panting from the effort of holding myself back, I lean on the table.

Whatever that feeling was, it didn't come from me. But it was *strong,* an urge unlike any I've ever felt before, so strong I almost ran right out the door and straight to Wulfric. "Uh. Lyall?"

A grunt answers me. It sounds like Lyall is rummaging around in a drawer.

"Can our wolves do other things? Like... talk to us?"

A chuckle. "Oh, aye! Being ulfhednar means sharing our bodies with the spirit of a wolf. Our instincts run strong. It's usually best to listen."

"So I'm being haunted by the ghost of the wolf I murdered?"

"What?" Judging by how perplexed he sounds, he probably thinks I'm an idiot.

"Never mind." Taking a seat at the table, I focus and try to home in on whatever wolfy instincts are swirling inside me.

I know how I feel. I want to leave and go home. And yet something else gnaws at me. A sense of *wrongness* almost like a gut instinct. It must be my damn wolf. I want to leave, but maybe *he* doesn't. Fuck. I'm the worst werewolf, *ulfhednar,* ever. Somehow, my stupid wolf thinks leaving would be a bad idea.

Because of Wulfric. I promised Wulfric. We had a deal.

He isn't who I thought he was. The past week while we trained, I saw a whole other side of him. He was patient with me. Dedicated to my survival, even if it was mostly for his own benefit. He needs me to stay sane, after all.

He saved my life when he offered to train me. How can I run away now and break my word?

But what was that feeling just now? My wolf whispered something to me. Something like... mate?

Is Wulfric my *mate?* I know he thinks I'm his because of whatever wolfy instincts he has, but I'm human. Except I'm not. Not anymore. I'm ulfhednar now. I have all the same instincts he does. And said instincts are screaming at me to go find Wulfric and hump his damn leg, apparently.

Oh god. No. No, no, *no.* This has got to stop. I've got to leave before I start believing in all this werewolf soulmate crap.

"All right. Think I've got everything. How do you like this shirt?" Lyall's in the doorway, a bundle of clothes in his arms.

I could ask him to find one in another color or style, then while he's distracted, I could try and find the branch.

"Kieran?" Lyall looks concerned at my indecision.

I smile and say, "It's... It looks great, Lyall. Thanks."

He grins. "Of course, but remind Helga to take it in for you!"

My heart races fast as I leave Lyall's house.

This is it. I've made my choice.

I'm mating with Wulfric tonight and then, I'm going home.

If my wolf even lets me leave at all...

Before I left, Lyall told me of some customs I needed to be aware of for the mating ceremony. Bathing is important. Cleansing impurities, that sort of thing. But also who wants to smell like ass at their own wedding? Once I'm at the longhouse, I lock myself in the sauna and sit anxiously in my own sweat. I leave feeling overheated and tired.

Inside the kitchen, thralls stir the contents of iron cauldrons and soapstone kettles full of food and roast various ingredients over the embers. They carry barrels of liquor out into the yard behind the house. They're working their asses off preparing a feast for Wulfric and me. I can't be with someone who keeps thralls, even if it is socially acceptable in this timeline. Everything here is too different, too backwards.

"There you are, lad!" Helga motions me over to a chair by the hearth and hands me one of the shirts Lyall brought over. "I took in your shirts like you asked. Let me know how they fit now."

In the bedroom, I dress in front of the mirror. The silk shirt is smooth against my skin, the leather breeches a bit long in the ankle but otherwise comfortable. My fur cape keeps the cold out, though the chill in the air doesn't bother me much anyway. Not now that I'm a wolf. The man staring back at me in the mirror looks like a different person, parts of his hair braided, bronze scruff on his jaw. I don't look like the man who came to Reykjavik and got lost in another time.

I look like the people roaming the streets outside the windows. Like I belong here. With them. My pack. If I go back to my time, would I be the same or would a beast still howl beneath my skin? How can I return to a normal life when *I'm* not normal anymore?

I invite Helga in to approve her handiwork.

Helga squeezes my shoulders. "Such a handsome lad. Are you ready, dear?"

A smile trembles on my lips. "I think so."

She grins, eyes alight. "Then let's go find your mate."

A mug of ale later, and she practically has to carry me out of the house. Not from the ale, though. My knees are shaking too badly to support myself. Moonlight spills from behind a cloud, and heat prickles over my skin. All of a sudden, everything is too hot.

"All right, lad?" Helga asks.

Lurching to a stop, I take in a shallow gulp of air. The night has gone from cool and pleasant to stiflingly hot. I grip my shirt and fan myself with it. "Is it hot to you?"

A frown wrinkles her brow. "No. It's quite a mild night. Are you sure you're feeling well?"

I have no idea how to explain the sudden ache in my balls, so I don't say a thing. What gives? Why am I so horny all of a sudden?

The pack awaits us in the woods. A band plays lyres, bone flutes, and drums, and blows horns in a toe-tapping cacophony of sound. Tables have been set up, covered with cloth, and laden with dishes. In a firepit there's the charred carcass of a whole goat.

Roast chickens rotate on a spit, dripping juices into bowls to be used for stock later, I'm sure. Bowls of meat are bathed in sweet red berry sauce. Boiled fish wait to be devoured, seasoned with herbs and stewed with turnips and butter. Mugs of ale and mead clutter every table. There's more food than a whole pack of ulfhednar can eat. All this effort, for Wulfric and me. I almost feel guilty for thinking I'll puke if I eat any of it.

There's a tugging in my soul and I know he's near. But where? Where is he? Where is *mine?* Flashes of heat roll over my skin as I weave through the crowd. I need to get to him. Wulfric can help me. He'll know what to do. I don't understand how I know this—it must be a wolf thing.

Shaking free of Helga, I move before I can rationalize a thing. Instinct drives me forward, following the scent that sings to me. Just like last night after my first shift, something lights up in my chest and this time I know what it is. A bond, a golden thread tying me to Wulfric and Wulfric to me. But it's incomplete. We're connected, but we're not one. Not yet.

Shaking free of the crowd, I catch my breath. When I see him, everything just... stops. The noise of the crowd fades to distant buzzing, and his scent fills the air around me. Wulfric waits for me in the clearing beneath the swirling northern lights, wearing tight leather pants and a tunic so white it seems to glow. Those eyes like shards of moonlight find mine, and he looks at me like I'm the aurora borealis that lights up the night sky.

Mine, my wolf howls.

"Are you well?" he asks, approaching me.

I stumble away from him, alarmed by the sudden surge of *want* that possesses me. "Am I... what?"

"Are you feeling all right? Your face is flushed."

Am I feeling all right? I don't know. Everything's gone sort of numb because I've just noticed the wooden arch behind him.

I'm getting married, mated, I don't even know what to call it. With my last boyfriend, Mark, I thought we would be together forever. As I've approached thirty, I've thought a lot about my future and when I pictured marriage, it was always to a man I loved, my dream partner in every way. And Wulfric couldn't be further from any of my fantasies.

I don't love him but here I am, about to do the werewolf equivalent of tying our souls together forever. My lungs seize, and I can't even suck in a pinch of air. As my heart pounds hard enough to beat out of my chest, I know I have to run and fast.

"Kieran!"

I ignore Wulfric's shout and bolt, tearing into the trees. I don't get far, struggling to breathe around the panic clawing at my chest. If I can just shift, I can run faster, get away before anyone catches me and forces me back.

I yank the fur hood over my head and lose my footing as the shift takes over. But it's so damn slow. My limbs jerk and seize, and to my horror, I lose all control of my body. Mentally, I scream at myself to run, but all I can do is twitch and jerk as my panicking body fights the changes. I end up stuck somewhere between man and wolf, my body covered in thick fur but still human.

Curling in on myself, I choke back sobs. What a nightmare. I wish this wasn't real. I wish I could close my eyes, open them, and find myself back in my bed. I miss my job. My family. Amanda. All I want is to go home.

"Kieran?"

Big hands grip my fur cloak and pull it back. The shift falls away from me, leaving me human once more. I whimper and hide my tear-stained face from Wulfric, but the bastard can probably smell my tears. As he leans over me, his body blocks out the light of the moon.

"Nervous? I was too this morning."

A sound between a laugh and a sob escapes me. I can't even manage words.

"Breathe with me. It will pass." He takes in a deep breath and blows it out.

My lungs are too tight to manage more than a shallow breath. Wulfric's hand, warm and soothing, glides up and down my back. "That's it. That's good. You're safe."

Is he... comforting me?

Wulfric rubs the nape of my neck, and a low, contented rumble escapes me. "Relax, little rabbit. We're going to be mated, but that doesn't change our deal. I will not force you to stay with a man you can barely stand." With every rhythmic breath and gentle touch of Wulfric's hand, my wolf settles. "Your wolf likes me, at least." He chuckles, a low and rusty sound that spreads warmth throughout my cold body.

My wolf's instincts tell me to trust Wulfric, so I do. I breathe with him, leaning into his comforting touch, and I can finally take a full breath.

Wulfric offers an unsure smile. "Better?"

Not really, but at least I'm not panicking now. I sit up slowly.

"I wish things were different," Wulfric confesses, heaving a low sigh. "In a perfect world, you would not have had to prove yourself to my pack. At a glance, we would have trusted our bond and fallen in love. I would have worshipped you the rest of our lives together. But that isn't what happened."

A lump rises in my throat. Why do I hate feeling like I'm disappointing him?

Wulfric scowls and looks away, scratching the back of his neck. "When I was a lad, my father took me hunting. I would not hunt and kill the prey we needed to survive the coming winter."

"Why not?" I ask, not really caring, just needing to keep my racing mind focused on something.

"Because I didn't want to harm an innocent creature. I knew where meat came from, but looking the rabbit in the eyes and knowing what I had to do... It was harder than I thought it would be. My father was not happy, but no matter what he said, I was stubborn. When I woke up the next morning, he was gone."

That catches me off guard. "Your dad left you alone in the woods? How old were you?"

Wulfric shrugs. "I hadn't seen my ninth winter yet."

"But you could have died!"

He nods. "If I was too weak to survive, then it would have been the gods' will that I die rather than burden my pack."

"That's messed up, Wulfric."

"It's the way of this world. I didn't like it, but I had to kill that rabbit so that I would have enough food for the journey back to the village. I did what I had to in order to survive, and so must you. I need you to do this, Kieran. It's obvious you hold no love for me. So do it for yourself. Do what you have to in order to return to your time." With a sigh, he rises and turns away. "Take the time you need. I will wait under the arch."

Before he can go, I ask, "How did you know how to help me?" I didn't mean to ask, but the question just slipped out. How had Wulfric known how to calm my anxiety attack?

Wulfric's steps falter. He looks back at me, opens his mouth, but seems to think better of it. Turning away, he disappears into the trees.

I remain where I am on the forest floor, breathing in slowly to center myself. As much as I hate it, Wulfric is right. I must do what it takes to get home.

I follow the tugging in my chest back to the clearing where a crowd has assembled before the wooden arch. Heart beating hard in my ears, I make myself take one step and then another. The crowd parts for me, revealing Wulfric beneath the arch. Music plays. I think it's a guitar, no, a lyre. Making myself breathe, I focus on his face. He's a handsome, moody bastard, I'll give him that. Of all the guys I could have been forced to mate with, at least he's good-looking—and kind, I guess, in his own surly way.

We stand toe to toe beneath the arch. Wulfric is un-characteristically fidgety, unable to hold my gaze for longer than a second. His heart races fast, his chest testing the laces on his tunic with each swift inhalation. I've never seen him so nervous before. It's kind of nice, knowing such a high-and-mighty alpha wolf gets as nervous as I do.

Cracking a smile, I reach out and touch his hand, teasing him. "Relax. Nerves aren't a good look on you."

He glowers at me.

The priest comes to stand between us. I'm focused on Wulfric's hand in mine, needing something to ground me, so I don't really pay attention to anything he's saying. Until Wulfric speaks, his deep voice cutting through the noise in my head.

"From henceforth, I vow to you that you shall have the protection of my pack. Be it with fang or claw, my blade or my body, I will protect you from my enemies, provide for you in times of hardship, and... love you until my dying breath." He chokes on the last word but to his credit, gets through it without looking too pained.

Shit. I have to speak now. It's a werewolf version of a wedding, so I figured there'd be vows, but I was also hoping I'd be drunk by now. Except werewolves can't get drunk. So instead of talking, my brain just... freezes. The silence gets thicker as the crowd waits with bated breath for me to honor their Alpha with loving words. My face burns hotter and my chest gets tighter.

Clearing my throat, I stammer, "W-Wulfric..." Shit, what's his last name? "Is your last name Wolf-Heart?" I whisper, then wince because everyone in this crowd's a damn werewolf and now knows I don't even know their Alpha's last name.

A smile twitches his lips. "Eriksson."

It's a good name. "Wulfric Eriksson, I offer you this... prey. That I hunted. For you. It's over there." I point to the table. Lyall is standing beside the reindeer calf we caught, which is roasting over the flames. He waves. "Um. I know I'm not the mate you expected." I wince. Way to air that in front of the crowd. "And I'm not a great hunter. Or much of a warrior. Or really anything special. But—"

"You will be."

"Huh?"

Wulfric squeezes my hand in his, his silver eyes never leaving mine. "Trust in the gods. They brought us together for a reason, no matter how unconventional we may be. You will do incredible things, Kieran, and I..." He swallows hard. "I can't wait to see it."

I must be having a rougher day than I thought because suddenly I want to cry.

Oh man. If Amanda could see me now. I wish she was here.

Wulfric's sudden kindness makes me forget the priest is here until he binds our joined hands with cords and asks us to repeat after him as he reads us our vows. The words fall from my numb lips, barely registering. I grip more tightly to Wulfric's hand and focus on all the shades of gray in his eyes.

The priest says, "Before the eyes of the gods, I declare this couple bonded for life. You may kiss."

Oh, right. The kiss. I haven't even had time to prepare myself. Shit. I haven't kissed anyone new since Mark and I started dating. Before I can overthink a thing, Wulfric pulls me in close. When his lips collide with mine, Wulfric is all I can taste and smell, his scent sweet and clean as a mountain breeze.

Closing my eyes, I breathe in his scent, lose myself in the touch of his hand on my cheek, calloused but surprisingly gentle. It's nothing like our vows, which were awkward and unrehearsed. No, kissing Wulfric feels... right. More than right. Heat spreads from where our lips meet all throughout my body. A sudden, powerful ache of want and need takes me by storm. Grabbing his face between my hands, I lose myself in kissing him, chasing his taste.

I need him. Need him to put his hands on me and possess me, body and soul. I need him to put his fangs in my skin and bite until I bleed. Need him to claim me as his and extinguish the raging fire coursing through me.

Alpha, the wolf whines.

I break the kiss, gasping and alarmed, and find Wulfric's eyes full of concern, like he knows something I don't.

What in the fuck is wrong with me?

Chapter 10
Wulfric

Damn it.

Kieran is in heat.

In all the excitement of the ceremony, I neglected to warn him. The winds change and his scent, spiced with arousal, floods my nose. Even if I couldn't smell it, I'd know at a glance by how flushed his cheeks are and how wide his pupils have dilated. On the full moon after a wolf's first shift, their body goes into heat and seeks a mate. If one has not found their mate before their first shift, then the hours until daylight can be agonizing.

The waves of arousal never end, even after rubbing your cock raw with your balls aching from spilling your seed over and over again. Nothing sates the primal hunger to bite, fuck, and breed. Except a fated or chosen mate. I would know. I went through it myself.

I can't let Kieran go through his heat alone. But will he let me be there for him? Even if the most he lets me do is bring him cups of cold water and a wet cloth to keep his body cool from the hot flashes, then I would consider it a privilege. This is a chance for me to show my feelings for him, that I've changed my mind about him. For however long I have him, that is.

Heads turn and others scent the air. They can smell his heat. A growl builds in my chest as the eyes of other wolves land on my vulnerable mate. When Gunnar shoves his way through the crowd and goes toward Kieran, my blood boils. Gunnar's wolf has been slowly taking over since he lost his family. The scent of another wolf in heat might drive him over the edge.

If he so much as touches Kieran, I will rip him apart. I'll have no choice, not when the berserker's rage still hasn't been soothed by my mate. Closing the distance in seconds, I slam my hand into Gunnar's chest. "Back off," I snarl, the words grating in my throat.

Gunnar's close to losing it, his eyes flaring bright, his fangs sharp. "Smells so sweet." His nostrils flare as he scents the air. "Are you sure you don't want to share him, brother? I'll be so good to him."

My fingers curl around his throat. Inwardly I'm horrified to be handling my brother so roughly, even if we've done worse in the past, but the fury throbbing in my veins eclipses everything else. "Touch him and I'll tear your arms from your body. Kieran is *mine*."

"I..." His eyes widen like he's waking from a dream. "My deepest apologies." He turns and flees into the crowd.

Kieran sways on his feet, panting softly. "Wh-what was that?"

Sweeping an arm over his shoulders, I urge him to my side. The way he curls into me, nuzzling into the furs around my shoulders, stirs every protective instinct I have. "Stay close to me until we're out of here."

"We're leaving?" He doesn't sound like he cares, too busy sniffing at my neck. "Fuck. You smell so good..." The little growl that edges into his voice makes my prick jerk and thicken in my trousers.

"Yes, little rabbit. I'm getting you out of here because if one more person looks at you, I might tear their eyes from their skulls."

"But what about the rest of the ceremony?" Sharp little fangs find the skin of my neck and nip.

I fight back the groan that nearly slips free. "It's just a feast to celebrate our union tonight. Nothing more. It isn't important." But Kieran is. I've got to give him what he needs, whatever that might be, whether it's the pleasures of the body or simply comfort. What I want is to throw him down on the nearest surface and have him over and over again until we're both howling at the stars. But my wants come second to his. We promised to complete our bond but there's a chance he may be too overwhelmed by his first heat. I should have anticipated this. If he's feeling too vulnerable to lie with me tonight, then I'll be there in any other way he'll let me.

"Come with me." I urge him away from the crowd. When he stumbles, weak on his feet, I bend over and hoist him up and over my shoulder. He yelps in protest but goes slack against me with a low moan of contentment.

"Where are we going?" he mumbles, speech slurred.

"Somewhere more private. You're mine tonight, little rabbit." Mine to care for, mine to protect.

Cool water can help with a heat, but in my experience hot water can aid in sweating out a heat faster even if it feels less pleasant. On the edge of my territory, I built a cabin beside a hot spring. It's much smaller than the main house, more private, meant for two rather than the master of the house and his thralls and farm animals. Once we reach the cabin, I set Kieran on his feet and grip his shoulders to steady him.

"Where are we?" he mumbles.

"My little hideaway." I motion to the cabin. "It can be yours, too, if you like." Steam clouds the air, rising from the hot spring near the house. The swirling lights in the night sky reflect on the pool's still surface.

"Cute. Never was really into any of that cottagecore stuff, but this is nice." Kieran sways and rubs his eyes. "Fuck. What is happening to me?" He tugs at his clothes, and I can only imagine how hot he is in them.

"You're going into heat."

He squints at me. "Heat? Like... like an animal?" His eyes widen in horror.

"Aye. Your body shares a wolf's spirit and all the primal needs that come with such a gift."

"How do I m-make it go away?" The flush on his face darkens. "Wait. Don't answer that." He turns away, muttering.

I guess he figured it out. The scent of lust only thickens, and I have to curl my fists so I don't reach out and pull him toward me. "There are other ways to get through a wolf's heat but they aren't as effective as... lovemaking." My face burns. "A soak in the hot springs can help you sweat out the heat. It works faster than most other methods I've tried. You're in a vulnerable state. You're welcome to stay in the cabin until you've recovered. I will be nearby to ensure your privacy. No one will get in or out without a bloodbath, I promise you."

Kieran's chest rises and falls faster, and he plays with the buckle of his belt. My eyes drop to his hand and primal hunger stirs in me as his cock strains the front of his pants. "You'd... stay with me?"

I fold my arms so I don't haul his lithe body against me. He would melt in my arms, so pliant and needy. The sounds he'd make if I ground against his cock would drive me to madness. "Of course. I wouldn't leave your side until your heat is through."

Nodding, Kieran wets his lips. His eyes are as dark blue as the deepest depths of the ocean. "And would we, uh..."

Gods, if he would just say the word… Drawing in a deep breath, I exhale around a growl. "If you let me, little rabbit, I'd have you on your back right now. I'd let you use my body as a tool for your pleasure until the sun comes up and we're too spent to continue." My prick throbs just imagining being sheathed in the tight heat of his body, hearing him cry out my name as I pound into him. Kieran's breathing quickens and, though he bites that supple lower lip, I don't miss the little whimper that escapes him.

The beast strains against every restraint I have. He wants Kieran. Needs him. Has to have him. But I can control it. I must.

Forcing myself to breathe around the throb of arousal, I grind more words out. "But if that isn't what you want, then I understand. It can be terrifying, losing control of your body in such a way. I need to stay nearby to ensure your safety, but I will not touch you. Not unless you ask me to. We can wait until you feel more in control to complete our bond."

I need to get away. Put some distance between us before I snap and go back on my word. "I will remain outside the cabin unless you need me."

I turn away and Kieran blurts out, "And what if I want to complete the bond now?"

I freeze in place, balling my hands into fists so I don't turn around and bolt to him.

Yes, the berserker snarls, and fur grows thick on my arms. *Fuck. Bite. Claim.*

"Kieran..." It's a warning growl. "You don't know what you're asking."

He takes a step, twigs snapping.

"Don't!" My roar echoes in the woods around us. "Kieran, don't. If you touch me, I can't promise I'll be able to control myself any longer." I've wanted him for too long, and my control hangs by a thread. Gods, if he would just let me have him, I would make him feel so good he'd never want another man in his bed.

He'd never want to leave me.

There's a soft laugh directly behind me. He's closer, prowling toward me as softly and silently as a skilled hunter. Pride warms me. "Shut up, you chivalrous asshole." Then he's whirling me around. His small yet strong body presses against me.

Gods. He's naked. Moonlight glimmers on his bare, freckled shoulders. His long, slender prick is trapped between our bodies. Calloused fingertips rasp over my jaw as he frames my face between his hands. His eyes are wolf-bright, a sliver of fang protruding when he smiles, sure and confident. I can scarcely breathe at the sight, my breath escaping me in shallow pants.

"Don't hold back. If your beast wants me..." Kieran breathes, his breath scorching against my mouth. "Then he can have me."

The thread snaps, and I devour Kieran's lips with mine. The sound he makes against my mouth, high and needy, awakens a hunger in me that will never be sated, not until I've heard him scream my name. His taste is sweet as spring water, and I thrust my tongue past his lips, dying to taste more of him.

I claim his mouth in hungry, eager strokes, and he returns my fervor with his own. My fangs cut his lip but before I can apologize, he's nipping at my mouth like he wants to devour me piece by piece. Gods, the sounds he's making.

"On your back for me," I snarl against his mouth. "Now."

Kieran squirms as I stroke his cock. "Whoa. Hold on a moment."

I take in a breath to calm my raging lust. "Aye?"

"Have you ever been with a man before?" He seems to be thinking more coherently now that I'm pleasuring him.

"I have." I kiss the side of his neck, making him sigh.

Wetting his lips, he asks, "And did you use protection? Or lube? Did you bottom, and if you did, did you clean out before?"

None of his words make any sense to me. "Protection?"

"From STDs." He grimaces. "Uh... illnesses you can get from sex."

"Ulfhednar are immune to disease."

He exhales. "Oh, thank fuck. Okay, have you bottomed? Uh, how do I say this... Have you been on the receiving end or have you given?"

"Given." Heat flames my cheeks. "But once I... received." I know it is considered shameful for a man to take a passive role in anything in this life, but I'd wanted to try it.

I expect him to ridicule me, but instead he grins. "Really? You bottomed? That's... whoa. That's hot as hell. So, when you bottomed, did you do anything to make it comfortable for yourself? Because I am *not* bottoming without prep or lubricant."

"It was..." I shudder, remembering. "Unpleasant."

He looks horrified. "Did it hurt?"

"Greatly. I told him to stop, so we did something else."

"Oh god. I'm so sorry you had that experience. I promise there are so many ways to make anal sex feel amazing."

It occurs to me I have no idea how to make this enjoyable for him. The last thing I want is to hurt him like I was hurt. "Tell me how."

He looks delighted. "Okay! I bathed earlier, so I'm clean down there, but we'll need oil or..." He makes a face. "Melted fat of some kind."

"Why?"

"To make things nice and slippery."

"Oh!" I head into my cabin and from my pantry I retrieve a vial of oil and bring it back.

"Oh good, you had some. Now, I believe you were about to order me to my back." Grinning slyly, he drops to his knees then lies back, sprawled obscenely on the grass by the edge of the hot springs. Kieran grabs his cock and strokes, moaning.

"Don't," I growl, and his hand freezes, his wide eyes gazing up at me full of awe and need. "The only one in charge of your pleasure tonight is me. Understood?"

His pale throat bobs when he swallows and then he angles his head back, exposing his neck to me. Submitting to me. "Y-yes, Alpha."

Alpha. I never asked him to call me that. He did it all on his own.

"Gods, you're going to be the death of me." The air gets hotter as I join him on the tundra grass. I tear off my clothes and toss them somewhere. Running my hand through the bronze fur on his heaving chest, I pinch one nipple, then take the other between my teeth and tug. Kieran's back arches and he chokes out a cry.

"F-fuck! M-more, Alpha." Kieran curls his fingers in my hair.

A growl rumbles through me and makes him gasp, squirming beneath me. Eager to taste his sweet flesh, I lick a line down his chest to his stomach. He raises his hips, trying to direct me to his cock. He's already leaking for me, drops of pearly seed smearing on his stomach. Dropping a kiss to his hips, I grab the head of his cock and squeeze. A hoarse cry escapes Kieran and he thrashes beneath me, trying to use my fist.

"I've barely touched you and you're already like this?" I smear away droplets of his cum on my thumb, then lick it. The salty, bitter taste of his seed makes me moan. "I bet you'll spill the moment I take you in my mouth."

Fisting his cock, I guide him to my lips, parting them. A litany of curses spills from Kieran, his nails biting into my scalp as he grabs onto my hair for dear life. The taste of him explodes on my tongue as I swallow him down. My eyes roll back as he moans, and I fight back the urge to grind my hips into the earth. Knowing I've pleased him gives me as much pleasure as if I'm the one getting my prick sucked.

Following the fervent tugging of his hands, I glide up and down his prick. When he bumps the back of my throat, I gag on him and he chokes out an apology and tries to soften his grip. I double down, bobbing my head with urgency until Kieran is moaning below me. Swirling my tongue around the head, I stroke the base of his shaft, hard as iron in my fist.

Panting, Kieran tosses his hips, plowing faster and deeper into my mouth. "Yes! Fuck! Yes!" he cries, and his seed floods my mouth. His grip in my hair softens and he strokes my hair almost reverently as his body goes slack beneath me—except for the part of him that's still in my mouth. Oh no, that part stays very hard.

"Wh-what?" Kieran pants, brows furrowed in confusion as I pull off his rock-hard prick. "Why do I still…"

I chuckle. "It's normal." I give his shaft a flick, enjoying how stiff he is.

"N-normal?" He covers his face with his hands. "I'm still hard! Jesus. Who needs Viagra? Just become a werewolf on a full moon!"

I don't know what Viagra is, so I ignore his question and focus my attention on his thighs, nipping and licking his soft skin. "What you need is my cock. My knot. Your body is craving it. Nothing else will truly satisfy you but that."

"Your… what?" He squirms when I rub my beard against his thigh.

"My knot." Sitting up, I squeeze the base of my aching cock, showing him the bulb at the base of my shaft. "Once I'm inside you, it will swell and tie us together. It's what your wolf is craving."

"Oh god," he says. "Will it hurt?"

"I've heard it's the most pleasurable experience a mated pair can have together. Second only to a mate's bite. A bite can end the heat altogether."

He mumbles something behind his hands.

"What?"

"Don't want it to end," he pants, hiding his face from me. "Not yet."

I grin, fangs sharp in my mouth. "Don't you worry. We've got all night, and I plan to spend every hour of it making you come for me. Now, lift your knees up. Show me that needy hole."

Shivering, Kieran obeys, drawing his knees to his chest. Seeing his hole, I begin to lose my nerve. What if I hurt him?

"You don't have to fuck me yet. You can do something else," he says reassuringly.

"I just... if I hurt you—"

"Use the oil. Get your fingers slick."

Nodding, I do as he says, coating my fingers. I curse as I spill too much, but Kieran says, "It's fine. You'll need a lot."

Exhaling, I press my fingers to his hole, watching him closely. "Can I?"

"Yes," he says, lifting his legs up toward his chest. "Do it."

I push one finger inside and groan. He's so tight and hot around me. Kieran groans with me, rocking his hips. "Fuck. That's good. Move."

Heart racing, I work my finger in and out slowly. He seems to enjoy it every time I stretch his rim.

Kieran moans. "Another. Give me another."

I add another finger and work him open more. "What else can I do?"

Panting, Kieran says, "If you want, you can... you can use your tongue, too?"

My eyes widen.

"Only if you—" But Kieran doesn't get the chance to finish. I grab his hips and flip him onto his stomach. He lifts for me, presenting his beautiful ass to me, and then I dive in, lapping at him from his swollen balls to his clenching hole.

"Oh my god! A-Alpha!" Kieran cries out, twisting his hips. "Fuck, you're so eager. More. Please!"

I plunge my tongue inside his slick hole. He moans when I slide my hands up to his plump ass and squeeze, holding him open even more. He's unbearably hot around me, clenching hard around my tongue as I lick and curl it inside him.

Gasping, Kieran rolls his hips and rides every flick of my tongue. "Deeper," he says with a groan. "Yeah, fuck yeah. J-just like that. Feels so good, Alpha. Fuck me with your tongue like you'll fuck me with your cock."

I go deeper until it's physically impossible to go any farther. I stretch my tongue out as long as I can make it, stroking, rubbing, and curling, and Kieran moans shamelessly. I may suffocate, but I can't imagine a more worthy death than on my hands and knees, pleasuring my mate with my tongue. Not even Odin's mead hall Valhalla holds such appeal.

A whine escapes Kieran. "Wulfric," he pants. "God. Put your fingers in me."

I do, sliding them into his clenching body.

"More. To the left a little. Yeah, yeah, good. Kind of stretch them like—"

Crooking my fingers, I find a spot that has him arching beneath me. "Fuuuck, yes! Right there!"

"Good?" I kiss the back of his thigh. "What did I do?"

"You found my prostate, that's what."

I'm not sure what this is, but it must be a good thing for him to be moaning like that. Feeling around again, I find that spot once more and he groans. "Don't overdo it. Feels good enough just having your fingers in me. N-no one's ever made me feel this good... not like this."

My blood boils at the idea of Kieran offering himself to anyone else but me. I roll him over and capture his gasping mouth with mine. I kiss him until my head throbs with the need for air. "There will never be anyone else," I growl against his mouth, curling my fingers against that spot that has him crying out beneath me. "Never again. You can feel our bond now. You know what it means?"

"Y-yes," he whines, rolling his hips, taking my fingers in faster, deeper.

"Tell me." I snarl the words against his lips, biting and nipping at his mouth. "Tell me who this hole belongs to. Who owns your pleasure tonight and every night."

"Y-you," he pants, and that single word lights my blood on fire. "I'm yours, Alpha."

The beast inside preens in primal delight. "Good." I smack a kiss on his mouth, thrusting my tongue inside to taste him, claim him. He moans around my tongue, his body tensing with his impending release.

"So close. Please, Alpha."

I know what he needs. I'm back between his thighs, spreading him wide open. My tongue spears his clenching heat, thrusting deep inside. He shouts my name as he spills, his hole spasming. I didn't even touch his cock. When I look up, Kieran is completely ruined, chest and stomach covered in pearly seed. Yet his cock is still a furious red, hard as iron against his stomach. Kieran gawks at the mess he made. "Holy shit. Never came hands-free before."

A pleased growl escapes me and I lean over him, licking up every drop, growling at his salty taste.

"Don't swallow. Want to taste it," Kieran rasps, face bright red at his admission.

I lean over and kiss him, spitting his own seed into his mouth. He whimpers as I squeeze his throat, and my cock throbs when he swallows. "Filthy," I growl against his mouth. "So insatiable, even after I've made you spill for me."

"Wulfric," Kieran says. "Not enough. I need you. Please. Fuck me."

I can't wait any longer. I've got to have him. "On your hands and knees for me. Now." He doesn't hesitate, crawling onto all fours on the ground, thrusting his hips back. My cock jerks between my thighs, aching to be inside him at last. "So good for me," I whisper, hands roaming down his quivering back. I grab handfuls of his perfect ass and squeeze hard enough to leave red prints behind.

"Wulfric," Kieran snarls, and my cock jumps to attention. "If you don't fuck me now, so help me, I'm climbing on your dick and riding you."

I growl my approval around a smile. "Some other time perhaps."

Dribbling on more oil, probably more than I'll need, I grip my oversensitive cock, guiding it to his slick hole. Slowly, I rock my hips and growl my satisfaction as pure heat engulfs my throbbing cock. Inch by inch, I fill him, my nails biting into his hips to anchor myself so I don't spill before I've made him scream for me. Peering down, I'm gifted with the view of his hole stretching around my cock as I disappear slowly inside him.

Nothing has ever felt so good, so right. But is it the same for him?

"Are you okay?" I ask him, heart racing.

Kieran swallows hard beneath me, raising his hips higher. "Yeah, I'm good. I promise."

As Kieran moans and rocks back on my cock, I know he isn't lying. I fit inside him so perfectly, there's no question in my mind that we were made for each other. Lowering myself to his back, I kiss his shaking shoulders, then bite the shell of his ear. "How could I have been so wrong about you?" I whisper, kissing his damp, heated skin with each roll of my hips. "You are perfect. My perfect mate."

A needy sound escapes him, and he pushes back against me, riding every thrust. My eyes roll back, and the pleasure that courses up and down my cock is too much for me to hold back any longer. I moan with him every time I drag along his tight walls, biting down on his shoulder as I work my hips against him faster and harder. It's not enough. I need more. Pulling out of him takes effort but I do it anyway, ignoring his disappointed whine. "Roll over. Need to see you."

Kieran's on his back in seconds, hiking his legs up, groaning with me as I bury myself back inside and fuck him with such urgency it's like we were separated for years, not seconds. His thighs lock around my waist, his claws raking up and down my back, his body quivering with mine as I slam into him again and again, each thrust taking us to new heights.

Our lips collide, stealing every gasp and moan that escapes us like they're secrets. Kieran kisses me like I'm the water of life and he's been lost in the desert.

I fuck him like we've only got seconds left to live, like this is the last chance we'll ever have to be together, like it's the end when I know in my heart this is only just our beginning. If the world ended around us right now, I wouldn't stop kissing him, fucking him, loving him for anything. I never want to stop.

Being inside my mate is the closest I've ever been to Valhalla itself. And, gods forgive me, I know that nothing else shall ever compare.

"Kieran." I say his name out loud and through the bonds that tie our souls together as my knot swells and makes our bodies one.

Now, the beast inside snarls, *bite. Claim. Now.*

As if reading my mind, Kieran offers his neck to me, his eyes flashing wolf-bright. "Please, Alpha."

I nuzzle into his neck, panting harshly against his skin with every slap of my hips. My knot's locked within him, ready to keep my seed inside. His sweet mountain flower scent calls to me, a call I can't refuse. I part my lips and bite down, tasting blood.

Kieran spasms beneath me, his head thrown back as he screams for me. My name fills the night air as he spills between us. His ass clenches around my knot, and I fuck into his tight heat, snarling against his skin as I fill him with my seed. Burning pain briefly eclipses my pleasure as Kieran bites down, and then waves of bliss wash over me. Kieran's pleasure becomes mine, and mine becomes his.

The aftermath of our lovemaking seems to last hours. I hold him and shiver with aftershocks. Kieran holds me tight, gasping against me. Sweeping his sweaty hair from his forehead, I kiss between his brows and hold him to me.

The berserker rumbles in my chest, his rage at last appeased by the man in my arms. A piece of me I never knew was missing is finally complete. "I'm yours, little rabbit," I whisper, leaning down to find his lips. A soft, tender sigh escapes Kieran, and he leans into the hand I rest upon his cheek.

There's much more I want to say, but it can wait until the morning.

Kieran nuzzles into my neck, eyes closing. Reaching back, I grab my furs and drape them over us.

All my life, I've believed that when I die, axes in my hands and covered in the blood of my foes, I would go to Valhalla. I thought there could be no greater glory than to drink mead with the warriors from our most ancient legends. The moment I saw him, though, I knew my soul no longer belonged to the gods. Not Odin, not even Fenrir.

My soul belongs to my mate, and from this moment on, I will fight, not to die with honor and glory but to live another day at his side.

Chapter 11
Kieran

Dawn's light glows golden and bright as I open my eyes. My body aches but in only the best way. Wulfric's heart beats in my ears, and his chest makes the perfect pillow, fuzzy, firm, and warm. His big arms cradle me to his body. His warm body, the furs draped over us, and the steam from the hot springs makes sweat break out across my skin. Despite the discomfort, I never want to leave his arms.

Memories of last night make my face heat and my cock thicken. What in the hell came over me? It was like a fire of lust was burning in me, and only Wulfric could quench the flames. What had he called it? Heat? I really could use a crash course in werewolf biology.

But I don't regret last night. No matter how surprising it may have been, or embarrassing. How many times did I beg him to fuck me? Too many. But I saw a side of Wulfric that I never expected. I knew he had it in him to be patient, but his tenderness and passion took my breath away. I feel terrible that he paid so much attention to me without my returning the favor. With Mark, it was all him, all the time. But Wulfric worshipped me with his hands, his cock, his mouth.

He's still inside me, soft but very much there, though his knot's gone down. The sensation of being knotted was strange for a few seconds, but as I adjusted, I loved how thick he was, lighting up all my nerve endings as my body stretched to fit him. Just remembering has my cock rock hard, ready for another go. Arching my hips, I wriggle on his cock, biting my lip when he starts to harden inside me.

Wulfric groans softly, his beautiful silver eyes opening. "Gods. Do you ever tire, little rabbit?" His calloused fingertips glide down my back and squeeze my ass, spreading me wide.

"Is being horny all the time a wolf thing?" I don't remember being this insatiable for any guy before I became ulfhednar.

"No." He flips us so I'm on my back, his big body blanketing mine and trapping my aching cock between our bodies. Grabbing the oil in the grass beside us, he coats his cock until he's dripping with it. A big hand grips my throat, squeezing. "That's you, being desperate for my cock," Wulfric growls right into my ear and thrusts. His hips smack my ass, and my eyes roll back in bliss. A groan shivers from him before I swallow down his guttural growls of pleasure with my lips.

Slipping a hand between us, he grabs my cock in his fist and strokes. His palm is dry and calloused, but somehow his rough touch is the perfect sleeve for me to fuck into while he fucks me.

"Fuck." I groan. "Damn it!"

Wulfric sucks a kiss into my neck. His hips falter. "Are you well?"

"No, no, fuck! What are you doing?" I squirm, trying to force his cock deeper inside me. "Don't stop. Please. Don't. I just—" I see stars as he hits that spot inside me.

He growls low when I clench around him. "Then what's wrong? Tell me. I'll make it better."

"I just..." It's hard for me to think with him pumping into me. Raising my hips, I meet his every thrust, crying out my pleasure to the open skies. "W-wanted to please you, too." I was supposed to take the initiative this time, not assume a passive role again. "Tell me how."

"This pleases me." He pulls out, leaving me painfully empty until the head of his dick notches against my hole. "Watching you take my cock." His eyes close, his teeth clenching as he pushes inside, a groan tearing from him.

Needing more, I raise my knees to my chest, biting my lip to stifle my whimpers as he fills me inch by inch.

"Those shameful sounds you make. How needy you are even after I made you spill your seed." With a snap of his hips, he bottoms out inside me. We both cry out as his hips pound the backs of my thighs. "Being inside your perfect ass. Knowing I'm the reason you're moaning for me. That's what pleases me."

"B-but... But I should—" Whatever I'm about to say is silenced when his lips crash down on mine. He plunders my mouth, nips and tugs my lip, sucks on my tongue.

"What you should do," he snarls in my ear, "is be quiet and take every inch of my cock." And though his words are crass, I understand. Wulfric's devoted to my pleasure. And maybe it's selfish, but after years of giving and never receiving, all I want is to let him take control and give me what I need.

So I stop worrying about what I think I should do. I let him pin my hands over my head and pound into me. My doubts crack and crumble and all hesitation disappears as I surrender myself to him.

"That's it," he says reverently, kissing my lips, my jaw, sucking on the bite he left on my neck. "That's good. I've got you."

The tenderness in his words makes my eyes sting. Every kiss and whispered word heals a piece of my heart I never knew was broken by years of never feeling good enough. In this moment, I'm enough. I don't have to prove anything, not to Wulfric. I can just be, and it's all he needs.

I cry out his name, spilling between us.

Wulfric moves through my climax, movements slowing as his knot locks inside me. With a snarl, he floods me with his release. He crumples to my chest and drops my wrists. I don't waste a second throwing my arms around him, hauling him even closer to me as I shiver and shake, overwhelmed.

"You are mine," he whispers, like he knows me from my soul to the depths of my mind. "Made for me. You will always be enough."

"Are you sure it's okay?"

Wulfric sighs around a mouthful of porridge. He brought us a couple bowls from the house, and we enjoy our breakfast in the hot spring. "Would you believe me if I told you that it's no hardship to fuck you until we're both mindless and spent?"

"Oh, I for sure believe that." I run my fingers through the hair on his arms. I was never really into body hair, not until I saw Wulfric naked. He's truly glorious, huge and muscular, chest covered in blond fuzz. So yummy. "I just... feel bad not reciprocating."

"Don't." He reaches for a flagon of ale on the rim of the spring behind us and takes a sip, licking his lips to chase the taste. "You had to do enough to prove yourself to my pack. To me."

A furrow appears between his brows and at the same time, a feeling stirs deep inside me. Guilt. But it's not mine. Mating with Wulfric has given me the ability to sense his emotions. He really is nothing like I thought. He does feel things, quite deeply. Of course he's not a machine, but he's also not the barbarian I thought he was.

"I don't often feel good enough." The confession falls from his lips. He tenses beside me, like he didn't mean to say that aloud. "I... wasn't ready to become alpha. Not really. I knew since I was a lad that I would succeed my father in the role. But I always thought I'd have more time to prepare, to learn from my father." He falls silent, his jaw working like he's fighting with whether he should say anything more.

I can't look away, mesmerized by the crack in his armor, by the shimmer of emotional vulnerability I'm seeing from him. I rub his arm. "Hey. You can tell me."

He blows out a quiet breath, heavy with dozens of unspoken feelings. "Losing him... it happened fast. His body wasn't even cold before all his duties and responsibilities were thrust upon me. Lives were put in my hands and I... I don't know if any of the choices I made after his death were the right ones." His throat works as he swallows, his eyes fixed on the horizon.

"What happened?" I ask, speaking quietly without even meaning to.

"Ulfheim has only been our home for a decade or so. Before that, we lived on the mainland. Some years ago, a group of Christian humans came to the shores of our village. We thought ourselves well hidden but somehow they'd found us. They called themselves missionaries, and they were led by a man named Thorald. He showed us miracles gifted to him by the power of his Christian god, offered us riches if we would convert. But nothing would convince my father to accept this new god."

"Because that would mean giving up the power you get from Fenrir?"

"Aye. If they'd simply allowed us to keep our own gods as well as theirs, there might not have been an issue. But they'd made it clear we would have to surrender our 'barbaric' gods. My father refused to renounce our gods and told them in no uncertain terms to get out of his town and never return." A shiver racks Wulfric's body, and his eyes lose all focus as he stares off at the horizon. Like he's trapped in the past.

"They were no missionaries, but hunters in disguise. They returned the next day and slaughtered my friends. Burned our village. Father and I beat them back to the shore, tried to make them retreat. Father fought them off as best he could, but—" Wulfric cuts himself off sharply. His trembling lips pinch into a thin line, and with his eyes bright with pain and fury, he stays silent for several long seconds.

The anguish he's feeling courses through the bond between us, bringing a lump in my throat. "Why would they do something so cruel? Just because you're shifters?"

Wulfric's voice quakes with fury. "It's... more complicated than that. When we were boys, Father rescued the lone survivor of a wolf attack. The lad called himself Soren, and as he'd been orphaned, Father raised him as one of us. Even made him ulfhednar when Soren asked to join the pack. He and Lyall became friends as boys and claimed each other as mates once they were grown."

My breath hitches. "Soren didn't... betray you, did he?"

Wulfric's low growl is all the answer I need. "The hunters came for him. From what Lyall could tell me after... everything, Soren's father had survived the attack and came to 'rescue' his son. We do not know how he was able to find us. Soren cozied up to us all those years for protection, only to betray us the second he knew his father was still alive."

"I'm so sorry." Before I can stop myself, I rub his arm. His fury and pain are eating me up inside. I'd do anything to make him feel better. "What happened to him? Soren, I mean?"

"Exile." Wulfric snarls the word. "Death was too good for him. We stripped him of his furs. Used a branch of Yggdrasil to send him away into a whole other time. May he rot and wolves feast upon his festering innards." He spits over his shoulder.

"That's... yeah, that sounds like a good punishment." Beneath the water, I squeeze his knee. If he feels my touch, he doesn't react. He's a thousand miles away, fighting painful old memories.

"I moved us to Ulfheim, thinking we'd be safe. And we are. For now. If my own brother doesn't turn my people against me." He looks so young in this moment. For as rugged and powerful as he is, he's still only a young man, hardened and aged by loss and war.

Suddenly, he splashes warm water over his face, then gives his head a shake, scattering water from his beard.

I sputter. "Hey!"

Clearing his throat, he says, "What I meant to say is when I'm inside you, when I've made you cry out in pleasure and spill your seed, I feel like I'm enough. It's not something I feel often. Of course, if you want to take control from time to time, that is fine. But I want to be the one in control of your pleasure. That is what pleases me, knowing I've satisfied you, more so than anything else."

I tilt my head, pretending to give it a good, long think. "Okay. If you *have* to, I guess I can endure it."

He chuckles when I elbow him, the sound deep and warm. Droplets run down his skin, trickling over the bite between his neck and shoulder. I did that. A pleased rumble rolls up from my chest, and I cover my mouth.

Wulfric grins. "What just pleased your wolf?"

"Um. Your bite mark. The one I gave you." Reaching out, I run my thumb over the scar I left on his skin. "I got this big rush of satisfaction just now. Or my wolf did."

Wulfric's smile widens, showing a hint of fang. "Oh, aye? It pleases you, knowing you've marked me as yours?"

I fold my arms. "Make me sound like a possessive caveman..."

He leans in, runs his tongue along the curve of my neck, then bites down on my earlobe. "Be as possessive of me as you like, little rabbit. I want to be your first thought when you wake and the last before you close your eyes. When you look at another man, remember me and how I've pleased you and know no one's cock will satisfy you like mine does. That mark on my flesh makes me yours now. All yours."

Suddenly, he pulls away and clears his throat. "For now, anyway. I... Imagine you'll want to return home soon now that the terms of our deal have been met."

"Oh. Yeah. Sure."

I can't believe I completely forgot about our deal. We've helped each other. Our obligations to each other are over.

So why do I hate the idea of leaving?

"Well, I could stay. Just a while longer."

His eyes widen, and something like hope lights up the bond between us. "Aye?"

I shrug. "Sure. There's no rush."

A smile teases the edge of his lips before he leans back in, cupping my cheek. "I'd like that, little rabbit. Very much."

"Me, too…"

His mouth claims mine, damp from steam, sweet from mead. I tangle my fingers in his hair and kiss him with everything I have. Every time I think I'm all used up, I find I have more of myself to give to him. It's frightening how easy it is to lose myself in his kisses, how familiar and comfortable I feel with this man despite how different he is.

Wulfric feels like home.

Home. When's the last time I thought about returning? The realization stuns me.

I don't *want* to leave. Not anymore now that we've bonded. Just the idea of leaving him makes me ache inside.

Is it possible Wulfric's past can be my new present?

Chapter 12
Wulfric

The rest of the day after our mating ceremony feels like a dream I never want to wake from.

The only time we leave the hot springs is to return to my cabin for food or rest in a proper bed. At night Kieran seems unsure as he goes inside. He glances at the hearth as if he expects to sleep by the fire like a dog.

"No," I say, "you will sleep in my bed from now on. Or, if the bed displeases you, then we shall sleep on the floor. But whatever we decide, we will be waking up together from now on."

Until he decides he's ready to leave, that is, but I force that thought away.

He smiles like that has pleased him greatly. He comes to my bed, and we curl up together beneath the furs. It's far, far too easy to let my guard down around him.

I don't talk about what happened to my father. There's no real reason to when those who survived the hunters still remember as well as I do. Besides, remembering that day still pains me greatly. Reflecting on it can be bad for my mind, causing more nightmares and sudden rushes of fear during the day. Like my mind still thinks I'm on that beach, watching my father, friends and neighbors die.

But talking to Kieran lifted a weight from my shoulders. He didn't judge me or think me weak. He just listened and offered what comfort he could. As I nuzzle into the back of his neck, I kiss the spot just below his hairline, enjoying the way he shivers.

"Sleep well," I whisper into his skin.

He curls back into me. "I will."

And I do, too, better than I have in years.

Something wakes me in the night. The room is dark, the fire nothing but embers in the hearth. Every bone in my body tenses. A growl builds in my chest. Has someone found our cabin? Holding my breath, I strain my ears. The house creaks as it settles in the dark. Owls call out in the night. The wind howls low and mournful. Claws sprout from my fingertips.

If someone comes for us, I will fight tooth and claw to keep Kieran safe. No one will take him from me. My heart races, my breath catching. Panic claws at me. So many emotions swirl inside me: fear and despair, loathing myself. So much loathing. Gods, it feels like I'm drowning, spiraling out of control. Then I realize what's happening.

These are not my feelings.

They're my mate's. Kieran isn't in bed beside me.

A snarl tears from me as I leap from the bed and run to the door. Knowing I'll move faster as a wolf, I pull my furs over me and let the shift take me. The cold wind courses through my fur as I rush outside and sniff the air. His scent is stronger in this form as I pursue him on four legs.

Deeper into the trees I run, nose bent to the earth. Why would Kieran run all the way out here? Was he trying to leave me? A stab of pain in my chest makes me whine.

A flash of white fur catches my attention. It's Kieran, sitting in a crouch by a tree, arms wrapped around himself. His little rabbit heart races in my ears, his shoulders rising and falling fast as he gasps for breath. The salty scent of his tears has me rushing forward, bumping my head against his back, sniffing around him.

He's hurting. I must find where he's hurt. Lick his wounds. Kill whatever or whoever has caused him such distress. When I push my nose against his ear, he shoves me hard. "Go away, Wulfric!" His body shakes like he's lost in a frigid storm. No sobs escape him, as if he's fighting them back.

Chest aching, I stumble back. My mate rejected me. Why, what have I done?

"*What's wrong?*" I ask through our bond. "*Tell me. Are you hurt? What's happened?*"

"J-just leave. Please."

I growl, nipping gently at his ear. "*No. Tell me what is wrong.*"

"Ow. Okay! I'm..." He sucks in a shuddery breath. "It's nothing. Really. It's stupid."

If it was bloody nothing, rage wouldn't be festering within me at the very idea someone has caused him such distress. *"Who did this? I will kill them. Lay their broken, bloody body at your feet."*

"Jesus!" He lurches back from me, wide-eyed. Did I not say the right thing? "No, you won't kill anyone. Nobody hurt me. I'm just... really fucking sad all of a sudden. And anxious and... God. I just feel like shit."

My rage calms enough so I can shift back. I squeeze my hand into a fist, fighting back the urge to reach out and comfort my hurting mate. For the first time since we mated, I haven't the slightest idea what to do, how to make him feel better. "You could have woken me."

Swallowing hard, Kieran shakes his head. "Didn't want you to s-see."

Scooting closer, I tentatively touch his thigh. "See what?"

Tears spill down Kieran's face. "Me! Like this. Fucking anxious and messy and—and—" With a broken noise, he hides his face in his hands, his nails scraping at his skin. Instantly, I grab his wrists and pull his hands away from his beautiful, tear-streaked face.

"Do not hurt yourself. Why wouldn't you wish for me to see you like this? We are mates, Kieran. We aren't meant to hide things from each other."

Lips wobbling, Kieran wraps his arms around himself, and I realize I want to be the one giving him that embrace, if he'd only let me. "I... I have generalized anxiety disorder."

I am not sure of the meaning of any of those words. "What does that mean?"

Sighing, Kieran gazes at his hands. "My brain, it—it doesn't work like normal people's brains. I have bad thoughts that don't go away. That repeat themselves over and over again."

Somehow, that sounds familiar. I think I know how he feels. "These thoughts... do they speak to you?" I know mine do sometimes. They tell me I'm worthless and weak. A disappointment to the memories of my parents. A horrible alpha.

Sniffling, Kieran nods. "It's like being in a constant argument with myself all day. The thoughts tell me that... people hate me. Or that I'm stupid. Or ugly. Worthless. That the world would be better off if I wasn't in it."

I open my mouth to interrupt. How could he think these things about himself? He's not stupid at all, or any of those horrible things. Biting my lip, I force myself to stay silent. My instincts tell me that Kieran needs to get all this poison out of his system.

"Or it digs up memories from years ago and forces me to replay them over and over again with different outcomes. It's fucking torture. I started taking medication a few months ago—that's stuff you eat to make yourself feel better," he adds to counter my confused look. "I guess here you'd take, what? Herbs?"

Ah, I understand what he means. "I see. And did this medication help?"

Nodding, Kieran says, "For a while, but then I ended up here and I left it in my time. I haven't taken the medication in a while."

Fear tightens my chest. "Are you in danger?"

"I don't think so. Just feel really emotional right now, and sometimes I feel dizzy. Some people have it really bad when they quit cold turkey. Others don't."

"But if you take this medication, you'll feel better again."

"Yeah. I should. It'll fix my stupid, broken brain."

Growling, I lean in and grip his chin. "Look at me, little rabbit." My stubborn mate resists, but I make him look up. His teary eyes and trembling lips make me ache inside. "You are not stupid or broken. Who told you this about yourself?"

With a shaky laugh, Kieran turns his face from my grip. "No one. It's just the truth."

Framing his face in my hands, I brush away a fallen tear with my thumb. "No. Nothing could be further from the truth, Kieran. I've never wanted anyone else like I want you. I wake up hard and eager at the thought of having you. When I left you in the springs yesterday morning to get us food, I wanted to be back at your side, fucking you, kissing you, food be damned. I can't get enough of you." Unable to keep my distance any longer, I wind my arms around his shoulders. "Must be witchcraft."

To my relief, Kieran doesn't push me away. With a shaky sigh, he relaxes into my arms, nuzzling his face into my shoulder. "Do you not like feeling this way?"

"I do," I admit. "But only if you tell me that you feel the same." I don't want to be alone in this. If he doesn't want me as badly as I want him, then it would hurt me worse than the deepest cut from a blade.

Angling his head, he parts his lips and I see the invitation for what it is. Leaning in, I kiss him as deeply as I can. Our tongues tangle as he opens for me, urging me in. Just kissing him isn't enough. I want his taste to linger on my tongue like the finest wine. Want to memorize every little sound he makes. Burn him into my heart and soul and wear his mark upon me like a brand.

"I want you," Kieran rasps, "more than I've ever wanted anything in my life. All the time. And I never want it to stop."

My heart squeezes in my chest like it will burst from joy. The smile on my face must make me look like a madman, but I don't care.

I never knew happiness like this could exist.

And I wonder then if this is what it feels like to fall in love.

"Then whatever witchcraft this is," I say against his lips, cupping my hand against his angular jaw, "I pray it never lifts. I want you tonight and tomorrow. I want you for always."

Something pained twists across his face but before I can ask, he's kissing me like he'll never get the chance to do it again. "Always," he whispers, like it's a promise. But from the sadness that twists through my heart, it feels like a promise he isn't sure he can keep.

For a long time, I hold my mate. We exchange slow, gentle kisses, and I let my hands glide up and down his back.

"My—someone I knew, he hated it when I'd get anxious."

I tighten my arms around him as pain thickens Kieran's voice.

"He made me feel like such a disappointment. Like he was embarrassed that I couldn't just be normal. That's why I—" Kieran's voice catches, and the salt of his tears hits the air. "That's why I didn't want you to see. I d-didn't want you to think of me that way."

Gods, just the fact that he could think I'd be so cruel cuts like a knife.

Brushing my lips over his cheek, I say, "You could never shame me. Or cause me disappointment." I wish I could find the words to tell him that, with each day that passes, I grow more and more proud that he is mine.

Sniffling, Kieran squirms out of my arms and I reluctantly let him go. "Ah, man!" Kieran scrubs his face stubbornly and when he drops his hands, he flashes me a smile. My heart squeezes in my chest. My mate is beautiful, even with his face red and splotchy, and his smile is big and bright. "Enough of this depressing crap. Let's talk about something else."

"Oh? Like what?" I take a seat in the grass beside him, back against a tree. The northern lights dance across the sky above us, coloring the snow in vibrant hues.

"This café down the street from my apartment. I seriously miss having breakfast there!"

I cock my head. "A café?"

He chuckles. "You look like a dog when you do that. A café is... kind of like a tavern, I guess? You can get food and drinks. Sometimes before I had to go to work, I'd go to that café and order a few scoops of Greek yogurt with honey, berries, and granola. Ugh. I miss that so much."

"Yogurt? Is that a food? I've never heard of it."

He purses his lips. "Uh... it's made from milk. Kind of tart and sour unless you eat it with something sweet like honey."

"Oh! That sounds like skyr."

A frown wrinkles his brow. "Skyr? Is that even a word?"

"We make it with soured milk, heated until it cracks and releases the whey. It can be eaten or drunk if you mix it with some water."

"Hm. Sounds similar." Resting his chin on his knees that are drawn close to his chest, Kieran sighs softly. "It's more than that. I miss my home. My job. My bed. I miss living in the city."

Propping my arm on my knee, I ponder what to do to cheer him up. "Tell me stories about this city. Where is it?"

"The city is New York. Where I live, Manhattan, is on a little island. It's a big city, though. There are five boroughs. Manhattan is one of them."

"Boroughs?" He's making my head spin.

Smiling, he says, "That's like... five villages, I guess, but big. Really big."

Trying to understand, I say, "So the city is New York and within that city are five villages, one of which is yours."

"Yeah. Pretty much. The buildings there are huge, way bigger than anything in your village."

"How big?"

He points to the horizon where the mountains reach toward the moon. "I'd say half as tall as that mountain."

My mouth falls open. "No." I can't understand why anyone would need houses that big. Unless... "Ah. I suppose that leaves room for your farm animals, then. Or perhaps a whole generation of family members."

He blinks at me, then snorts laughter. "No. Okay, maybe the farm animals part makes sense. Some people hoard weird shit in their apartments. There's nothing like New York. People from all walks of life infuse the city with their culture, so you can get different food from all over the world. It's expensive as hell, dirty, loud... but I never want to live anywhere else. No matter what you're looking for, you can find it there."

It sounds incredible. "Like what?"

"If you're into nature, you can visit Central Park or ride a train upstate to find some good hiking trails. See a ballet or a musical on Broadway, go to a concert or go clubbing. I wish you could see it for yourself. I think you'd love it. Although it might be hard for a werewolf to live there. You'd need lots of room to shift and run." He pauses, worrying his lower lip. "Man. I miss it there."

Even though I'm having trouble picturing this world of the future, I can understand his yearning for the familiarity of his home—even if I wish there was some way I could make my world feel like his home so he'd never want to leave. But he will, soon. He's said so.

Are we destined to part ways? Are our worlds too different for us to be together?

"What is a... a concert?" I ask, trying not to think about him leaving.

A smile blooms over his face. "Somewhere you go to see live music. A band like the one who played at our mating ceremony."

"I see. Do you still have skalds in your time?"

"Huh?"

"A storyteller, someone who crafts poems of great heroes and their deeds."

He shrugs, tearing up some grass. "Sure. I've never been into poetry, but I've always loved playing and writing music."

Kieran, a musician? I wouldn't have expected that. "What instrument do you play?"

"I *played* a guitar for years—that's a stringed instrument."

"But you don't play anymore?" To my dismay, Kieran's shoulders slump, his scent souring with sadness.

"I don't know if I'll ever find the passion to. Ever since I was a kid, I wanted to be a singer-songwriter. Like Ed Sheeran. He's one of my favorite artists. Oh man, his album, X? That's a damn masterpiece." His face lights up when he speaks of this musician. It almost makes me jealous.

"If you love music so, then why did you stop?"

"Because I wasn't any good anyway."

For some reason, I can't imagine Kieran not being good at something. He's so stubborn, and he learned to shoot a bow in a week. He's dedicated, smart. "Why? Did someone tell you that you weren't skilled?" My fingers flex. I'd like to find whoever insulted his pride and cleave them in two.

When he nods, his lips quiver. "Oh yeah. When people important to you don't believe in you, it makes it hard to believe in yourself. So, I stopped. The world's better off without my music."

"Kieran—"

He shakes his head. "Let's go back to the cabin. It'll be dawn soon."

I let him leave without argument, but I want to find a way to cheer Kieran up—and I think I know just the thing.

Chapter 13
Kieran

WE HAVE TWO DAYS of bliss. Two days of waking up in Wulfric's arms, two days of nothing but kissing, eating, and fucking like rabbits on any surface we can.

When we're not going at it like horndogs, Wulfric goes off into the woods and disappears for a few hours. He comes back smelling like sawdust, which makes my nose itch but also makes me swoon at the woodsy aroma permeating from him. He never tells me where he's been, as if wherever it is, it's a closely guarded secret.

I asked him, jokingly but also a little seriously, if he was meeting some mythical woodland creature to sate desires I couldn't satisfy. He pinned me to the table and showed me just how insatiable he really was by rimming me until I was begging him to just fuck me already. He gave me what I wanted but only after the bastard edged me for a whole hour.

My mood slowly stabilizes. I have some mood swings, going from highs to sudden lows, and some dizziness still. When my mood drops, Wulfric is there to hold me and kiss me. He doesn't magically make things better, but having someone by my side who doesn't think I'm a burden or criticize me for not being neurotypical is... It's more than I could have hoped for. Wulfric accepts all of me, even the parts I hate the most. Somehow, I went from not being able to stand this guy to wondering how I ever could have hated him. Okay, I know why I hated him—he was kind of a prick with all the growling and kidnapping and *mate, grrr, claim* stuff.

But that's not all there is to him. He's sweet and gentle with a kind soul behind that tough alpha mask he shows the world. I'm so privileged to be the one he's chosen to share that soft heart of his with.

On the third sunrise, I wake to an empty bed, my body aching from last night's amazing activities. Wulfric stands nude by the hearth, stirring something in an iron kettle. The motions of his arm make the scars on his back stretch. I've noticed them before but never asked about them. I know ulfhednar can heal faster than any human can. When I'm on my back with Wulfric's cock buried inside me, our animals surge to the surface. His fangs cut my lips; my claws scrape his back. The cuts heal in seconds.

So why haven't these scars healed?

"Where'd you get the scars on your back?" I ask.

His shoulders stiffen, and I regret asking. He ladles some porridge into a couple of wooden bowls, sprinkling green onions over them and adding a spoonful of butter to each serving. He's a good cook. Despite the limited ingredients of this time, Wulfric's meals never lack flavor. Settling into bed beside me, he pulls up the furs and we sit shoulder to shoulder and eat.

He's quiet beside me, his brow furrowed. I'm about to apologize for ruining his mood when he says, "After my father was killed, my people hungered for blood and I for vengeance. I led a raid on the hunters that still lived, and though we slaughtered many of them, their new leader got the upper hand. He took me captive. I woke up in silver chains that burned my flesh. The leader of the hunters wanted answers about our kind."

I drop my spoon into my bowl, my appetite fading as I imagine Wulfric in chains at the mercy of the men who killed his father. "What did he want to know?"

Wulfric shrugs his shoulders, staring into the depths of his bowl. "Everything. It became very clear to me he was interested in becoming one of us. He wanted to use our power for himself. I knew if I told him our secrets, he and his hunters could become unstoppable. As hunters, they were already deadly. As ulfhednar, they would destroy us."

The hand squeezing his spoon shakes.

"I wouldn't talk. I knew if I did, I might as well execute my people myself."

"And he... did that to your back?" I grip his trembling arm before I can stop myself. Wulfric flinches at my touch, like he's back in chains, at the mercy of his captors.

A ragged breath saws out of his trembling lips, his eyes unfocused. Abruptly, he rises from the bed. I feel cold without him pressed next to me.

"I got away," Wulfric says, but it's quiet, more to himself than to me. "And what's more, I killed the bastard. Tore his throat out with my teeth and put an end to their terror for good. That's all that matters." He grabs his clothes. "I'm going to bathe. We have been away long enough. I need to return to the village and check on my people. *Our* people." He kicks the ashes in the hearth, extinguishing them. "I'll wait for you outside."

The door closes behind him and I sit in the silence.

Shit. What have I done? I shouldn't have asked. Stupid! Why did I ask him that?

Scowling, I lurch from the bed and get dressed, my fingers trembling as I lace up my boots.

My guilt fades and fury takes its place.

I'm not a warrior, but for Wulfric, I would be one.

Wulfric is *mine*.

No one will hurt him. Not ever again.

Outside, Wulfric has just finished his bath in the hot springs. He rises naked and dripping from the pool and dries himself with a cloth. His wet hair clings long and sleek to his back, and his muscles flex as he tugs on his trousers, then laces his tunic. Tying his hair up, he turns and finds me. Though our eyes meet, he looks right through me like he's thousands of miles away. Back in chains. Separated from his pack. Hurting.

There's so much I want to say, but nothing feels good enough. When he turns away, I go to him and follow him through the trees toward the distant smokestacks rising over the village. He doesn't look at me, doesn't say a word. He might as well be a ghost as he wars with the demons that lurk beneath his skin.

I don't want him to fight alone. Reaching out, I grab his hand in mine and squeeze.

The breath hitches in his chest, but he doesn't pull away.

"I'm here," I tell him and ignore the voice inside that whispers, *But for how long?* "Okay? Whatever you need. Whenever you need it. I'm here."

Wulfric finally looks at me, and something I can't read breaks through the haze in his eyes. His throat bobs when he swallows, but he stays silent.

Slipping my fingers between his, I hold on tight. "I won't let anyone hurt you again."

Maybe I can't promise that I'll always be here. Our worlds are simply too different. But for as long as I remain a part of his world, this is a promise I will keep.

No one will hurt my mate.

Not as long as I'm around.

Howls echo over the trees the closer we get to the village.

A chill runs down my spine, the human in me unnerved, but my wolf tries to howl. I barely swallow it down.

Wulfric tips his head back and howls to the pack, and that nearly makes my control over my wolf snap.

"What are they doing?" I ask, rubbing my throat.

He smiles. "Our pack is welcoming us home."

Our pack. The words fill me with pride and surprise.

As we walk into the village, everything looks the same. But I don't feel like the same person I was a few days ago, and Wulfric's people don't treat me like the outsider who came into their lives. People smile at me, even angle their heads to expose their necks, a gesture my wolf inherently recognizes. It pleases him.

"They're... accepting me?" I ask, my words low and meant for Wulfric.

"Aye, lad. They're welcoming you to the pack. Acknowledging you as one of us."

My stomach flutters with anxiety. "Oh. What is it they expect from me?"

"To stand beside me and lead. To offer me counsel and guide in times of strife. To question my authority if I lead us astray."

I swallow hard. "What if I..."

"Hmm?" He arches a brow, silver eyes curious and devoid of judgment.

"What if I can't be any of that?" My worries threaten to swallow me up. "I just became a wolf. I don't know how to be any of that to you."

I can't meet his gaze, worried he'll only reaffirm my own insecurities. "You will learn," he says easily. "And so will I. We'll learn how to work together as a whole. If you decide to stay," he adds, some of his certainty wavering.

He speaks with such confidence, like he believes in me. I wish I could feel as certain as he does. "You think I can do that? Stay here? Fit in?"

Wulfric nods. "Aye. I do. We will hold an Althing today."

"What's that?"

"A meeting. Our kin will come to us for guidance. They will look to us to ease their hardships, and we will make decisions that benefit our pack together."

A meeting? Oh great. Those already made me anxious enough in my timeline where I already knew how everything worked.

A low chuckle rumbles from his chest. Wulfric takes my hand and squeezes. "You will not be alone. If you like, you can stay silent and observe."

I'm still undecided as we near the longhouse. There's already a line of people outside waiting to see Wulfric...

and me, too, since I'm an extension of him. The idea of meeting with all these people makes me want to lock myself in our bedroom. Inside the house, thralls bustle around, setting the table with bowls and plates, carrying heavy platters of mead and various dishes to the table. The sight of their dirty, tired faces makes my heart squeeze in my chest. I wish I could help them. It isn't right.

"Where do the thralls sleep?" I ask.

"We have housing out back for them," Wulfric answers, his brows furrowing at the distaste surely visible on my face.

"Does everyone in the village own these people?"

"No. Only the wealthy."

My fists curl at my sides. "If they're wealthy enough to own thralls, they're wealthy enough to pay them for their labor."

Wulfric's brows shoot up. "Pay them? Is that what you do in your time?"

"A person is always paid for their hard work. It's despicable not to." I try to rein in my anger. Wulfric is a good man, but he's still a man of this time. I can't hope for him to understand how much slavery upsets me.

Leaving his side, I go and stand by a bubbling kettle. A thrall quickly averts her gaze. "Do you need any help?" I ask, offering her a smile.

She shakes her head rapidly. "N-no, Alpha-Mate. Do not trouble yourself." She walks over to chop up some rhubarb, then winces. She seems to be favoring her right leg.

"Are you hurt?"

Grabbing a knife, she chops the vegetable into thin slices. "Aye. It's the gout in my toe. Always acts up when it gets cold like this."

"Is there anything you can do for the pain?" I know they don't have any over-the-counter meds in this time, but surely they must have some herbal remedies to ease her pain.

She shakes her head. "I have asked for help, but I don't believe our overseer ever told Alpha Wulfric."

Of course not. "Who is your overseer?"

"Brynjolf."

I would be having words with this Brynjolf. "I'll make sure to tell Wulfric. What's your name?"

"F-Freda, Alpha-Mate."

"Call me Kieran, Freda." I march back to Wulfric. He's talking to Helga over a mug of mead. "Did you know Freda has gout?"

Wulfric frowns. "Who?"

I roll my eyes skyward. "Freda! One of your thralls. She has terrible pain in her foot. Brynjolf, her overseer, never brought it up to you."

Understanding clouds Wulfric's eyes. "Oh."

"Why don't you know the names of any of the men and women that cook your meals and clean your house?"

He averts his eyes. "Knowing their names has never seemed important to me."

Disappointment tastes sour in my throat. "Because they're objects to you, right? They're people, Wulfric. They deserve respect and decency. Why can't you see that?"

My mate hangs his head like a scolded dog. "What would you have me do?" he says, challenging me with a glare. "They live on my land for free. They have safety from their enemies. A roof over their heads. Food."

"When the overseer remembers to feed them," I add, looking with disgust at how thin the thralls are.

Throwing up his hands, Wulfric rises to his feet. "Sorry to be such a disappointment to you, but this is the way of life. If they're too weak to fight, then the least they can do is serve."

Shaking my head, I back away from him. "You're better than this, Wulf. Start acting like it." Ignoring his frustrated sigh, I stomp past him. Turning to Helga, I say, "I need to help Freda with her gout."

"Of course." She leaves Wulfric and me looking anywhere but at each other, then returns with a basket full of herbs. "Here you are." She hands me some kind of gourd. "Cherry gourd. It can be boiled, then crushed into a paste. If she puts it on her foot, it should help with the pain."

"Thank you." Rising from the table, I grab a soapstone kettle and fill it with fresh water from a pitcher on the table. I stew in my annoyance while the water comes to a boil over the fire. Somehow, I have to convince Wulfric that keeping thralls is inhumane. Dropping the gourd into the boiling water, I watch it float around amidst the bubbles.

Someone comes to stand beside me. I don't have to look to know it's Wulfric since I can smell him.

"Freda's condition should have been brought to my attention," Wulfric rumbles beside me. "I will be having a word with their overseer. Mayhap they are not great warriors, but the thralls are still hard workers, and they cannot work if they are in pain."

"Can you free them?"

Wulfric's eyebrows shoot up. "*Free* them? I rely on them for their labor. They do the work I myself don't have the time to do. Besides, for many of them, it is all they know."

"That doesn't make it right." I turn toward him, needing him to understand. "They should have a choice to stay or go and forge a new life for themselves. Freedom is a right we all deserve, no matter what caste we're born into."

Moving his jaw from side to side, Wulfric stares into the bubbling water. "This is important to you."

"It is." I grip his arm. "Wulfric, I..." The words get stuck in my throat, but this may be the only way he'll listen—if he cares about me at all. "I can't be with a man who treats other people like property."

Wulfric's shoulders stiffen. A rush of panic flares through the bond connecting me to him but then all feeling disappears. Like he's shut me out. "This is no simple thing you're demanding of me."

"I know. It's your way of life, but it's cruel and it isn't right. If our values don't align, then I can't see this relationship working out."

A muscle in his jaw twitches, like he's grinding his teeth. "How am I to broach this to my people without causing trouble for all of us? Not everyone would be pleased. Some might challenge my authority."

"It's possible some of the villagers have already considered freeing their thralls. Think about the ones you know who treat their thralls more kindly than others. They may be more open to the idea."

A sigh makes his nostrils flare, and his lips thin to a straight line as he weighs what I'm asking of him. "If I'm to bring this up at the Althing, then we need a plan."

Hope lifts my sinking heart. "You'll consider it?"

Dragging a hand through his hair with a sigh like he's going to the gallows, he says, "I will broach the idea at the Althing. Before then, if you have any ideas, share them with me."

"I do, actually," I say, unable to keep the smile off my face. "But I'd rather hear what they need first."

Wulfric nods, stirring the gourd in the water. Then he adds, "You're a good man, Kieran. Far better than I am."

The praise takes me by surprise. Such surprise that I lean up and kiss his cheek, curling my fingers in his hair. "Thank you for hearing me out."

He grunts but leans into the touch of my lips. A warm flare of contentment blooms in my chest. I like that I can feel how I affect him.

Heart ten times lighter, I hurry out into the yard and go in search of the thralls' quarters.

An hour goes by while I visit with the thralls. They enjoy the idea of being paid for their work, their faces lighting up with hope at the prospect of building a future for themselves.

When I return to the house, Wulfric is at the head of the table, waiting to meet his people. A feast has been prepared, the table piled with dishes. Sliding into a seat beside him, I grab a flagon of mead and take a sip.

"Did you speak with them?" Wulfric asks.

"I did." I go over what I learned, watching him with my heart in my throat.

Wulfric sighs. "It seems there's much to be done." He glowers into his stew. "How could I have let their living conditions get so bad?"

"Isn't it the overseer's job to report stuff like that to you?"

"Aye, and he hasn't been doing his job." He massages between his brows. "Neither have I. My mind has been elsewhere. What else have I let slip my notice?"

Seeing him troubled makes me feel troubled, so I lean in and bump my shoulder against his. "Good thing you've got me to remind you, huh?" I mean it as a joke, but a soft smile hooks the corner of his mouth.

"Aye. Very good indeed." He leans in and claims my lips, cupping the back of my neck in a firm, possessive hold that makes me shiver. "It's fortunate the Norns brought us together when they did."

"So you'll really do this?"

"I will announce it at the Althing. The Norns brought you to me for a reason. It's their way of telling me that the time for change has come. I will free those who want to be freed to do as they wish, and if any would prefer to stay, then they will be paid for their work. I don't expect many others to follow along. The opposite, in fact. But I will do this. Have I pleased you?"

I kiss him in answer, framing his face between my hands. "So much." Beneath the table, I slide my hand over his thigh then farther up, curling my fingers over his clothed cock. "In fact, I wish this meeting was over now so we could make good use of this table."

A low growl rumbles from his chest. "I take it that means you'll stay with me and I don't have to tie you to my bedpost."

My breath hitches as a realization takes hold of my heart. I could have a place here with Wulfric. In my timeline I'm nothing, a nobody, but here? Here in Wulfric's time, I can use my knowledge from the future to make a difference in the lives of Wulfric's people.

But more than that... I don't *want* to leave Wulfric. As much as I miss the familiarity and comfort of the modern world, for everything the future has, there would be no Wulfric. Is that really a world I want to be a part of?

"Oh, you can tie me to your bedpost any time you want," I purr into his ear.

Taking his hand in mine, I hold tight beneath the table as the doors open and the villagers come in. Lyall and Gunnar are among them... and so is Anders. Great. My stomach twists at the sight of him. Those green eyes find mine, narrowing in contempt. I still remember him rushing me, claws extended, fangs sharp. He got me in trouble, but everyone still thinks I attacked him, though it seems they've forgiven me. I doubt Anders has just let things go.

"All right?" Wulfric asks, no doubt sensing my anger and fear.

Humming, I lift his hand and kiss his knuckles.

The meeting begins once everyone is seated. Wulfric squeezes my hand where it lies on his thigh and says, voice low and clear, "Kieran and I thank you all for helping us celebrate our union. We are aware our mating is not conventional. Outsiders, especially humans, are rare in our pack. But I believe this is a sign from the Norns that the times are changing, and that we must change with them."

Anders's narrowed eyes bore into me, his whole body taut and radiating contempt.

"Kieran and I have talked about changes we'd like to make going forward." He looks to me expectantly, and I realize with a lurch in my stomach that he wants me to speak.

Clearing my throat, I open my mouth, but my brain shuts down mid-thought. "I..." I take a breath and fight through the panic fogging my brain as everyone's eyes land on me. "I talked to Wulfric about the, uh... the thralls he keeps in his service. Um." *Come on, me. Say something!*

"I'm right here." Wulfric's voice fills my mind.

Squeezing his hand so tightly his breath hitches, I continue speaking. "People are not property. We all deserve freedom, no matter our status in life. So, from this day on, we will free any thralls in our service. Those who choose to stay will be paid wages for their work." Whispers spread among the villagers.

Lyall doesn't look troubled by the notion and neither does Gunnar. "I think that's fair," Lyall says. "Keeping men and women in chains has never felt right to me. I'm glad this is changing."

Gunnar chuckles. "Seems to me our brother's gotten soft."

Wulfric growls, but Lyall and Gunnar laugh at him.

Anders continues to glare at me. "First, you'd have us free our thralls, and then what's next, brother? Shall you have us roll over and take it up the ass from our enemies, too?"

Wulfric grips my hand so tight, I wince. "If you have a problem with my leadership, then speak plainly."

"Your so-called leadership is a bloody sham!" Anders slams his palm on the table, his claws raking the wood. "First, you take this *human* as your mate. Then you free the thralls we depend upon for our survival. This outsider wants to change our very way of life! And you're rolling over and allowing it! You and your foolishness will lead us all to our deaths!"

Wulfric just shakes his head, laughing his disbelief.

Heart racing, I say, "The thralls wouldn't all leave. If we offer them an honest wage and improve their living conditions, and you know, treat them like actual human beings, many will likely stay to work."

Anders points a clawed hand at me. "I did not tell you to speak, *human*! Speak to me again, and I will—"

Wulfric rises so fast, his chair falls backward with a crash. "Think very carefully about what you're about to say to him." The ice in his voice makes me shiver, and Anders's rage sputters out of him. "Insult me all you wish, but speak that way to my mate again, and I will not hesitate to draw my blade in his defense."

A rush of warmth spreads throughout my body. *My mate.* I never dreamed he'd defend me so fiercely. No one's stood up for me before. All too well I remember the night when he snarled that I would never be the mate he'd have chosen. The shame in his voice had cut right through me. I don't know why it hurt—I wouldn't have chosen me either, some nervous wreck who wasn't good enough for his own boyfriend.

Now here he is, that very same man, ready to draw his weapon against his own brother in my defense. Choosing me. Letting me take up space at his table and govern his people alongside him. Like I'm someone special to him, like I *matter.*

Anders looks ready to tear him apart for it, and my wolf snarls beneath my skin. Before I can stop myself, I go to Wulfric's side where I belong, wrapping my arm tight around his waist.

No one will hurt him. Not ever.

CHAPTER 14
WULFRIC

ALL MY PROTECTIVE INSTINCTS surge to the surface as Kieran comes to stand at my side.

Anders stares me down, claws out and fangs sharp.

I don't want this, but this storm between us has been brewing for a long time. Anders has always coveted the title of alpha, and he's made it plain that in his eyes, I am a piss-poor choice. Lyall rises and goes to his twin, murmuring to him, his eyes wide and pleading.

Anders shoves him away. "You will be the death of us, Wulfric. Our parents are watching us from Valhalla. The shame you bring their name... it must tear them apart."

I tense my stomach muscles like I'm preparing for a punch. When Anders is pissed, every word cuts deeper than a knife. He's right. I'm sure my parents are disappointed in me. I try, gods, I try to be the man, the son, the leader they would have wanted. And I'll never know if it's enough.

Like he's sensed an opening, Anders strikes again. This time, he goes deep. "If I'd been on that beach when the hunters came, our father would still be here."

I can feel the blood drain from my face, my hands curling into fists sharp with claws.

Anders's voice shakes, his eyes wild with emotion. "I could have saved him. If he'd just let me go in your stead, but no. It had to be you, didn't it? His *precious* heir! You're the one who should have died that day, not him!" Spittle flies from his lips.

His furious roar drags me down to that damned beach where my world crumbled. Blood dyes the foaming waves red as they splatter over the rocks. The lifeless eyes of men and boys I know by name stare right through me as I lie face down on the bloody shore, too terrified to move. Warriors utter prayers to Odin through throats thick with blood. Others in the throes of death whimper and beg for their mothers, their loved ones, their children.

Arrows soar over my head, barely missing my skull. Weapons crack like thunder against shields. My people are dying or dead, and I *can't move.* I can't because if I move I know that I will be cut down and my life will be over. *Just be still. Be quiet. Live.* They can't hurt me if they think I'm dead.

A huge black wolf charges through the clashing bodies. With a single pounce, he brings down a hunter and tears into his throat. When he looks at me, blood drips from his snout.

My father still lives. When he sees me, his fear and relief surge through the bond. He runs to me, shaking the ground.

And he doesn't see the archer on the cliff above, not until the arrow has flown loose. With a roar, my father stumbles, biting at the arrow lodged in his shoulder.

Get up.

Get up.

Get up.

I can't move. I'm too fucking scared. If I run fast enough, I can make it. I can save him.

Another arrow pierces my father, this time in his throat. He goes down, shaking the earth.

A hunter comes toward my father, stepping over the corpses of my slain kin, bedecked in armor with the Christian cross painted across the metal in blood. A silver dagger gleams in his hand. Slamming a boot down on my father's skull, the hunter lifts his weapon and—

"No!" The roar tears from me. Stumbling back, I crash into the hearth, clutching the mantelpiece so my buckling knees don't give in. "It wasn't my fault. I tr-tried." I'm panting but no matter how fast I breathe, I can't get in enough air. My heart slams against my ribs, racing so fast I know it will rupture in my chest. I should be dead. Anders is right. I'm the one who should have died.

"I r-ran as fast as I could. I was almost there. I could have saved him. I—"

If I hadn't been such a coward. If I'd just been stronger, braver...

Gasping, I press my face into the stone floor, unsure when I fell to my knees in the first place. *Just lie down. Be still. Be quiet. They won't hurt me if I'm dead.* The screams and pleas of dying men tear at my brain. Red waves smash over the rocks. Arrows puncture the ground around me. I close my eyes and wait to die.

"But you didn't. You didn't save him. We lost him." Anders's voice shakes with grief and fury. "It should have been you. Why couldn't it have been you?"

The sound of flesh hitting flesh and a pained grunt silence Anders's tirade.

Gasping for air, I look up.

Kieran is inches from Anders, and from the angle of his clenched fist, I think he just punched my brother in the mouth. Anders's split lip and blazing eyes confirm it.

"Shut the fuck up," Kieran snarls, his body vibrating with fury. White fur sprouts on his arms, his fur cloak bristling like it's about to come to life. "How about you look past your own fucking grief and understand that he's hurting, too! He did the best he could."

Anders's chest rises and falls quickly, his hands in fists. If I don't get up now, he's going to hurt Kieran. "You weren't there."

"No, I wasn't," Kieran snaps, staring him down without a fear in the world, "but if I know anything about Wulfric, it's that he would have given everything he had to save his father. He cares about this pack so deeply, he mated a man he barely even knew because he wants to be the best alpha he can be. Because he cares about you, you asshole, and your brothers. So if you really think you can do a better job than him, then how about you shut up and prove it?"

For a moment, I'm stunned out of my panic. I've never seen Kieran so furious, and it warms me that it's on my behalf. My knees shake too badly to stand, but I need to go to him and make sure my brother doesn't hurt him.

"That's enough." Helga gets between Anders and Kieran. "This Althing is concluded. Get out, all of you."

"But, Alpha, someone stole my goat!" a man shouts.

"To Hel herself with your goat. Out!"

"Yas, queen," Kieran whispers. I have no idea what that means, but he looks at Helga like she hung the moon.

Helga motions wildly for everyone to clear the room. "And you." She rounds on Anders. "Your parents would be ashamed of this. You're fighting among your brothers when you should be coming together."

Anders flinches. "Apologies, Aunt." But from the glare he gives me, I know this isn't over. Good. I've had it up to here with Anders challenging my authority. If he thinks he'd be a better alpha, then he should prove it just like Kieran said.

The house empties except for my family. My mate kneels at my side, rubbing my shoulders. My breathing is choppy, and my head swims as spots dance in front of my eyes. If I close them, it feels like I'll fall into nothingness.

I should have tried harder to save Father. I could have done more. All the guilt I thought I'd locked away for years now has returned with a vengeance, threatening to eat me alive.

"I'll make you that tea, Wulfric," Helga says, like she knows I will be in for an especially bad night. Her tea keeps the nightmares at bay and helps me sleep.

Lyall approaches and tousles my hair. "I'm proud to call you Alpha, brother. Anders is hurting, but he's wrong."

Gunnar nudges my boot with his foot. "We know you did the best you could. You fought to save him with everything you had, I'm sure of it."

Bile rises in my throat. If they knew... oh gods. They would hate me. Anders is right. He's right.

Kieran shakes his head, tucking his face between my neck and shoulder, nuzzling me like a wolf would. "I think he needs to be by himself, guys."

"I'll stop by in the morning," Gunnar promises.

"Good evening," Lyall says, offering one more smile.

"Wulfric?" Kieran asks, his voice soft in the silence. "Do you need something? What can I do?"

I can't speak. It's like I'm trapped on that beach, terrified to move even a single muscle.

"Hey." Gentle hands frame my face, but I flinch out of his touch. I don't deserve kindness nor understanding. I should be dead. "Wulfric." Kieran's voice is far away. I can't even look at him. He deserves so much better than me. A sigh rattles from my chest. Closing my eyes, all I want is to curl in on myself and never wake up.

If I'd just been stronger, been a better warrior, a better son, I could have saved him.

I can't take it. The pain. The guilt. Every time I think the wound has healed, something tears it open all over again and I bleed out. I need to escape. Yanking my furs over me, I let the shift drag me under. All my emotions are pushed to the back of my mind as I run, crashing through the front door and out into the cold. My mate calls after me, his bond compelling me to turn back, but I ignore it.

My paws carry me forward, leaping over fences and startling livestock until I'm surrounded by overgrown forest. I run until the breath tears from my aching lungs, until the demons from my past can no longer catch me. When my body is too sore to keep running, I collapse at the base of a tree.

In this form, my worst thoughts are only distant whispers, easily carried away by the wind.

Head on my paws, I close my eyes and finally know peace.

The moon rises and falls seven times. It's been a long time since I've stayed away from the village. In the days after my father's death and my escape from captivity, I stayed away for weeks at a time. Being a wolf was simply easier. I could be another person and not the coward who'd lain on the shore and watched as his enemy drove a blade into his father's neck. Like a gods-damned coward.

I'm not Wulfric. All I am is a wolf, and all wolves have to do is eat, hunt, and sleep.

But every so often, a howl echoes over the trees, and notes of sorrow and loneliness make my heart break. I long to return my mate's song, to reassure him that I will return, but I can't bring myself to acknowledge him. I closed myself off from the bonds connecting me to my pack, needing privacy. I can't hear them or sense them, nor can they do the same to me. I need to be alone.

I never wanted anyone to see me like that. Never wanted my people to see the real me, the scared boy who couldn't save his father. But they did. They saw how deeply I am still scarred by his death. Kieran saw that.

A low whine escapes my throat, and I curl up more tightly into a ball on the forest floor.

How can I ever face him again? I can never be the mate, the *man,* he deserves.

Best to simply stay as a wolf and let Wulfric the man die.

Anders would be a better leader. He would have saved our father.

It's better if I disappear.

The sun rises on another day alone in the woods. My mouth waters for the reindeer I killed the other day, so I rise, shake off my pelt, and set off at a trot into the woods. Twigs snap behind me and the winds blow familiar scents to my nose.

Oh no.

Spinning around, I bare my fangs as Lyall and Gunnar emerge from the trees. Lyall, a white wolf, whines, lowering his head submissively while still wagging his foolish tail. Gunnar, a mottled gray wolf, growls at me.

"Go away," I tell them, turning my back and walking away.

"That's enough of this nonsense, Wulfric," Gunnar says, loping up beside me. *"Get off your hairy asshole and come back to the village."*

"Gunnar, take it easy," Lyall scolds, nipping at his brother's flank.

Gunnar snaps at Lyall in retaliation. *"When has easy ever been good enough? Did you lot let me take it easy after I lost Leif or my boy? No. If I had been allowed to 'take it easy,' I wouldn't still be alive."*

"Wulfric, come back to the village. We're worried about you."

"I know!" Lyall's ears perk up. *"How about we go for a swim? That always makes you feel better."*

Gunnar rolls his lips back from his fangs. *"No, let's take him hunting, work out all that negative energy!"*

Lyall nips at his ass again. *"Swimming!"*

"Hunting!" Gunnar pounces on him and the two engage in a fierce sparring match.

Gods, give me strength. They are like oil and water, Gunnar's hotheaded impulsiveness a contrast to Lyall's even-tempered, soft-spoken nature.

Satisfied, I lope away into the trees. I have my peace and quiet back... for fifteen minutes, until they catch up to me.

They don't approach me, but it's easy to see them through the trees, stalking me like prey. Every time I think I've shaken them, Gunnar's dark coat stands out against the snow or Lyall's tail wags above a bush. I'm forced to change direction multiple times to try and evade them until I realize what they're doing as the path becomes more and more familiar.

The trees thin the closer we get to the village and smoke rises over the woods. If I go east, I could be there in moments. I could see Kieran. I have no doubt he's angry and worries for me. Instead, I go west when I spot the glimmer of Gunnar's eyes from beneath a cluster of trees near the village pathway.

My feet lead me onward, my brothers hot on my trail. I know where they're guiding me. It's somewhere I haven't been in a long time. The burial mound looks like an ordinary hill from this distance. Towering stones erected to form the shape of a ship encircle it. I don't know why they've led me here, but I suspect it's in some misguided attempt to help me. The fools. A plague on the pair of them.

Still, it's been some time since I paid my respects, so I seek the entrance to the barrow. Inside, Gunnar and Lyall wait for me as men. They must have come from the other side of the hill while I hesitated. They've already lit the torches, illuminating the chamber within. Stone slags conceal the ancient remains of the alphas and their mates who came before me, but I find my father's and mother's remains easily. Even in death, my heart knows my pack.

Many of our ancestors' remains were desecrated when the hunters burned our childhood home. After we burned my father on the pyre we gathered his ashes and bones, dug up the graves that hadn't been destroyed, and brought their remains to their new resting place.

Offerings lie upon their coffin: arrows, my father's sword, my mother's shield and her favorite steed's saddle. If I'd known I was coming, I'd have brought something for them. I wish to this day I'd had the chance to get to know my mother, but she died giving birth to me. Our father and Helga raised us.

Gunnar steps away from Lyall and me and crosses over to the coffin where his chosen mate lies buried with their son. They were both killed in the hunter attack. Gunnar kneels by the coffin and hangs his head. I look away, unsettled by the scent of his pain.

Lyall stares down at the coffin, sighing softly. "Father was a great man, Wulfric. But I think you forget he had his imperfections."

Gunnar growls, "Like trusting Soren."

Lyall rounds on him. "Do not speak his name! Soren didn't betray us!"

I haven't heard Lyall speak that traitor's name in years and yet the anguish in his voice is still as heavy as it was all those years ago.

After Father took him in, Soren grew up alongside us, Lyall's constant companion. When Soren confessed himself that he'd known about the hunters' plans, it had shocked us all.

Gunnar says, "He confessed so himself, Lyall. He gave up our location to the hunters. He chose his father and his hunters over us."

Lyall shakes his head furiously. "He lied to protect me, so the rest of the pack wouldn't think I was in on the attack! You all wanted someone to blame for father's death, so you took it out on him! You never even questioned the things he said."

Mayhap he's right. I don't know. The days after the attack are such a blur in my memory.

Gunnar gives us an icy look over his shoulder. "Still you defend that traitorous craven!"

Lyall winces, grinding his teeth. I can see he longs to protect Soren, still, after all this time. As much as it irritates me, I can understand. It was clear to all of us that he loved Soren. I'd thought Soren loved him, too, but it was all a lie. He'd used us for protection, then stabbed us in the back when the hunters came to save him. When Soren was exiled, Lyall disappeared into the woods for days and didn't return. When he did, he smiled less and the light in his eyes had ceased to shine.

Clearing his throat, Lyall carries on. "I'm only saying that Wulfric bears too much responsibility for Father's demise. Our father knew what he was doing. He was a man, a warrior. He knew the costs of war."

Lowering myself to my belly, I rest my head on my parents' coffin. Even if I were human, I could never find it in me to tell them my role in our father's death. If they knew I'd given in to fear and watched our father die, they would hate me. I've lost both my parents. I cannot lose any more of my family, but I fear the guilt inside will fester until it eats me alive unless I tell them the truth. The fear of losing their love and respect wins out over my guilt, though. I stay silent.

"Kieran misses you deeply," Lyall says.

A whine escapes me before I can choke it back. I miss him, too. It's only been a handful of nights since I last saw him, but it feels like months since I held him in my arms and kissed him.

"Won't you go back to him? It isn't fair to make him worry."

"I can't face him," I say through the bonds. *"Not after showing such weakness."*

Gunnar scoffs. "He doesn't give a shit about any of that, you pigheaded oaf. He misses you."

Why would Kieran ever want a broken wolf with scars carved upon his heart and soul? No matter how much time passes, all it takes is a harsh word from my brother and I'm back on that beach, cowering in terror while my father dies in front of me.

Gunnar comes to kneel beside me and rests a hand on my head between my ears. "Our village needs their Alpha. Anders is getting more brazen with each day you're gone. He'll stage a coup. You've got to come back."

"We need you, Wulfric. We need you to be strong for us."

I tire of being strong, of fighting battles outside and within myself. All I want is the space to fall apart and the time to put myself back together again. Aren't I allowed that much?

Panic erupts in my chest. No. Not again. I can't go back to that beach. I can't...

"What *is* that?" Lyall gasps, clutching his chest. "Is that... By the gods, something's wrong!"

It's not my panic, not my terror that's coursing through my chest.

It's Kieran's fear, his *pain* that courses through me like the bite of a blade.

Something horrible is happening to him.

I'm up on my paws and tearing from the barrow. For the first time in days, I find my voice and hurl my head back to the skies.

A song of war pours from my throat and echoes into the vast open sky above.

Chapter 15
Kieran

Damn it, I miss Wulfric.

It's been days since I've seen him. If I wasn't sure he needed his space, I'd have followed his scent and found him myself. I felt like that's the opposite of what he needs. So, I stayed away, even if it killed me inside.

I spent the nights in the bed we'd shared, hoping that when I woke, he'd be there. He never was. At night, I went into the woods, shifted, and sang my heart out for him, hoping he'd hear my song, that he'd come running home to me. But the nights have been silent without his answering song.

I miss him, so much.

More than anything, I'm scared for him. I've been to some really low places over the course of my life. I know what a breakdown looks like, that eruption of emotion that happens when something has been building and building. I've been there before. What happened with Wulfric was bad. I don't know how to help him, so all I can do now is give him the space he needs.

I just hope he doesn't shut me out. We were finally growing close. Wulfric had let his walls down and given me a glimpse of the kind, thoughtful man behind them. I don't want to lose that, lose *him*. When did that happen? Were my feelings so gradual they snuck up on me without me even noticing? Or were they there all along, hiding behind a mask of contempt?

Somehow, I've gone from despising the man to needing him with a desperation I've never felt for anyone before. Did I ever despise him? I was always attracted to him, I know that for sure, but I couldn't stand feeling that way toward him when he was such an asshole.

But now that I've seen him, the *real* Wulfric, I can look back and see moments where his true self shone through the grumpy façade. When he cooked me breakfast because he knew I wasn't eating the food the thralls prepared. How dedicated he was to my survival and my training. The way he saved me when we met.

I hope he comes home soon.

In the meantime, I'm trying to keep myself busy around the house. I help prepare meals and train with Lyall and Gunnar. To my knowledge, they don't know where Wulfric is either.

Gunnar told me this has happened before. Wulfric falls into a dark place and retreats for days, sometimes weeks, at a time. He always comes out of it. I wish I could feel reassured, but all I can remember is the way the blood drained from his face as his knees buckled, how this giant of a man curled in on himself, trying to make himself small in the face of whatever horrors tormented him.

It still makes my heart hurt just thinking about it.

I swear, if Anders ever fucks with Wulfric again, I'll make him regret it.

He's been lurking around the village. I've seen him in passing in the marketplace, sensed him watching me while I train with his brothers, but he doesn't approach me. I wish the feud between him and Wulfric would blow over already but somehow Wulfric's absence feels like the calm before the storm.

On the seventh day of Wulfric's absence, I go in search of Lyall and Gunnar in the training yard. From the open kitchen window, Helga calls, "They went looking for Wulfric."

My heart leaps. "They did? Do they know where he is?"

"Oh, they've known all along. They wanted to give him space, but I told them enough's enough. Knowing Wulfric, he's been shifted the whole time he's been gone. It's not good for the mind to stay as a wolf so long or we risk getting stuck in that form."

Has Wulfric been shifted this entire time? What if something had happened? Fear has me curling my hands into fists. "Why would he risk that?" I snap, frustrated and worried.

Sadness steals the light from her eyes. "He can't help it, Kieran."

Sighing, I kick a rock across the yard. "I know, I just… I'm worried about him."

"I know you are, dear. In the past, it's taken all of us to bring him back but now he has you."

I shake my head. "What about me? I've barely got a handle on my own problems."

"You're very put together. You've kept this place afloat while he's been away."

I'm only put together because my anxiety won't let me be any other way. Inside, I'm a damn mess. I wouldn't come back for me if I were Wulfric. Now that I've depressed myself enough, I say, "I want to go for a walk. Do you need anything?" I've got to stay busy. If I'm busy I can't think things like, *What if he never comes back?*

"We're running low on eggs. Could you trade for some from Hilda's farm? Give her this."

Through the open window, she hands me a sack of grain. "Sure." I set off down the road and into town.

I wish I were in a better mood because today is a beautiful day. Snowy mountains on the horizon reach toward a clear blue sky and while it's chilly, it isn't freezing. It's a gorgeous day but without Wulfric by my side, I can't enjoy it. There's a void in my heart. Wherever Wulfric is, I hope he's okay. I can't sense his emotions but Helga told me that's normal, that he closes the bonds to give himself privacy. Worry twists my insides into knots.

Someone small crashes into me. I stumble and almost drop the grain in my surprise. "Whoa! Watch it, bud!" A child with red hair, blue eyes, and cute freckled cheeks tugs urgently at my sleeve.

"Alpha-Mate, my friend is hurt!"

Why is he coming to me? Where are his parents?

"Please, come quick! You have to help him. You must!" He tries to tug me off the main path through the village.

"How badly is he hurt? Does he need a healer?" I think I remember where the healer's hut is. She should tend to the kid's injuries, not me.

"Please, hurry!" The kid takes off before I can stop him. Damn it, I have to follow him. I can't get the healer if I don't know where his friend is.

"Hey, wait up!" I jog after him, leaving the bustling street behind as I pursue him. The buildings thin until we're surrounded by woodland. What were these kids doing out here alone? It doesn't seem safe, especially since they can't shift and defend themselves yet.

The kid waves at me from a cluster of trees, pointing wildly at someone out of sight. Shit, is the kid passed out? This is bad. I'll have to carry him back to the village and to the healer.

Bracing myself for the worst—lots of blood, a broken bone or two—I peer around the trees. But there's nothing there. I look around, but there's no sign of another person, not even a scent. Except the winds change, carrying the scents of other people to my nose. Four of them, and they're right behind me.

I whirl around in time to see four men burst from the cover of the trees they were hiding behind. One of them hurls something powdery in my face that burns my nose. Silver. My face ignites with scorching heat, my eyes blazing in their sockets. My howl of pain becomes a grunt as a knee slams into my stomach. Cramps rack my body, bringing me to the ground. I choke on sour bile, curling into a ball to protect myself.

My eyes water, spilling tears down my face so I can't see the men attacking me. But I've got their scents in my memory now. One of them smells like horseshit. Two of them reek of ale. The third has notes of green onion and angelica wafting from him. Hopefully, I'll live long enough to do something with that information.

"Think you can come into our village and change everything?" one of them snarls.

"You've weakened our Alpha!"

A boot slams into my jaw, cracking it. Blood fills my mouth as a tooth gets ripped free. I roll over, hiding my face in the ground as I groan pitifully.

"Anders is right. Outsiders like you are a threat!"

Anders. That bastard!

Fear and fury light up the dormant bond in my chest.

Wulfric. It's him. He's coming for me.

Terror eclipses the brief joy at finally feeling him for the first time in a week.

"Don't. Don't come. Stay away, Wulfric. Stay away!"

This is what Anders wants. He's going to lure Wulfric out of hiding by hurting me. I'm going to be used as a weapon to harm the man I love.

No. No, no, no!

"W-Wulfric," I croak, and then another kick hits me across the face. My nose crunches on impact, and hot blood spurts down my face. Waves of agony leave me paralyzed. One of them took away my furs and without them, my healing won't kick in. All I can do is gasp for breath through a chest that feels like it's been shattered.

Laughing, the men leave me by myself, blinded and too injured to move.

Curling into a ball, all I do is wait for the pain to end.

"Kieran? Oh gods... Kieran!"

That voice pulls me from the depths of my agony.

My eyes are too blurry to see him, but I would know that voice anywhere, even if I can't smell him through my broken nose.

Tears of joy and pain sting my eyes.

Wulfric is here. He came for me. I don't care what happens next, just so long as he's here.

"Oh, little rabbit." Emotion makes his voice quake. "You're going to be all right. I promise. I'm here."

Big arms wrap me in a tight embrace as he hoists me from the ground. My body aches, and I stifle my whimper by hiding my face in his shoulder. A rush of sound comes at me as we return to the village. Voices rise in panic and confusion, the noise making my aching head throb.

"Move, all of you!" Wulfric roars.

Gnashing my teeth, I gasp at the pain that cracks through my skull.

"Shh, love. I have you." Tender lips find my forehead, the scratch of his beard a comfort I've missed.

We move fast, and I spiral into a throbbing abyss of pain and nausea. A door opens and Helga cries, "Thank the gods, you found him!"

Wulfric says, "Get the healer. Now!" Another door creaks, and I'm laid on something soft. Our bed, I think.

Big hands take hold of my hand, rubbing and squeezing. His hands are so warm, but I feel like a block of ice. Shock. That must be it. I can't stop shivering.

I fall back into the abyss.

Pain pulls me from the nothingness, a scream tearing from my lungs.

"Don't hurt him!" Wulfric's furious roar makes me tremble.

"I-I'm so sorry, Alpha!" an unfamiliar voice says.

"Wulfric, it was a mistake. Calm yourself," Helga snaps. Her hand is warm and leathery in mine.

A rough hand brushes my cheek. "Shh. Rest. The healer is making you better."

I close my eyes and...

When I open them next, I can see. My face throbs like a brick smashed it in. The windows are shuttered and the room is dark, but shards of sunlight illuminate enough of the room to make out my surroundings. I'm in our bed, but Wulfric isn't with me. Panic squeezes my chest. *Please, don't be gone.*

I try to reach out to him through the bond but only encounter an empty space in my head and chest. My furs are gone, and I can't sense the pack, can't sense Wulfric. Wulfric is gone. He left again. He—

The door creaks open and I wince as the light from the bright room burns my eyes. I guess they aren't as healed as I thought. Blinking until my watery vision clears, I gasp as Wulfric comes into view. Joy warms every part of me and my eyes dampen again, this time from the happiness of seeing him.

When our eyes meet, he slams the tray on the table and bolts to my bedside. On his knees, he carefully frames my face in his hands, guiding me in for a kiss that's painfully chaste for how desperately I want him. He has to be careful of my injured nose, I guess.

He shakes against me and when I taste the salt on his lips, I realize he's crying.

"Kieran," he croaks. His fingers curl in my hair, his nails scraping over dried flecks of blood. There's pain, but it's nothing I can't handle, not when he needs me like this.

I try to put my arms around him and gasp, grinding my teeth at how stiff and achy one of my arms is. Praying it isn't broken, I wrap my good arm around his shoulders and squeeze tight.

"Gods. Forgive me. Please, forgive me." He sucks in a shuddery gasp, kissing the mark he left upon my neck again and again. "I shouldn't have left you alone."

"S'okay, Wulf," I say, my voice gravelly from dehydration. All that matters is he's here. "Long as you don't do it again, you bastard."

His body shudders against me, his trembling arms holding me tighter. "Never in this life or the next."

"Can I... have some water? Or Advil or something?" I really miss the convenience of modern medicine right now.

"Yes. Yes, of course." Releasing me from his arms, Wulfric grabs the tray and carries it to me. "Hardly a warrior's meal, I know, but the healer said you need liquids until you can chew comfortably."

Wulfric doesn't look good. Bags hang under his wet, bloodshot eyes and his hair is disheveled. Lifting the spoon to my lips, he helps me take a sip of hot broth. "She said you could have porridge too. I can make some if you like."

"Stay."

He smiles but it doesn't reach his eyes. "I will."

The broth warms my stomach, chasing away the cold. We don't speak until the bowl is empty and I've had my fill. My aching eyes long to close.

Wulfric takes my hand and squeezes it. "Who did this to you?"

My throat tightens, and I feel so damn useless. "I don't know."

"What did they look like? Did you see their faces?"

"No," I snap. "They rushed me. I didn't even have time to react. I couldn't even fight them off. I..." Shame overwhelms me, and I bow my head.

"Because they were godless cravens who didn't have the balls to face you man to man. Not because you were weak, Kieran. You are the very opposite of weak."

Tears burn my eyes and I wish I could stand up and break something to pieces. I feel so goddamn weak, so powerless, so fucking ashamed. "I only got their scents. Can you do something with that?"

Wulfric leans in, his eyes intent upon me. The eyes of a hunter. "Tell me."

Closing my eyes, I try and recall, fighting through memories of pain and terror. "Two of them smelled like ale.

One of them smelled like horses. The other like he'd been cooking green onions and angelica."

"Horse dung. I will ask the stable master who was working the day of your attack. The ale you smelled, were there any notes in the brew that stood out to you?"

"I don't know." Frustration surges within me. "Uh... yeast. Hops. Some kind of... berry? Juniper?"

Wulfric growls softly, like that makes sense to him. "I will have the innkeeper give me a list of every drunken lout he served juniper ale to that day. As for the scent of onion... I know a farmer who grows them. I will be having words with him." A lot more than words, by the sound of the fury in his voice.

Accepting the mug of water he passes me, I take an eager sip. "There's something else." I hesitate, knowing this will hurt him but maybe not surprise him. "One of them mentioned Anders. Is it possible he... I don't know, put them up to it?"

A muscle twitches in Wulfric's jaw, and his lips press into a thin line. "I don't want to believe it. Our parents raised us to be men of honor!"

"It's not the first time he's attacked me."

I wince when horror widens his eyes. "What? When?" Then it hits him. "The night you tried to escape..."

"He set me up. Planned to make it look like I'd attacked him so the village would turn against me. He ran right into that silver knife he gave me."

"That bastard!" Snarling, he lurches to his feet and paces, jerking his fingers through his blond mane. "Gods! How far has he fallen? He is not the man I once knew. Envy has blackened his heart. Once he would have challenged me, man to man. Instead, he used you to... to carve right into the heart of me." Pain makes his voice crack. Shaking his head, he comes to me and gingerly takes my face between his hands. "He will never hurt you again. I will make sure of it."

My breath hitches. "You're going to kill him."

A cold smile tugs at his mouth. "When I'm through with him, he will wish I had."

"Wulfric, don't do this. I'm not—"

"Not what?" he growls, gripping my hair between his clawed fingers. "Don't you say you aren't worthy. I would go to war for you, Kieran Grove, and lay every enemy of yours broken and bloody at your feet. You are *mine*. My pack. My heart. My soul. And *no one* harms what is mine."

I'm terrified for him. If he challenges Anders, I don't know who will walk away alive. I can't lose him, but I know nothing I say will change his mind. Neither of us will be safe until Anders has been dealt with.

"If you die, I'll dig you up and kill you again," I growl against his lips.

A dark chuckle rumbles through him as he claims my lips with his. "Then I won't die."

It's a promise I pray he can keep.

Chapter 16
Wulfric

Kieran's bruised face and bloodshot eyes haunt me as I spend all day chasing down leads.

I checked the onion farmer's home and found only his wife and children. She had no idea where he had gone. The innkeeper had been helping himself to his juniper ale and couldn't remember who he'd served, so he was of no help. Two of the stablemaster's apprentices were missing, a couple of men named Horri and Thorin. He didn't know where they might be, though.

Fury thunders through my heart at the cravens who harmed Kieran, but so much of the rage I feel is at myself.

I never should have left him alone. Gods! What a fool I am. I must make this right. I will not rest until the godless bastards who harmed my mate beg for my mercy. And then... then I will confront Anders. This rivalry between us was fine when he was only snarling at me. But for him to have conspired to attack my mate... A part of me doesn't want to believe it was him. Somewhere deep down below his grief and envy, the man I grew up with must still be there.

How could he have harmed me in such a grievous way? In attacking Kieran, he has attacked me. And if those men really attacked Kieran on his orders... then I will do whatever I must to ensure it *never* happens again.

In the center of the village, I howl to the skies above, calling all my people to me. In minutes, the streets are full of my kinsmen. I must learn all I can about the attack. There must have been witnesses. Someone must have seen where the bastards went. They wouldn't stay in the village, not after attacking the Alpha-Mate. They'll be on the run now.

"There are traitors among us," I say to the gathered crowd, my hands in fists at my sides. "Four of them attacked Kieran and stole his furs so he can't heal his injuries." Gasps and alarmed whispers spread through the crowd. "I need to know if anyone saw anything. These men must answer for their wrongs against my pack."

To my dismay, no one comes forward with any information, just murmuring to themselves in shock and confusion. "Please. Anything at all. What they looked like. Where they fled."

Suddenly, a little boy stumbles from the crowd. His mother, Elisabet, grips his shoulders. Softly, she says, "Go on. Tell Alpha everything. It's all right."

Tears streak his face, and his little shoulders heave. Going to him, I kneel in the mud at his feet. "Something to say, lad?"

Gasping, the boy wipes his eyes. "M-my brother Olav made me do it. Told me he'd b-beat me if I didn't."

"Do what?" I'm careful to keep my voice calm even as the berserker within roars for blood.

The lad wipes his nose on his sleeve. "He and his friends were really angry at the Alpha-Mate. S-said he was changing things too much. So he made me lure Kieran away from the village and... and attacked him."

Grinding my teeth so I don't snarl my outrage, I meet Elisabet's stony gaze. She says, "I knew nothing about my fool son's plans, Alpha. I swear to you."

"I need to find him," I tell Elisabet.

"If I had to guess, he's with a girl he's sweet on in the next town over. Issfjord." I'm pleased she doesn't try and shield her son from the consequences of his actions. She hugs her little son to her. "Find him, Alpha. Make him pay. I don't care what happens to that lout."

With vengeance in my heart, I saddle up my horse. Gunnar and Lyall follow me to the stables.

"I've looked everywhere," Lyall pants, sweeping his long blond waves behind his shoulder. "Anders is gone."

I don't like that his whereabouts are unknown when I'm about to leave the village.

"Will you need help?" Gunnar asks, leaning on a box stall.

"Yours, aye." Gunnar's an excellent tracker. "Lyall, I need you to stay with Kieran."

Lyall thumps his chest. "You got it. I'll look after him, brother. I promise." He swallows thickly. "And if you find Anders, what will you do?"

Turning to him, I say, "I don't know yet. If you catch even a whiff of Anders, you howl and I will return." Slinging a leg over the saddle, I tug the reins and urge Fenna out the doors. Gunnar follows me on his black steed. Together, we ride to the edge of the village. I hate leaving Kieran again, but I know he'll be safe with Helga and Lyall.

My brother rides up beside me, dark eyes fixed on the horizon. "Issfjord is a day's ride from here. They're ahead of us, no doubt, but they'll have to stop and rest themselves."

"We have to move quickly. We can sneak up on them at night."

Gunnar urges his horse to move faster until we're galloping down the road. "They will suffer for this, brother. You have my word."

"I know. That's why I brought you."

I love Lyall, but his heart has always been the softest of us all. It's his greatest strength, but not one that suits my needs now. Gunnar, though... ever since he lost his chosen family, his control has dangled by a thread. I need his cunning, his brutality.

"These bloody cravens don't know who they are messing with," Gunnar growls, leaning forward in the saddle. "They think we're weak, but what they don't understand is that the losses we've endured have hardened our hearts. Father. Mother. Leif and little Bjorn." His voice shakes when he mentions his chosen mate and his child. "Our losses have only made us more protective of what is ours."

He's right.

"Leif was a good man."

Gunnar doesn't speak. I can still remember the dark days after Leif's and Bjorn's passings like they were yesterday. Gunnar disappeared into the wilds for a whole winter and when he returned, he was a different man, one who smiled less, laughed little, and was ready to rage at the slightest threat to those he cared for.

I don't know if he will ever move on and find another who speaks to his wolf, but I hope so.

We ride on until the skies darken and the moon glows full.

"Do you see that?" Gunnar points west.

A column of smoke rises over the woods.

"Fools," I growl. "They truly believe they aren't being followed."

Gunnar bares his teeth in a smile. Hitching the horses to a tree, Gunnar and I descend into the darkness of the woods. The distant light of a crackling fire gets brighter. As the scent of the traitors gets stronger, my blood burns hot with fury. We approach from downwind so they won't scent us, our steps quiet. They are gathered around a fire, laughing and drinking ale. Unaware that tonight is their last night in this world.

Gunnar's voice echoes in my mind. *"How do we play this? Do we wait until they're asleep or strike now?"*

My wolf hungers for blood, but these cravens are not worthy of an honorable death. They will not earn their place in Valhalla. They will die choking on blood while they sleep.

"We wait," I tell him.

Gunnar nods, then settles back on his haunches.

The clouds roll by, concealing the moon. The men disperse one by one to their bedrolls around the fire. When they begin to snore, I know the time has come. A single look at Gunnar and he is on his feet, his claws sharp. From the shadows, we advance on the campsite. With a jerk of my head, I motion Gunnar left. I will go right. We will each take two.

Turning my back, I prowl toward my prey.

Behind me, there's a wet choking sound, and blood sours the night air. Looming over one of my targets, I raise my claws to his throat. He is not Olav, but I can see him across the fire, sleeping unawares. And they call themselves ulfhednar. Pathetic.

With a single slash, I split the craven's throat open. His eyes go wide, and blood bubbles from his mouth. He clutches his neck but cannot stop the flow of his life's blood as it oozes between his fingers. Behind me, Gunnar deals a killing blow to his final target. I set my sights on Olav. He begins to stir, his brows furrowing.

I throw myself upon him, claws at his throat, my other hand grabbing hold of his balls. He wakes with a shriek, freezing when he sees me. The fear in his eyes gives me such a thrill.

"Don't bother screaming for help, Olav. All your friends died choking on blood, and you will be next."

A whimper escapes him.

"Do you know why I'm going to kill you, Olav?" I twist his balls between my claws, and his agonized howl shatters the night air.

"S-stop. Please! I didn't do nothing! Honest, I swear, Alpha! It was them who did it. They wanted your mate dead, n-not me!"

"I can hear your cowardly heart thundering beneath all that meat and bone, Olav. You *lie.*" I dig my claws into his throat, drawing beads of blood. "Someone threw powdered silver in his eyes. Could have blinded him. Broke the fingers on his right hand. Was that you?"

"N-no. I swear! It wasn't!"

But oh, how his heart trips in his chest. I don't know if he threw the silver or broke Kieran's fingers. It doesn't matter.

"Too bad I killed your friends, Olav. You'll have to bear the punishment for all of their actions."

His begging is cut off when I pull him to his feet by his neck and drag him to a boulder.

"Hold him," I snarl at Gunnar. "Lay one hand flat on the stone." Gunnar pins him down just like I asked. Ignoring Olav's pitiful screams, I seize a rock from the forest floor. Weighing it, I decide it's heavy enough. I draw it back and smash the stone down against Olav's right hand. I crack his fingers beneath the stone again and again until his hand is nothing but mangled, bloody flesh.

Grabbing his jaw, I give his face a few smacks so he doesn't pass out. "Did Anders put you up to this? Hmm?" I shake him roughly. "Answer me!"

Eyes rolling back, Olav nods. "T-told us to beat him up. Wanted to piss you off."

Gunnar growls low in his throat. "He's challenging you, Wulfric."

I had my suspicions, but knowing my brother would stoop so low makes me see red.

"Where is he?" I scratch my razor claws against the thin skin of his throat.

"D-don't know. I swear. He... he just said he'd be waiting 'where the end began.'"

At first, I think maybe he means the beach where my father met his end, but we haven't returned to the land we were born and raised on since Father's death.

Gunnar meets my gaze, and understanding passes between us.

The burial mound.

"L-let me go. Please. I promise I'll never hurt your mate again."

A dark laugh rumbles from my chest. I tighten my grip on Olav's throat and smile through a mouthful of fangs. "I'm not finished with you, Olav. My mate's eyes have yet to fully heal. Mayhap I'll pluck yours from your skull and give them to him as a gift?" His pleas cut off as I dig my claws deeper into his throat, piercing the skin. "No one harms what is mine and walks away alive."

What Anders has done can never be forgiven.

His betrayal haunts me as Gunnar and I ride back toward the burial mound where Anders awaits us. The only outcomes are death or exile. Even through the red haze of fury that clouds my eyes, I doubt if I will have it in me to kill my brother.

When I voice these thoughts aloud, Gunnar sighs. "He is not the boy we once knew. Father's death changed him."

"It changed all of us." Once I might have been more empathetic. I can't find it in me to make any more excuses for Anders.

Gunnar nods grimly. "Aye, but it changed Anders especially. He has to be stopped."

I stroke the white wolf fur in my lap, Kieran's fur I took back from the cravens who stole it. "Should I kill him?"

"Do you want to?"

I almost say yes, but the word gets caught in my throat. I want to hurt Anders, yes, make him suffer as he made Kieran suffer. But kill him? As furious and betrayed as I am for the wrongs he committed against my mate, I don't think I could end his life.

Sometimes, I look at him and remember the boy who comforted me after a nightmare. The boy who taught me how to catch a fish, who helped me practice my sword work. The brother who helped me through my first shift and held my hand through the pain. However, those fond memories are tinged with cruel, biting remarks and sudden bursts of violence that only got worse over the years.

"What do you plan to do?" Gunnar asks.

I grip the reins tighter, the dried blood cracking on my knuckles. "I will challenge him to a duel. If I win, then I will decide his fate."

"And if you lose? It's too risky. Let me fight him in your place."

I shake my head. "I have to make him pay for what he did to Kieran. I won't lose."

I can't afford to.

The village comes into view, but we detour and gallop toward the barrow where our parents are entombed. Anders's scent hits my nose, and fury boils my blood. I leap from Fenna's back before she has completely stopped and barrel toward the barrow. Gunnar runs after me.

The door crashes open and I stumble into the barrow, claws out and fangs sharp. "Anders!" My roar bounces off the walls and fills the chamber, ringing in my ears. "Come out, you skirt-chasing craven! Can you smell the blood of your lackeys on me? I cut their throats and now they rot in Hel's domain. Don't make me do the same to you."

A low chuckle echoes in the dark. "You should have been a skald, brother. Why don't you take out a lyre and strum me a little song to go with your dramatics, aye?"

"Do not test me," I snarl at the shadows. "Come on. *Now.*"

He glides from the shadows, teeth bared in a grin. With a little flourish, Anders bows. "At your service, *Alpha.* Took your time to find me. I was getting bored in here. Started eating the offerings."

He dares to stand before me cracking jokes when he ordered my mate bludgeoned near to death?

Anders cocks his head. "Oh. Are you expecting an apology? Did my men go too far? I told them to bloody him up, not kill him."

My claws snap around his throat, and Anders grunts as I slam him against the wall. "You will never hurt him again! You have wronged me for the last time." Tightening my hold on his neck, I stare into his wild green eyes and snarl, "You have challenged me, and I accept. Tomorrow at sunrise, we duel."

A vicious grin slashes across Anders's face. "And if I lose? You won't have the stones to kill me. You've always been soft, but that mate of yours has weakened you even more."

"No," I growl into his face, "he's made me strong enough to recognize that I don't need anything from you. Not anymore." Letting go, I turn and stalk from the barrow.

Come tomorrow, this life-long rivalry of ours will finally come to an end.

Chapter 17
Kieran

When I wake to an empty room, my body throbbing, the fear is worse than the pain. Wulfric still hasn't returned. I can't feel him without my wolf furs. Why hasn't he returned yet? Oh god, has something happened? What if—

I have to get out of bed and go find him myself. He's been gone too long. If he died trying to avenge what happened to me, I'll never forgive myself. The door opens just as I force myself to sit up.

"Whoa. Whoa. Easy, little rabbit."

The sound of Wulfric's voice makes my breath catch. When he kneels by my bed, it's like a dam breaks open, and I throw my good arm around him, burying my face in his chest. "You asshole," I choke out, "you were gone for days!"

That low, raspy chuckle I love so much vibrates in his chest. "Careful, you almost sound worried."

"I was, you dickhead." I rub my nose against his neck, eager for the scent I know and love, but I can't detect anything through my aching nose. "Is it over?"

"First..." Wulfric pulls back and reaches for something behind him. When he hands me thick white wolf furs, tears sting my eyes. I haven't been a wolf for long, but it's become such an important part of me. It's what helps connect me to Wulfric and this world I'm beginning to call my home. Wulfric drapes the furs over me and I gasp as the broken bones mend and the bruises begin to disappear. "Feel better?"

"Like new." I tenderly touch my face and find my nose has healed, too. "Did you find who attacked me?"

His lips thin, the scent of his anger pungent. "I did. They will never harm you again."

"Was... was Anders behind it? What happened to him?"

"The sun rises in only a few hours." Wulfric turns his gaze to the dark sky outside. "I will face him then and end this feud between us for good."

My heart breaks for him. He sounds resolute in his decision, but I can smell the sadness. "I'm so sorry." I take his hand and loop my fingers through his, squeezing. Wulfric just grimaces, but not at me.

"This has been coming for a long time now. It will be good to finally end it."

"But he's your brother."

Wulfric shakes his head. "The boy I once knew died with my father, and then he died again the moment he hurt you. This must end, and I have to be the one to do it."

I feel terrible for him, and I hate Anders for making him do this. "You're allowed to mourn him, you know. The person he once was. The relationship you two could have had. I think you're doing the right thing. I... I'm proud of you. I really am. What you're doing is the hardest thing a person can do. We're told we have to appreciate our family, even if they're crueler to us than anyone else. But family isn't always who we share blood with. It can be the ones we find along the way."

"Am I your family?"

A smile tugs at my lips. "Yeah, you are. You and Helga. Lyall and Gunnar. It's crazy I had to go back in time to find the people who see the best in me, but I wouldn't have it any other way."

Wulfric leans in and touches his forehead to mine, his hands big and warm against my jaw. "You are a part of my pack, Kieran. A part of my very heart and soul. You will always have a place here. I..." He clears his throat gruffly. "I was wrong about you. I could not see the strength of your spirit. I thought your humanity made you weak, but I see now it's your greatest strength. I was cruel to you. I promise you, I will spend the rest of my days worshipping you, body and soul."

I forgave him a long time ago. I'm not sure when. Maybe when he trained me to fight. Maybe when he cooked for me. I forgave him for everything he'd done and everything he'd ever do.

Twining my legs around his waist, I urge him closer. "You can't die today," I pant into his ear, nipping the lobe. "You can't promise me forever and go off and die on me. Got it? I'll never fucking forgive you." Rocking my hips, I grind on his cock, moaning when he hardens against me. "Promise me," I pant, fangs sharp as I nip his neck. "Wulfric, you promise me."

He kisses me fiercely. "Promise."

It's not enough. I want the promise of his body against mine, his cock hard and throbbing inside me, his knot tying us together. Without having to say a word, Wulfric knows this, he must. Because he devours my mouth with his. Our tongues clash in wet, urgent strokes. Every time I catch my breath, it's driven out of me when he grinds his big cock against mine.

"Make me feel good. Make me forget everything but you."

A shiver runs through him and when he kisses me, it's slow, tender. "I will, little rabbit. Promise."

All I'm wearing is a thin white tunic, no pants, so when he shoves the tunic up to my chest, there's nothing stopping him from devouring my cock in one go. Clutching at his hair, I groan my delight to the ceiling while he bobs his head up and down in slow, toe-curling pulls.

Nobody has ever been so devoted to my pleasure before. It makes my eyes sting.

"*Yes*. That's perfect, Wulfric. Feels so good."

Pumping my hips, I fuck the tight, wet heat of his mouth. My stomach muscles clench with every hard pull of his lips over my throbbing flesh. When he cups and squeezes my balls, my eyes roll back. Wulfric taps two fingers against my lips, and I open for him and suck. Those same fingers press inside me, and I see stars as he works me open while he sucks me off.

"Y-yes. Shit! Want your cock. Hurry."

He growls around me, and the vibrations have me arching up.

Grabbing fistfuls of his hair, I tug him off me. "Please, Wulfric."

Wulfric kisses my thigh. "I'll take care of you. All of you."

Gasping, I draw my knees to my chest. With both hands, I grip my cheeks and spread myself open. Wulfric's chest rises and falls faster, his eyes locked on the most intimate part of me.

On his knees, Wulfric approaches me. "Keep your hands there." He opens the dresser and grabs a vial of oil, which he dribbles over the length of himself. I whimper when his pelvis bumps the back of my thighs. When he pushes inside, the burn has my eyes rolling, a moan escaping me. For the first time in days, I finally feel complete.

He doesn't fill me up, not completely. Rocking his hips, he drags his cock along my walls, pulling out until the ridge of his cockhead catches on my rim, then pushing back in an inch at a time.

A whine escapes me, and I writhe on his cock, trying to take him deeper. Grabbing my hands, he pins them to the bed. "Easy, my heart. You don't deserve a quick fuck," he says against my mouth, hips rolling in slow, shallow pumps. "You deserve reverence, Kieran Grove."

Reverence. God. Tears sting my eyes, and I tug him down into a kiss I want to drown in. No one has ever made me feel so sacred, not until him.

I can't look away from his face, his eyes hazy with pleasure, his jaw clenched tight, as he fucks me slow and deep. One hand grips the back of my knee, hoisting my leg up high, giving him deeper access. Golden hair falls around his face, muscles clenching with every rock of his hips. Just the sensation of being filled by him leaves me a panting mess, but when he hits my prostate, I moan his name so loudly I'll be surprised if no one else in the house hears us.

I know when he's close as every thrust comes faster, harder. As his guttural groans fill the air, I'm not sure who is louder, him or me. My own release bears down on me, stealing all my reason. I'm closer to him than I've been in days and I never want it to end.

Suddenly, he stops all movement. Yanked from my bliss, I whine, "No, no, no, come on, please."

He grins, chest heaving. "Not done. Not yet." Tightening his grip on my wrists, he stays inside me but doesn't fucking move. To my dismay, my climax slips out of reach. His abs are tense and his jaw is tight, like it's taking every ounce of control he has not to pound me into the bed.

"Wulfric," I whine, wriggling on his cock, trying to fuck myself on him, but he just pulls back. I go rigid, not wanting him to pull out and leave me on the cusp of my orgasm.

Taking in a slow breath, Wulfric moves his hips again. Pleasure arcs throughout my body as he slowly brings us back to the peak. Reaching between us, he grabs my aching cock and strokes. A cry of bliss escapes me and I buck my hips mindlessly, chasing the pleasure building with every thrust and stroke.

"Don't stop," I beg him. "Don't you dare stop. Not now. Please. So close. Oh fuck. Wanna come. Please, let me come."

He captures my pleading lips in a kiss, fucking my mouth with his tongue while he pounds me with his cock. I lose myself to sensation, closer to heaven than I've ever been, a slave to the pleasure that overwhelms me.

Until he stops. Again.

I'm going to kill him.

"No," I say with a groan, slapping the bed in my frustration. "Fuck, no. Please. Why would you—"

"Apologies." His voice is choked, like he's barely holding himself back from filling me with cum. "I just... I don't want this to end. Not yet. Never. Want to stay inside you for hours. Never want to stop fucking you."

And I wonder if it's because he thinks this is the last time we'll be together.

Despair threatens to choke me. I throw my arms around him and guide him down into a kiss. The desperation he kisses me with steals my breath, and I realize to my horror that he must think this is our goodbye.

"No," I pant against his mouth. "This isn't it for us. You hear me?"

Burying his face in my neck, he kisses and sucks on my skin. A shudder racks his powerful body.

"You aren't dying, Wulfric. You can't." Fear and pain make my throat tighten. "You're coming back to me. You're mine, and you're not allowed to leave me. You'll win this fight and you'll come home to me, and we're going to be happy together. For the rest of our damn lives, we're going to be so happy, just to spite all the demons in our heads that tell us we don't deserve this. Because we do. We fucking deserve this."

His arms tighten around my shoulders and he trembles against my chest. Gasping, he moves inside me, eyes bright and wild. He kisses me again and again, swallowing my gasps and moans as he fucks me, loving me hard and fast and so deep I know I'll feel him there for hours. Pleasure eclipses everything else and nothing outside this room matters, just Wulfric above me, Wulfric's lips on mine, Wulfric inside me, his thick knot stretching me to my limits, and yet still it's not enough.

I beg him not to stop, for more, to please, please never stop.

"Never," he whispers in the space between our lips. "I'll never stop. I'll never leave you, Kieran. Gods. *Kieran*."

I say his name like a prayer as I start coming, spilling over my chest and stomach.

Wulfric's teeth find my shoulder, biting down as he fills me again and again.

We catch our breath together, wrapped in a heavy blanket of bliss unlike anything I've ever felt before.

Exhaustion makes it hard to hold my eyes open. Wulfric's lips brush over my forehead, sweeping my sweaty hair from my face.

"I'll fight with everything I have to come home to you," he whispers to me, and his promises lull me to sleep.

Chapter 18
Wulfric

The sun rises over the village, and the time has come.

Hand in hand with Kieran, I walk the streets. Memories haunt me. Everywhere I look, I see a place where Anders and I used to play or sit together and laugh. I know I'm doing the right thing. This rivalry between Anders and me ceased to be a squabble between siblings the moment he ordered an attack against the man I love.

My people have gathered in the square, forming a circle. Helga stands by Gunnar, her eyes wide with worry as she looks my way. Lyall stands alone, his arms wrapped tight around himself. "Hold a moment." I drop Kieran's hand and go to Lyall's side. "Are you well?"

Lyall nods at the ground, blond hair swaying around his cheeks. "Anders has had this coming."

"He's still your twin. You're allowed to wish things could be different."

Lyall grits his teeth, eyes narrowing. It's rare to see him without a smile. "I don't wish things were different. I wish he weren't such a gods-damned asshole."

That's the same thing, but I don't correct him.

Scowling, my brother tugs a hand through his hair, eyes bright with anger. "How could he try and tear our family apart like this? Why is he such a selfish prick?"

"I don't know." I'm aware he isn't expecting an answer, but that doesn't stop me from wishing I could give him one. I wish I could fix this. "If I'd been a better alpha…"

But Lyall shakes his head wildly. "No. You've been an amazing leader. End this, brother. Just…" His throat works hard as he swallows. "Will you have to kill him?"

A shiver goes through me. "If he surrenders, no. But if he doesn't, then I will do what I have to in order to keep our pack safe."

My brother looks away, his arms squeezing his middle. He doesn't speak. My fingers twitch, longing to reach out, but what good would that do? Turning my back, I go to Kieran and put an arm around his narrow shoulders. The crowd parts for us, revealing Anders in the middle of the throng of people. Claws sharp at his sides, he paces like a caged beast waiting to be set free. Black war paint smears around his eyes like a mask.

Kieran grips my hand. "Be careful."

Turning to him, I fold my mate into my arms. "I will. The gods won't fail me now."

"You're sure about that?" He squeezes me tight.

"Aye. I trust in them. How can I not? They brought you to me."

"Hey. Don't you get sappy on me. I need you tough. Strong. Pissed." He yanks me back by the shoulders and glowers at me. "Take this seriously."

Bumping my forehead against his, I say, "Worried for me?"

He clenches his jaw. "No. I think this is stupid, and that you're stupid, and—"

I silence his ramblings with a kiss, sighing my approval when his arms fly around me. "I'm fighting for you, little rabbit. Keep your eyes on me, and I won't lose."

Kieran parts his lips, eyes wide and full of fear. "I will."

Words rise from the depths of my heart, three words I've never told anyone, but I keep them locked inside. I won't tell him now. Later. After I've won. He must know how I feel about him, and I will fight even harder so I can tell him once the battle is through.

"Enough!" Anders bellows. "Face me, Wulfric. I will prove who is the rightful alpha after I've snapped your neck between my jaws."

I hate him for making me raise a claw against my own flesh and blood. "Your cowardly attack against my mate has only proven how unworthy you truly are. You will never be Alpha."

"That is for the gods to decide, here and now!" Face to the skies, Anders howls, "Odin, Thor, Fenrir—bear witness to Ulfheim's true Alpha!" He drops before me, furs writhing as they cover his body. When he looks up, it's through the eyes and face of a snarling wolf that prowls toward me.

Throwing up my furs, I let the shift possess me. My paws slam the ground, my lips rolling back from my fangs as my brother advances on me. Ulfhednar can heal all but the most lethal of wounds in seconds. I will have to bite deep, down to the bone, and often enough that his body won't be able to heal one wound before another opens. If he expends too much energy healing, he'll weaken and be easier to bring down.

Gods. This is how I would fight an enemy, not my brother, but Anders has left me little choice. How I hate him for that.

"Do not hold back," I growl into his mind. *"I will send you to Valhalla with honor, brother."*

With a furious snarl, Anders charges at me. Our bodies crash into each other, the collision winding me, but there's no time to recover before Anders drives his fangs deep into the side of my throat. My dense coat protects me, and my brother rips away a clump of hair and flesh. Stinging pain makes me yelp and retaliate with a claw across his snout. My claws skin away the flesh, narrowly missing one glowing green eye.

He stumbles back, pawing his eye, and I'm upon him. My fangs burrow into his coat and latch onto the back of his neck. Anders is strong, but I've always been the biggest of my brothers. Lifting him by the scruff, I hurl him into a tree. He yowls as his spine cracks against the bark. Pawing blood from my eye, I wait for him to rise.

Whining, Anders tries to force himself to his feet. *"What... are you waiting for? Don't you dare hold back on me!"* The fury inside him surges through the tenuous thread that still binds us.

"I won't attack you when you're down. Unlike you, I still have honor."

The furious snarl that escapes him tells me I hit a nerve. He's on his feet, shaking himself free of the pain. *"That self-righteous attitude makes me gods-damned sick! All our lives, you've looked down on me. Father never saw my potential! No matter how hard I tried, no matter how strong or fast or smart I was, I was never good enough! No, all he cared about was his precious Alpha-heir!"*

I take a step back, shocked. *"That's... that isn't true. Is that really how you saw our childhood?"* All I remember is Father taking him into the woods every morning to teach him how to hunt. Helga telling him stories by the firelight when he was unable to sleep at night after a night terror. He was as loved as any of us. Wasn't he? Did I really steal our father's attention from my brothers? If I did, then it's no wonder Anders hates me.

"It wasn't enough, was it?" Anders lunges toward me. He slams his body into me and when I fall, his jaws crunch around my ankle. The world spins around me as I fly backward, slamming into a tree. Snow rains down on me,

blinding my vision. *"Being Alpha, commanding Father's attention. You had to steal Mother from me, too!"*

The fight goes out of me, shocked and appalled by his accusations.

"I never got to know her." Pain tears across the bond that ties us, such pain it's almost too much to bear. *"Because she died bringing you into this world. I was too young. I barely remember her face, her scent. You robbed me of our parents! You killed them both!"*

He tears through my defenses with his words, then hurls himself upon me. I have no time to react. He bowls me off my paws and bites down, tearing into me again and again while I thrash to try and free myself.

"I didn't!" Kicking out, I claw him in the belly, raking into his flesh. Blood rains from his fur and spatters the snow crimson. Anders stumbles off me and I leap at him, slamming my paws into his side. He tumbles over, spraying snow, and then I pounce.

"You should be the one who died on that beach!" Anders struggles beneath me as I fasten my jaws into his neck. My teeth dimple his windpipe, and his ragged pants become choked. *"You robbed me of my father and mother! I hate you. I will always despise you for that!"*

"I know it should have been me!" I roar through the bonds, and then his fangs find my throat. We pant and snarl, knowing that the wrong move will result in both

our throats being torn out. *"I wish every day I had died in Father's stead. It should have been me. I know."*

Frozen, all we can do is catch our breath, bleeding out into the snow from the cuts to our bodies and souls. I remember him then. My big brother, lifting me up on his shoulders so I could pick an apple from the tree. How I delighted in the stories he told me of the gods and their golden apples of immortality. All this time, he hated me. All these years, I hurt him simply by existing.

"Why?" If a wolf could cry, there would be tears in Anders's blazing eyes. *"Why wasn't I given more time with them? It isn't bloody fair."*

He's right. It isn't fair. He deserved more time with his mother and father, but so did all of us. He can't see beyond his own pain to the pain of others.

"I want them back." Anders's voice shakes. He lets go of my throat and collapses into the snow. I stand over his quivering body, at a loss for what to say or do. *"I thought challenging you would make it all go away. That your death would silence the grief, the guilt, the rage that consumes me. And I just feel nothing. Because of you, I'll drown in these feelings for the rest of my damn life. So just kill me. Put an end to it."*

I can't move. I can't do it.

Pulling myself from my shift, I kneel in the snow before him. "It doesn't have to be this way between us. We can start over and move past this."

A growl rumbles from the black wolf curled at my feet. *"Either you kill me now or someday I will kill you. I will not lose anyone else I love because of you."*

I barely avoid flinching at his words. "I can't kill you." Even though I know I should. I still look at him and see the boy I grew up with. I can't separate the broken man at my feet and the boy who carried me on his shoulders through the woods.

There is only one option left and for many ulfhednar, it is a fate worse than death itself.

When I open my eyes, Anders is a man. Blood and sweat streak his face as he glares up at me. Rising to my feet, I speak loud enough for the crowd to hear.

"Anders, son of Erik and Matilda, I sentence you to exile. From this moment on, you are no longer a part of this pack."

Wide green eyes gaze up at me, blazing with hatred and fear.

Lone wolves never last long, and packs never take in exiled wolves. Death by my fangs would have been kinder.

With a strangled snarl, Anders turns his face into the snow and refuses to meet my gaze.

Closing my eyes tight, I hold fast against the guilt that tries to drag me under.

I'll never know if this was the right choice, but what's done is done.

From this moment on, my brother is dead to me.

"Are you okay?" Kieran asks softly.

We wait at the outskirts of the village for Anders to be escorted to us. The sun touches the horizon, staining the forest red and orange.

"I do not know," I answer.

Any moment now, Anders will come to us. The sword he named Wolf's Tooth when he was a lad will have been taken from him. He will have a sack with enough provisions to keep him full until he arrives at his destination. "I'll never see him again." I blink fast against a sudden rush of sorrow.

"He won't be able to challenge you anymore, or threaten me or anyone else in the pack," Kieran says, coming to stand beside me so he can rub my shoulder.

"I know." Grinding my teeth to anchor me, I hold on fast to the memories of all the times he hurt me with his words and with his actions. "It is a relief, but... it also pains me." I feel foolish admitting it out loud, but Kieran just leans his head against my shoulder.

"Yeah, I get that. He's your brother. You're allowed to be upset he couldn't be who you wanted, even if it's good he's gone."

I want to pull him into my arms, but my pack emerges from the trees. Gunnar and Lyall walk on either side of Anders. Without his weapons, Anders looks smaller than before. He still has his furs. He will need them if he is to survive. A sack swings from his shoulder, loaded with everything he'll need. Hopefully, it is enough. I will never know.

Without a word to any of my kin, I turn and lead the way to the beach. The grass turns to stones that crunch beneath my boots. Waves lap at the shore before they're drawn away. A single rowboat awaits, moored on land. Anders stops before the boat, jaw tightly clenched.

Blinking fast, Lyall puts a hand on Anders's shoulder and pushes. The pain in my brother's eyes makes me look away toward the horizon. This is the second time Lyall has had to exile someone so important to him. Anders sinks into the boat without a word. I know what happens next without having to look: Gunnar and Lyall will take each hand and tie them to the oars, and then I will push the boat into the water. My heart is heavy in my chest.

Eyes on the horizon, I come to stand behind the boat. Anders doesn't speak or acknowledge me, just stares toward the setting sun with me. "Farewell, brother. May the Father Wolf guide your path." As the tide comes rushing in, I push the boat toward the ocean. The tide carries the vessel out to sea.

Helga steps forth, unwrapping a cloth in her hands. A branch of Yggdrasil rests within the fabric. As she holds the branch to the skies, the wind picks up, billowing around us. A bright light flashes on the horizon. Beside me, Kieran gasps. Squinting through the light, I can make out Anders's silhouette as he rows toward the portal. The light burns my eyes, but I can't look away, desperate for one final look at my brother.

Before I'm ready, the light fades along with the setting sun as it disappears beyond the ocean.

Anders is gone.

If I didn't have the scars upon my soul to tell me otherwise, I'd have thought he'd never existed at all.

Chapter 19

Kieran

"Where did Anders go?" I ask Wulfric later that night.

Wulfric swirls his spoon through his boar stew. "I am unsure. Anywhere in the nine realms."

I don't like how shuttered his face is, his voice devoid of emotion. It makes me worried he's closing himself off again.

I blow on my food, hot from the cauldron and delicious. "Is it completely random?"

"Random? Do you mean does one have any control over their destination through the portals? It is unclear. Some think we can choose our destination. Others think the gods choose for us."

"What do you think?"

Wulfric sets down his mug of ale, foam in his beard. "I think that we go wherever we are needed. By our choice, by the gods' choice, who can say? All I know is you materialized right in front of our ships."

A smile tugs at my mouth. "Are you saying we were destined to meet?"

"Yes," he answers without hesitation. "And it's my hope that Anders has gone wherever he is destined to be. Or to who he is destined to be with. I hope so." Sadness falls like a veil over his face.

I can't imagine how hard it must have been for him today. Reaching across the table, I try to take his hand, but he jerks out of my reach. Damn it. He *is* pulling away. "Hey. Listen to me."

Wulfric takes a sudden interest in the contents of his mug, swishing it around.

"You did what you had to do for your pack. Anders was never going to stop challenging you. He was never going to be who you needed him to be. You did the right thing."

"He hated me." I've never heard his voice so soft before. "All these years, he blamed me for our mother's death and for stealing his time with Father away from him. I never knew. I never understood how hurt he was." He swallows audibly, his eyes taking on a sudden sheen. "That *I* was the cause of all that hurt."

I wish I knew the right thing to say to ease his guilt. I think it's something he'll just have to work through.

"Kieran?"

"Yes?" My heart skips when I look up and find Wulfric glowering down at his food. His hand is curled into a fist on the table. Whatever he wants to say, it can only be bad news.

"Do you—" Wulfric cuts himself off, his lips pressing into a thin line.

My mouth is dry. "What is it?"

Wulfric's heart races fast in my ears, and then he shakes his head. "Nothing. Never mind." He grabs his empty plate and carries it away. Then he goes to the door, tugging on his furs. "I'm going out."

"When will you be—"

The door slams behind him.

A sick feeling churns in the pit of my stomach.

What was Wulfric going to ask me?

I clear my plate and get ready for bed. Crawling beneath the blankets, I lie awake and wait for him to come back. I can't feel him through the bonds, which means he's closed himself off. It hurts that he can't be open with me about how he feels, but I don't know how to ask for that without pushing him further away.

Sighing, I close my eyes. He'll come back when he's ready. Won't he?

From far away, howls light up the night. I know Wulfric's howl without having to guess, even though his bond is muted. Two other voices harmonize with him. They can only be his brothers. The song the brothers sing is so full of heartbreak that it makes my eyes sting. It's a song for the missing, for the man they once called brother.

At least he isn't alone out there.

I stay awake as long as I can.

Come morning light, Wulfric still hasn't returned.

Helga and I both jump when Wulfric marches suddenly through the door during lunch. I want to be relieved, but I'm also pissed. Where does he get off leaving for hours and stomping back in whenever he feels like it?

"Where have you been?" I snap, lurching to my feet.

Wulfric averts his gaze like a scolded dog. "With Gunnar and Lyall."

"Why did you..." I glance at Helga.

She coughs and clears her throat. "Well, would you look at that? I've got to tend to the garden!" She hurries outside.

Taking in a slow breath to calm myself, I say, "Why did you close our bond again?"

Wulfric scratches the back of his neck. "I needed space."

"From me. But not your brothers."

His nostrils flare. "It isn't like that."

"Yeah? It sure feels like *that,* Wulfric. It feels like you don't trust me to understand what you're going through or to help you."

Shaking his head, Wulfric says, "I do trust you, Kieran."

"Then why do you shut me out?" The shout escapes me before I can strangle back all my anger and hurt. "We're mates and where I'm from, that's equivalent to marriage. In a marriage, you trust each other. I know you're going through a lot right now, but running away into the woods and keeping the people who lo—who *care* about you at arm's length isn't the answer."

His eyes narrow. "I didn't *run away*. What are you calling me, a coward?"

"No!" I snap, slamming a fist down on the table.

"And how do you expect me to deal with all these feelings you claim I have? Talk about them? Cry about them? Like a child? Is that how men do things where you're from?"

"I'd prefer that to you shutting me out!"

"Enough. I'm not talking about this anymore."

I throw up my hands. "Oh, okay! Yes, Alpha, whatever you say. Want me to shine your boots or pull the stick out of your ass while I'm at it?"

Grinding his teeth, Wulfric looks away from me. There's a defeated slouch to his shoulders and before my eyes, the fight goes out of him. Like he's given up.

Fuck. I'm being an asshole. "I'm sorry." My throat thickens. "I get it. You needed space. That's fine. I was just worried about you. It's good you were with your brothers instead of by yourself. I just wish you'd let me be there for you, too."

"I can never do the right thing, not even with you. Maybe—" Blowing out a sigh, he shakes his head like he's fighting an internal war with himself. "I don't know how to be what you need, or what my pack needs."

"Wulfric—"

Suddenly he says, "I'm going to get firewood."

There's already wood by the fire.

He leaves again before I can stop him.

Unwilling to sit around and worry, I leave the house to perform some of my Alpha-Mate duties, which are... Honestly, I still don't know what my duties as Alpha-Mate entail, but I would imagine helping out around the village would be a start.

I go from home to home, checking in and making sure my pack have what they need. I write a list of things each household requires, and then I check in on the former thralls, now employees since Wulfric has started paying them wages to take care of the chores.

Their conditions are slowly improving. For starters, they are no longer in chains and the overseer is more diligent in reporting back to Wulfric and me about what they need. I walk among them and learn their names, checking in to make sure their needs are being met. We have a long way to go in improving their quarters and eventually I want them to earn enough to start building their own homes off of our property.

They seem happier and healthier now that they're getting more nutrient-dense meals and having their medical needs met. Who would have thought? It still bothers me how poorly they were neglected before, but I'm hoping we can keep improving.

Horse hooves clop behind me on the village road. "Hail, Alpha-Mate." It's Gunnar, riding atop his horse.

Of all the brothers, I've interacted with him the least. He's always gone out of his way to avoid me.

"Hey. Going somewhere?"

"For a hunt. Join me."

Like Wulfric, he's a gruff man of few words. "Sure." I don't have many plans anyway.

Once we're in the woods, Gunnar hitches the horse to a tree, then calls upon his furs to change shape. Pulling up my fur hood, I morph into my white wolf and follow Gunnar's big gray wolf into the trees.

Gunnar scents the air. *"Smell that? A reindeer."*

The meat will make a good meal for the village. Together, we weave through the trees, following the musky scent and the hoofprints in the snow. Gunnar is stoic and silent as we lope along, his breath streaming in clouds from his snout.

"So, you hunt a lot for the village." My small talk skills are truly terrible.

"Aye. I do. I prefer being among nature than in a popu-lated area. Have my own cabin a few miles from the vil-lage."

"That's nice."

I pause to sniff a tree where the reindeer rubbed itself against the bark, leaving behind a tuft of hair.

"You and Wulfric hunted down the guys who hurt me, right?"

Gunnar growls, his lip rolling back to reveal sharp white fangs. *"We did."*

"Thank you. You didn't have to do that for me."

Gunnar swings his big head toward me. *"Of course I did. You're one of us. Pack. I didn't see it at first. Humans have a bad history with our kind. My little brother has been hurt enough, and I did not wish to see him hurt again by your kind."*

"I know. I understand that. If anyone hurt Wulfric, I'd rip them to pieces."

Gunnar makes a pleased growling sound. *"And that is how I know the Norns were wise to bring you together. When you stood up for him against Anders, I knew my brother's feelings for you were not misplaced."*

The lone reindeer comes into view between the trees. It's a young male, grazing from the forest floor.

"Keep low and quiet." Gunnar lowers himself to the ground, and I imitate his stance. We advance slowly from behind the reindeer. I tread on a stick, snapping it. The

reindeer bolts. Gunnar huffs beside me. *"You still have much to learn."*

I flatten my ears. *"Sorry."*

Gunnar bumps against me. *"Don't be. I will make a hunter of you yet!"* He takes off into the trees, and I follow.

We wind up catching and killing the reindeer, but it takes over an hour. I'm exhausted when I shift back and help Gunnar load the reindeer across his horse's back.

"Good hunting. You did not hesitate to go for the throat," Gunnar says with admiration.

"Thanks." I'm still picking reindeer hair out of my teeth, though. "Think I feel more at home around the village, though." I wince, hoping he won't think less of me.

Gunnar frowns thoughtfully. "Mayhap if more people valued the comforts of home over their bloodlust and greed, the world would be a kinder place." We're quiet for a time as we walk back to the village. As the familiar huts and chimney stacks come into view, Gunnar says, "I apologize, Alpha-Mate, for the way I treated you when you first arrived."

"You thought I'd attacked your brother. It was justi-fied."

"Wulfric explained what truly happened. Another trick from Anders. Still, I was too hot-headed. And then again, during your heat, I..." His cheeks redden and my own face burns. "Behaved inappropriately. I apologize for that as well."

I cough. "Don't worry about it."

"I admit, I envy my brother. No one has spoken to my wolf since... Leif." Gunnar looks away, becoming distracted by picking a leaf out of his horse's mane.

"He was your mate?" I guess.

"Leif was not fated for me, but he was the one I chose. I doubt there is another out there for me. It's just as well. I prefer my solitude." For all the surety with which he speaks, I get the feeling he's trying to convince himself. "Sooner or later, the berserker rage will take me. It's for the best I keep my distance."

"Hey, come on, don't think like that. You'll find someone."

He just shrugs. "I'd better get this butchered. I will see you later, Alpha-Mate. It was a pleasure." A smile, surprisingly soft and warm, forms beneath his rugged beard, and then Gunnar turns and leads his horse away.

I watch him go, sympathy squeezing my heart. I'm worried about him. It sounds as if he's resigned himself to being alone forever and eventually becoming consumed by the beast within. I hope there's someone out there for him, someone who can be to him what Wulfric is to me.

Unwilling to return to the village and mope around waiting for Wulfric, I decide to walk along the beach. I'm enjoying the cold wind on my face and the roar of the ocean when a sudden flash of light blinds me. To my surprise, Lyall rows to shore. There's a defeated slump to his shoulders as he leaves the boat, boots sloshing in the waves that laps at the stony shore. He pockets a branch of Yggdrasil, drags his boat the rest of the way ashore, then freezes when he sees me. Panic makes his eyes widen.

"K-Kieran. I... I was just going fishing! Didn't catch anything, though. Better luck next time, I suppose!"

"Do you travel to the future a lot?"

Suddenly, he marches toward me. "Don't tell Wulfric." He grips my shoulders hard. "You can't. If he knew, he'd never approve. I know it is unmanly to beg, but I will do it if I must."

"Whoa, whoa! Hold up. I'm not telling Wulfric anything. I promise. What you do is your own business." But I am curious as to why he goes so often and why Wulfric would take issue with his time traveling. "I really won't tell Wulfric. Your secret is safe with me. But why do you go to the future? Why would he be pissed at you for that?"

Lyall gnaws his lower lip. "Because it's the only way I can see him. My mate."

"Oh," I say a little breathlessly. "You have a mate in the future? But why would Wulfric be angry about that?"

Lyall parts his lips, then takes a step back from me. "I can't say. I'm sorry but I can't risk anyone knowing who it is I'm seeing."

Now I'm really curious, but I don't want to push him. "Okay. I get it."

He smiles. "Thank you. Do you plan on returning to your time?"

"I did," I answer. "Not anymore, though."

He cocks his head. "Why?"

Smiling, I say, "I guess you guys aren't so bad—dog breath and wet fur smell aside."

"Hey!" He punches my shoulder. "Well, you should probably tell Wulfric that. He's been quiet, and when my brother gets quiet, he's usually thinking. And Wulfric thinking isn't good for anyone, but especially not himself. He can take himself to these dark places, and it's difficult for even Gunnar and me to pull him out of them."

His words make worry churn in my stomach, and I want to rush home and see Wulfric now. "I will. Thanks, Lyall."

I jog home, eager to see Wulfric. I need to get through that wall he builds around himself and get him to tell me what's wrong before he does something stupid.

Wulfric's scent carries to me on the wind, and so I follow it toward the stable. Inside, Wulfric stands in front of Fenna's box stall. He brushes her white mane and strokes her nose, murmuring gently. My heart all but melts at the sight.

Those stormy eyes find mine. "Will you ride with me?" There's something I don't like in his voice, heavy and forlorn.

"Sure." My heart sinks to the bottom of my stomach.

Wulfric leads the horse from her stall and stops her in front of me. Once I've climbed up, Wulfric sits behind me. The warmth of his powerful body compels me to relax, but I've got a sinking feeling something is wrong.

With a click of his heels, Wulfric urges the horse into a gallop from the stables. The village blurs around us as we run until we're out among rolling hills and rugged wilderness. I don't know where he's taking me, but my heart sinks more the further we get from the village.

"Wulfric, where are we going?"

His hands tighten on the reins.

"At least tell me what we're doing."

"Something I should have done sooner." The resignation in his voice only makes me more nervous.

The trees clear, and we arrive on the same beach we visited yesterday. The beach where we saw Anders off into the unknown. Icy fear falls into my stomach like a chunk of ice. I know what he's doing, and I don't like it.

Wulfric dismounts from the saddle and approaches a rowboat. "I made you a deal, Kieran. If you mated with me, I would keep you safe until you could return home." He stares out over the rolling waves. Wulfric is a big man but against the endless horizon, he looks smaller than I've ever seen him.

"But I confess, I've been selfish with you. I haven't wanted you to leave. When that happened, I cannot say, only that I dread waking up without you beside me, never eating meals with you…" His hands curl at his sides. "But I cannot keep hurting the people I care for. You deserve to be back in your own time. If that is what would make you happy, then I cannot keep you here. No matter how badly I wish for you to stay."

My hands shake, so I squeeze them into fists. I haven't been cold in a long time, but the wind off the water cuts right through me.

When he turns around, Wulfric holds a branch of Yggdrasil. I want to smack it out of his hand. "One of Yggdrasil's roots twists far beneath the water. The branch will react to Yggdrasil's magic and take you home."

My eyes sting, and there's a lump in my throat. "You want me to go?"

"No." The word breaks on his tongue. "The idea of parting from you cleaves my soul in half. But I cannot keep you here if you would rather be somewhere else. So if you still desire to go home, then I will not stop you." His eyes glisten wetly, but the stubborn man refuses to shed a tear.

Relief bowls over me, making my knees shake. Wulfric wants me. That's all that matters. In a few short strides, I throw my arms around him. He's completely stiff, like he doesn't know if this is a goodbye hug or an I'm-never-leaving-you hug.

"You are my home. You, Wulfric."

The breath catches in his chest and then his arms are around me, crushing me to his body.

Curling my fingers in his hair, I tug him down and his lips find mine.

"Thank the gods," he whispers, voice trembling.

Wrapped in each other's arms, we stand on that beach together until the sun sets into the ocean behind us.

Chapter 20
Wulfric

Kieran chose me.

I don't know how or why, but I will forever thank the gods that he did.

Once we return home, we lie beneath the furs, hands intertwined. The wind howls outside, but otherwise the world is quiet and still. "Why?" I ask.

Kieran makes a curious sound as he kisses the back of my knuckles.

"Why did you choose me?"

Kieran stretches out on his back. "I got to know the people here. Adjusted to this new place. Realized a certain moody, broody Alpha wasn't as cold-hearted as he seemed." His leg bumps mine beneath the furs.

"I'm... broody?"

"So broody." He rolls over and kisses my shoulder. "So broody, in fact, you've been agonizing over whether you should be selfish and make me stay. That must have been killing you. I wish you'd just said something."

I wish I had, too. "I tried." My throat feels tight. "Every time I thought to ask, I would lose my voice. Like... in a nightmare, where you try and scream but you can't." Kieran's gentle fingers run down the column of my throat, then curl in the hair on my chest. "It felt like... terror. Because what if you had said yes? What if you had left?" Just thinking about it makes me feel cold all over. "I've never been scared. Before a fight, aye. But not like this. Not until you."

I can't look at him, worried I sound like a fool.

Kieran curls into my body, laying his head on my chest. "I know what you mean. The thought of losing you terrifies me."

I exhale all the breath I didn't know had been stuck in my lungs. "It's good I'm not alone in these feelings."

"No. You're not." He takes my hand and holds it tight. "You aren't alone, Wulfric. Never. And it isn't your fault Anders was hurt. You didn't do anything wrong."

All the warm, fluttery feelings turn to ash in my chest. I did. But if I tell him my greatest, most shameful secret, will Kieran change his mind about me?

"You're a good brother. A good alpha. Your parents would be proud."

I try to breathe, but my chest is too tight. It's like chains have wrapped around my lungs.

"Wulfric?"

I need to get out. Kicking off the furs, I stumble from the bed.

"Wulfric, don't!" Kieran's bare feet slap the floor, and then his hand is around my wrist, tugging me back. "Don't do this. Tell me what just happened. What did I do wrong?"

My eyes burn and my throat aches.

"Talk to me."

I can't speak. I couldn't bear for him to know the worst part of me and hate me for it.

"Was it... your parents? Wulfric, you have to know they'd be proud of you."

"Stop!" I wheeze. My chest feels like it will tear open. I hunch over, protecting the most vulnerable parts of myself from the claws of guilt and grief. "Please. Stop."

"Why?" Kieran asks, voice shaking. He lets go of my wrist, but I've lost the will to run. Instead I fall to my knees beside the fire and curl into myself, trying to be small. Praying they don't see. That they won't kill me like they just killed my father.

I can't keep the poison inside any longer. It's been building for years, eating me alive. If I don't tell someone, anyone, then it will keep on sickening me.

"I killed my father." It's like a dam breaks. The memories crash over me, drowning me.

"What?" Kieran whispers, and the shock in his voice makes me flinch. Oh gods. He hates me.

"A-Anders was right." I suck in a wrenching gasp. Something wet streaks my face. Blood. The blood of the dead and wounded lying all around me will always stain my skin. "He's dead because of me. Because I—" A strangled noise escapes me.

I can feel Kieran's presence beside me, kneeling close by, but I can't see him through the ocean spray that clouds my eyes. All I can see is the masked hunter towering over my father, blade drawn back. And I can't do a damn thing about it.

"I watched him die, and I did *nothing*."

I robbed my brothers of their father. Anders would never have turned on me if I hadn't taken our father away from us.

"I should have died. It should have been me."

A gentle hand touches my shoulder. I jerk back without meaning to, gasping through the tightness in my chest.

"You can feel however you want." Kieran's voice shakes. "I'll never understand the kind of guilt you're feeling. But I know you, and I know you did everything you could."

"I didn't!" I snarl at him, hardly feeling any guilt when he flinches from my outburst. "I did nothing but lie there and watch him die!"

"Okay." He squeezes my shoulder. "Take some breaths for me, Wulfric. Okay?"

"C-can't. Chest's too tight. I—"

"Tell me something you can see. Something you can smell, or touch, or hear. Anything."

Spots pop in front of my eyes. "I... Uh... You. I smell you."

"What do I smell like?"

"I don't know! Plants."

"What kind?"

I growl at him. "Too many."

"Name a few, come on." He rubs my shoulder, the gesture soothing.

Breathing in short starts, I pant, "Lupine. P-poppies. Pinecones and sweet sap. Grass."

"Something you can hear?"

Nothing at first, not around the blood roaring in my ears, but I've got to try for him. My own heart drowns out everything at first, but then I hear it. *Thump. Thump. Thump.* Steady and low. Soothing. Craving more of that sound, I lean into Kieran's body, my head to his chest. "Your heart. The birds outside. The wind. The fire crackling. Your breathing."

"What can you touch?"

My shaking hand glides over the floor. "The ground. The w-wood." Then I grip his leg. "Your clothes. Your thigh. Your hand." I find his hand and squeeze tight. As I start to concentrate on things outside of my anguish, the storm inside me slowly blows over.

When I open my eyes, I'm lying with my head in Kieran's lap, staring into the dying firelight. Gentle fingers sift through my hair, scratching my scalp. My face is wet, and I realize I haven't cried since I was a small boy, still soft to the ways of the world. I thought I would feel shame but something inside me is lighter. I told Kieran the worst part of me, but he didn't push me away.

"You didn't kill your father, Wulfric."

I swallow hard. "Not directly."

"You *didn't*. He died in battle, defending his people. If he was a good father—"

"He was."

"—and you had died in his place, he would have never forgiven himself. He knew the risks. He died for you and your pack willingly, not *because* of you."

Swallowing hard, I croak, "I was so close to him. If I'd just had the courage to stand up, I could have..." Tears spill down my face before I can fight them, and I hide my face in his lap. Kieran strokes my back and my shoulders. "I couldn't move. I was petrified. All I did was watch as that bastard ran him through."

"It wasn't your job to die for him."

I don't agree at all, but I can't seem to speak anymore.

"You stayed alive for your pack, to be the alpha they needed. Have you ever talked to Gunnar and Lyall about this?"

"No!" I look up at him, wide-eyed. "They would despise me."

Framing my face in his hands, he thumbs away my tears. "How do you know that?"

I can't say how I know, only that I do.

"I don't think Lyall is capable of hating anyone. That guy's a golden retriever in a man's body. And Gunnar's a hard-ass, but he's a big softie. Talk to them, Wulf. You've been carrying this pain around since you were a kid. It must be killing you. And you guessing how they'd react can only make it worse. Tell them how you feel and let them decide how they feel. Don't decide for them."

I can't promise I'll do any of that. Reaching up, I trace the shape of his jaw. "You are a wise man, Kieran Grove."

He chuckles. "Good to know all my years of therapy paid off somehow. You know, what you're dealing with sounds a lot like PTSD. That's post-traumatic stress disorder."

"What is that? A sickness? Ulfhednar can't get ill."

He rubs my chest. "It's a sickness in the mind, not the body. You survived a traumatic experience, Wulfric, something your body can't comprehend you lived through."

I swallow hard. That doesn't sound good. "Is there a cure?"

Stroking my hair, Kieran says, "In my time, some people take medication or go to therapy. But here... that stuff doesn't exist yet. You've suffered enough without keeping all those feelings to yourself."

"It's not the same as what you have? Generalized anxiety disorder, right? What is that like?"

Kieran bites his lip. "I don't know. It's like... I'm never certain of anything. I second-guess everything. Myself, other people."

"Do you second-guess me?"

He blinks fast. "Sometimes."

Reaching up, I cup his face in my hands and draw him close. "Then you should know the moment I saw you, it was like the universe righted itself. Everything I've ever done, all that I'd been through, was so I could meet you. For the first time in my life, my survival no longer felt like a mistake. There was a purpose to it, a design. I lived when my father died so I could find you, Kieran. I know it makes me selfish, because I cannot bring myself to regret it."

A shivery exhale escapes Kieran. "Wow." Sniffling, he quickly wipes his eyes. "Sorry. That was... a lot. Nobody's ever said something like that to me. Ugh. I'm a mess. Hang on." He scrubs his eyes with his sleeve.

"No, you aren't." Speechless, I can only gaze up at him. Kieran is strong. I'd never have guessed he had such demons inside him. "You're the strongest man I've ever known."

"So are you." He massages my cheekbones, then my brows, and my body relaxes into his touch. "All that messy stuff on the inside doesn't mean we can't be strong."

I've never thought about it like that before. "I... I'll think about it." Maybe he is right. Talking about it might help. "I wish there was another way. That the demons that plague you could take on a physical form."

"Why?" he whispers, his lips inches from mine.

"I'd fight them all for you, and I wouldn't stop until I'd won."

A smile lights up his face, and he draws me in, claiming my lips with his.

"So would I."

And if by some miracle I hadn't been in love with Kieran Grove before, I am now.

And I pray I'll never stop.

A month passes. It's a blissful one, full of mornings spent in bed worshipping every inch of my mate's body, working around the village, and drinks by the fire with my brothers and my mate. Most days I spend time at my cabin, whittling away at a gift I started making Kieran before I disappeared into the woods. For the first time in a long time, it's easy to feel at ease.

Despite showing him the weakest side of myself, being around Kieran hasn't been a hardship. There have been times I've wanted to run away from it all, but Kieran pulls me back from the edge. We do some ridiculous breathing exercises every morning. At first, I found them boring, but there's something special about simply sitting quietly with him, neither of us expecting anything from the other but his presence.

I have never felt for anyone the way I do for Kieran.

Gods above, I love him. Deeply. I just wish I could find the right time to tell him. Words have never been a skill of mine, so I aspire to prove my love with actions and focus on finishing his gift.

Laying down my whittling knife, I breathe a satisfied sigh. After several days of carving, at long last Kieran's gift is done. I only hope he likes it. I leave the solitude of my cabin and trek back to the village. As much as I hate to admit it, Anders's absence has been good for the pack and for me. I can breathe more easily knowing I don't have to worry about him challenging me every chance he gets. All these years I've been anticipating an attack from him and now the threat has passed.

The longhouse is warm and quiet but not devoid of life. The former thralls are bustling about in the kitchen, but there's a different air about them. They talk quietly to each other, laugh and smile with an ease that was missing not long ago. I need to remember to pay them later for their work. Construction has begun on a proper bunkhouse for them. It will be a bigger and more comfortable place for them to live in.

"Everything all right?" I ask them. I like to think I've been better about asking their names and inquiring after their needs.

One of the women, Hekla, nods. "Oh yes, Alpha." She goes back to talking to the cook.

In the bedroom, Kieran has his back to me as he adjusts the quiver of arrows over his shoulder. "Oh, there you are. I was about to go and train the kids. Where'd you go?"

Making sure my hands are behind my back, I just shrug. "Out for a bit." I clear my throat, suddenly nervous. I hope he'll like my gift. "I've, uh... been working on something for you."

Those bright blue eyes sparkle with interest. "Really?"

Suddenly, I'm second-guessing everything. What if it isn't good enough? Should I have spent longer on it, refined it more, mayhap? "Never mind."

"What?" he squawks. "Seriously? You can't tell me you got me something then just walk away!"

"I just realized it's not very good."

Rolling his eyes, Kieran reaches toward me. "It's my present. Let me decide. Give me!"

"Fine," I grumble and shove the object at him.

Kieran's eyes widen. "Is that a... an instrument?"

"It's called a lyre." I hand the instrument to him. "You said you played a stringed instrument, so I thought..."

Kieran swallows hard, his eyes shining. "You want me to play it?"

"That's what it's for, isn't it?" I huff, face burning. "I made it myself. Wood, some bone, and horsehair for the strings."

Kieran's mouth falls open. "You *made* this?"

"Aye."

Shaking his head, Kieran runs his hand over the sanded wood surface, then gingerly plucks the strings. "My god. Wulfric. I can't believe it. This is beautiful."

"I can teach you—if you like. If you don't want to, I can just—"

Kieran crashes into me, wrapping an arm around my back. He buries his face in my chest. "I'd love that. Thank you. Thank you so much. This is..." Pulling back, he wipes his eyes. "Wow. This is amazing."

Relief glows bright and warm in my chest. "You like it?"

"I love it! I can't wait to play it." Grinning, he plops down on the bed and cradles the lyre in his lap. I sit behind him and position his fingers over the strings. Following my movement, Kieran strums them, producing a gentle melody.

Kieran leans back into my body, and peace unlike anything I've ever felt settles over me. For so long, I thought the greatest glory in this life would be to die in battle and go to Valhalla. Now that I have Kieran in my arms, I can't imagine anywhere else in this world I would rather be. Soon Kieran familiarizes himself with the strings and creates a beautiful melody.

"I've never heard a sound so lovely," I whisper into his hair.

The strings squeak as Kieran suddenly stops playing. He shivers against me and I think he's cold until the scent of his tears hits my nose.

"What is it, little rabbit?" I press my lips against his hair and stroke his arms.

Sniffing, Kieran laughs shakily. "Sorry, sorry. Don't know where the waterworks came from." He wipes his eyes, then turns in my arms and huddles into me. His beard scratches my skin as he kisses my neck, then peppers kisses along my jaw. "You really mean that? It sounds okay?"

"Have I ever said something I don't mean?" I rub his back.

He huffs, his breath warming my skin. "Okay, got me there. I used to write music with my ex-boyfriend."

Anger heats my skin. "This boyfriend... what was his name?"

"Mark. We'd just broken up in my timeline before I came here. We'd been together three years."

"That's a long time." Is it possible Kieran still has feelings for him? I tighten my grip on him, growling low in my chest. "And you don't still care for him? At all?"

A soft chuckle escapes Kieran. "I did at first. He encouraged me to write songs and pursue my passion."

"What made you leave?"

"I found him in bed with another guy."

My fingers freeze in his hair.

"So I left. Went to Iceland with my friend Amanda to get over him. He kept texting me, trying to make me take him back, saying how much he misses me." He sniffles, and his tears drip onto my shoulder. "He t-told me I was nothing without him. That people only liked my songs because he'd helped make them, and I... I believed him. So I stopped playing. I let him destroy the only thing in life I was ever passionate about."

Rage makes my blood boil. Gripping Kieran's face in my hands, I make him look me in the eyes. "You will not take him back. Whatever he is to you, whatever he could have been—it does not matter. The moment I claimed you and you claimed me, you surrendered the right to lie with any other man again, and so did I. The names of any who came before me are never to be spoken in my presence again. They no longer matter, because they were unworthy of you."

"Really?" Kieran's voice shakes, and his cheeks are splotchy. He blinks quickly, his eyes damp. "He sure did a good job of making *me* feel unworthy."

I wonder if I ever made him feel that way. The thought makes me sick. "If I have ever made you feel that way, then I will spend the rest of my days making it up to you. I'm the one who was unworthy of you. You came into my world and made me see things differently. I'd never thought to think of thralls as people. It was never something I'd questioned until you showed me another way of thinking. You showed me a human can have the heart of a wolf. Helped me accept the fragile parts of myself I hate the most. You are a beautiful soul, Kieran Grove, and so is your music."

I love his music, and I... I love him, too. By the gods, I wish I had the courage to tell him.

Wiping away the tears flowing down his cheeks, I say, "The man who hurt you was but a stepping stone in the river of life that led you to me. You belong to me, little rabbit, and I belong to you. The only way we shall ever part is in death and even then I will find you in the world beyond this one." I brush my thumb over the scar from my bite in the crook of his neck.

Kieran shakes his head, gazing at me in the way one might gaze up at the stars. "I'm never letting you go. I had to cross a whole other time to find you, someone who appreciates and supports me when no one else could. I wouldn't change a damn thing." His lips find mine, urgent and so full of passion, I feel as if I will float away. "Wulfric, I—"

My heart knows what he will say, and the answering words soar to my lips, ready to be set free. But then Kieran says, "I do want to go back to my time, though."

A cold rock falls into my stomach. "O-oh." My voice sounds so feeble, I have to clear my throat.

Kieran snorts. "What? Don't look at me like that."

"Like what?"

"Like you're a kicked puppy."

"Not a puppy," I snap at him.

"Just let me explain. Geez. Someone's clingy." Kieran runs his fingers through my hair. "I wasn't lying. I want to stay here. This place is my home. You are my home. But I have people back in my time who probably miss me. Or might even think I'm dead. I need to go back and let them know I'm okay. It wouldn't be for long, just long enough to reassure them. Then I'd come back to you. I promise."

The knot loosens in my chest. I believe Kieran. I trust him. "If that's what you want to do, then I will have Helga give you her branch of Yggdrasil. Just..." I've loved and lost so many times. It's hard to say goodbye and trust that it won't be forever. "Say it again."

Pressing his lips to mine, Kieran whispers, "I'll come back to you. I promise." Closing my eyes, I lean into the press of his lips and let his promise wrap around my heart.

Chapter 21
Kieran

Even though I know I'm not saying goodbye forever, my heart is still heavy in my chest as the ocean waves roar. There's a rowboat moored on the shore, ready to spirit me away to my timeline. I found my way here once before—surely I can make it back in one piece. Unless something goes wrong and I get stuck in my time or—

"All right, little rabbit?" Wulfric comes to stand behind me, rubbing my cold shoulders. Nuzzling into my neck, he drops kisses over my skin. His beard tickles, and I fight the urge to laugh. Fuck. I'm going to miss him, and I won't even be gone very long.

"No one's ever... I don't know, exploded or lost a limb going through a portal, right?"

"I am not sure."

I groan, hitting my head back against his shoulder. "You're supposed to say no!"

"Oh. Is that sarcasm, too?"

Turning in his arms, I smack a kiss on his lips. My wolf whines at the thought of being apart from him. We belong here on Ulfheim with our mate and Lyall, Gunnar, and Helga.

Helga clears her throat softly. "Ready, lad?"

No, but the sooner I get this over with, the sooner I can come home. "Yes."

Wulfric walks me to the boat, his hand gripping mine tightly. Nerves writhe like snakes in my stomach. "So, um... how will this work exactly? Do you have any control over where you send me?"

Lyall chimes in, "Aye. Don't fret. It's quite simple. You came to us because of your bond to Wulfric."

"But I didn't know him yet."

"No, you didn't, but that doesn't matter. Through your connection, you had a link to this place. To travel back to your time, you'll need the branch, aye, but also a memory that ties you to the place where you're going."

I think I understand. "So, just think of something that reminds me of New York?"

"That should do it."

I stop beside Wulfric. The rowboat awaits to take me on my journey.

Coughing to clear the suspicious lump in my throat, I say as casually as I can, "I'll see you soon."

"You better." Wulfric grips my arms, eyes narrowing as a growl builds in his chest. "I'll tear the world apart to find you and bring you back where you belong."

"And where do I belong?" I twirl the end of his beard.

He rests his forehead against mine. "Here with me. Always."

I don't know how it happened or when, but I found a home here in this world so far from the life I once knew. In my mate's embrace, I found myself again.

He hands me a wooden statue of a wolf, just like the one Helga gave me. "Use it whenever you're ready to return."

I accept the little wooden wolf, blinking fast as my eyes sting. "I will. I promise."

Then I'm in his arms, and he's holding me like he never wants to let me go.

And damn it, I never want him to.

Throat tight, I lower myself into the boat. The horizon stretches ahead of me, as vast and overwhelming as it is beautiful. Wulfric stands behind me. "Ready?"

I swallow hard. "Yeah."

As the waves crash upon the shore, Wulfric gives the boat a shove and before I'm ready, the waves carry me away from him and out to sea. Helga begins to chant behind me and with a flash of light, a portal yawns into existence ahead of me.

With shaking hands, I row toward the light.

I think of New York. Central Park, my favorite spot in the city. Yellow taxicabs. The salty smoke billowing from a pretzel cart. The way the Hudson River looks at dawn. An image flickers in the portal, and it looks familiar. My arms burn as I row faster toward the image that gets clearer with each passing second.

The tip of the boat disappears into the portal, and this is it. Heart pounding, I look back. The silhouettes of Wulfric and our pack watch me go. Tears sting my eyes.

I forgot to tell him that I love him.

Closing my eyes, I find our bond and whisper, *"Wulfric, can you hear me? Wulfric, I—"*

And then I'm consumed in blinding light, and everything inside me turns upside down.

The boat overturns, and I'm plunged into murky water several degrees warmer than it should be in medieval Iceland. I break the surface with a gasp, shaking my head to get my wet hair out of my face. I'm in the middle of a huge lake with orange leaves drifting on the water, a lake I vaguely recognize. I'm in Central Park. Familiar skyscrapers tower over autumnal leaves, reaching toward a cloudless blue sky.

Oh my god.

It worked. I'm back in NYC!

My eyes are wet with water and stinging with tears. I'm really back home.

"Sir, are you okay?" A mom, dad, and their young son watch me wide-eyed from a rowboat they're piled into.

"I'm fine," I assure them, but I must look strange. I can't wait until they see my outdated clothing. "My boat tipped over."

"Come on in!" The dad leans over and I swim to him, and he helps pull me into the rowboat. Sure enough, when they see what I'm wearing, their expressions morph into curiosity rather than alarm.

"I was... at a Halloween party."

"In November?" Their son looks bewildered.

Huh. I lost track of time in the past. They paddle me back to the boathouse where they rented the rowboat. People stare at me in my wet, outdated clothing. I'm sure I look bizarre, especially with my long hair and overgrown but neat beard, but I don't care. It's New York—there have been stranger sights.

I've got to get back to my apartment. Mark shouldn't be there since he's usually at work around this time. I lost all my belongings when I first time traveled, including my wallet, keys, and phone, so I've got no way to buy a MetroCard or pay for a cab. Once I find the nearest subway station, I look both ways, jump the turnstile, and jog to catch the first train.

Dressed outlandishly and with my furs smelling of wet dog, I plop into a seat, smiling at the people who scoot away from me, and watch the platforms fly by. I missed riding trains. Even the annoying people who play music on the train don't bother me like they usually do. I spent so long wishing I could be anywhere else but now that I'm back, it might be hard to leave.

Except there's a void inside me where my pack and my mate should be. I can't feel them or hear their songs. As much as I love New York, I love Wulfric more.

Once I'm off the train, I make a beeline for my apartment. I follow a delivery person through the door. Jumping up the stairs two at a time, I arrive outside my door, breathless. Good thing I always keep a spare key under the mat. I shove the key in the lock and turn it—only to nearly fall on my face when the door opens.

"What the—" The words die in my throat.

Mark, my ex-boyfriend, stares back at me with wide eyes. Shit. What day of the week is it? It must not be a workday for him.

"Kieran?" My name is a croak on his lips. "Oh my god. Where have you *been*?" He goes to hug me, and I lurch out of his reach.

He's the last person I wanted to see. Ignoring the hurt on his face, I say, "It's a long story."

His hurt hardens into a scowl. Crossing his arms over his chest, he says, "That's all you have to say? I had to track Amanda down to figure out why it was taking so long for you to come back. She thought you were dead!" His voice shakes.

"Well, I'm back. Can I borrow a phone? I need to talk to Amanda." I hate that she's been so worried all this time.

"Yeah. Sure." I recognize that petulant tone. I didn't give him the answer he wanted, so now he'll try and make me feel like an asshole about it. He hands me his phone, and I squeeze past him and hurry into our bedroom. I put the phone on speaker and change out of my wet, chilly things.

"I told you to stop calling me, Mark!" Anger heats her voice.

Emotion stings my eyes at hearing my best friend's voice after so long. "It's not Mark. It's me. I'm back."

She gasps. "K-Kieran?" She sounds close to tears. "Oh my god. Kieran, is that you?"

Wiping my eyes, I say, "Yeah, Amanda. It's me. I'm so—"

"You fucking asshole!" she screams, then bursts into tears. I deserve that. I wish I could hug her. "How dare you! You scared me to fucking death, you absolute craphead!"

I clutch the phone close. "I'm so sorry. I'm giving you a hug. Can you feel it?"

Sniffling, she takes in a few deep breaths. "I've been so worried about you. The b-boat crew came back and said there'd been a wreck, and all the passengers were accounted for except you. I thought you'd died, Kier."

"I'm so sorry," I say again. "I promise I'll explain everything. Let's meet up." My brain short-circuits. "What day is it?"

"Saturday."

She's off work today then. "Can we grab a coffee? My treat."

She laughs wetly. "Yeah, of course. Ugh. I hate you so much."

"I know. I promise I'll tell you everything."

"You better. Meet at the usual at noon?"

"Sounds good." Amanda has a great bookstore slash coffee shop a few blocks up from her apartment. I check the time on Mark's phone. Noon is only an hour away.

I hang up and throw on some dry clothes, packing up my wet Viking-era clothes. After I'm dressed, I call my psychiatrist and tell her about quitting my medication. She tells me I'm fine to just start taking my regular dose again.

While I'm in the bedroom, I throw together a suitcase of stuff I want to take with me to Wulfric's time. Now that I have time to prepare, I want to bring some modern conveniences with me, like my toothbrush and toothpaste. And maybe a sex toy or two. I go through my nightstand, grab my Zoloft and swallow a pill dry. Hopefully, I'll start feeling better soon. Good thing I had an extra prescription tucked away at home. This should last me a few weeks, then I can come back to the future and get another refill.

In the living room, Mark's scowling like a petulant child, his arms crossed and foot tapping exaggeratedly. "Kier, I made a mistake."

I snort. "You accidentally sat on your friend's dick? Yeah. Sure."

Groaning, he says, "Because you're so perfect, right? You know, maybe you should try and see things from my perspective! It wasn't exactly easy dealing with your crap."

"My crap?" Anger heats my blood.

"All your anxiety. You could never just chill. You over-thought everything. You never wanted to go out with me and my friends on the weekends. It was like I didn't even have a boyfriend. Have you ever thought about how your anxious bull crap affected *me?*"

I almost apologize, like I would have done before we broke up. Before I met a guy who makes me feel like I am good enough, warts and all. I don't need Mark, and I don't owe him any more of my time.

"If you were unhappy, you should have just said so."

His cheeks redden in anger. "So you're just going to dump me? I don't get a say?"

"If you really cared so much, you should have thought about that before you went behind my back." Shouldering my bag, I shove by him.

"You'll be nothing without me, Kier!"

I freeze, my hand squeezing the doorknob.

"The only reason you had any success is because of me. People who liked our YouTube channel liked us because we were a couple. People liked our shows because it was my name on the billboard."

Once I'd believed exactly that. But I know better now. I don't have to settle for some half-assed version of love, because I found the real thing.

"It's over, Mark. Piss off. By the way, this is me moving out. Sure hope your boyfriend is down to cover my portion of the rent." I walk out into the hallway and let the door slam on my old life for good.

The train ride to Brooklyn flies by and before I know it, I'm outside our favorite bookshop and café, Moon Beans and Books Café. Through the window of the bookshop, I can see Amanda sitting at a table. At the sight of me, she springs from her seat and tears outside. She crashes into my arms, and I hold my best friend tight. I don't know if we're laughing or crying or both as we hold each other for what feels like ages.

"I almost didn't recognize you," she says, drying her eyes. "What's with the beard? I like it!"

"I do too." For once, I like who I am.

With my arm around her, we go inside the familiar bookshop. The bookshelves are divided into different sub-genres of romance, from historical to paranormal to fantasy. Amanda's already got a bag full of new books under the table.

"Hey, Kieran!" It's Jamie, the owner of the bookstore. He's got a smile like a sunbeam. Every time I come in here, he's always in the best mood. "The usual?"

"Yes, please."

Jamie gets to work on my iced matcha latte.

Amanda and I sit at our favorite table by the window. I'm not much of a reader by any means, but I still enjoy coming here with Amanda. We studied here several times a week throughout college. "Okay, spill. Tell me every-thing." She clutches my hand. There are bags under her wide eyes, and I hate that I've worried her.

She deserves the truth, no matter how crazy it sounds.

Jamie stops by to deliver our drinks and once he's gone, I start talking. The whole story takes me an hour to tell. Amanda, amazingly, stays mostly quiet except for the oc-casional gasp or exclamation of, "Get the fuck out of here, no way!"

"I've got the furs to prove it in my suitcase."

She's silent a long time.

Pulling out the wolf furs, I hand them to her. She blinks, her eyes unfocused as she strokes the white pelt.

"Hello, earth to Amanda? Yoo-hoo?" I wave my hand in front of her face.

"I'm sorry, I just... You went back in time? You met that Viking we saw in the painting at the museum, except he's a werewolf. *You're* a werewolf. And you two have some weird imprint Twilight bond?"

"Yes?" I don't understand the whole imprinting bit, but she's mostly right.

She exhales. "Whoa."

"You don't believe me, do you?"

"I... I believe that you're different now. I think that whatever happened in Iceland changed you, but only for the better."

I swallow hard. "Really?"

"Yeah, really." She laughs softly. "You're different, Kier, but only in a good way. You're happy, that much is clear. And that's all that matters to me. I think I just need time to wrap my head around the whole time-travel werewolf stuff."

"Fair enough." Smiling, I squeeze her hand.

And then a voice growls, "Tyr's balls. It's you!"

A chunk of ice falls into my stomach because I *know* that voice. But how?

The man standing behind me is tall and lean, dark-haired where his brother is light, green-eyed instead of gray. He wears tight jeans and a black T-shirt with a green apron like Jamie's. His hair is short now and he's clean-shaven, revealing a jawline a guy could cut himself on, but I still recognize him.

It's fucking Anders.

A smirk tugs at his mouth. "Well, well. Seems like Loki is having a laugh at my expense today. What happened? Did my brother get tired of his new pet and send you packing? Need a consolatory belly rub? Oh, how about a little scratchy behind your ears?"

I gnash my teeth. What a dick.

Amanda gawks. "Whoa. He's hot. And a huge jerk. How do you know him?"

"He's Wulfric's brother, the one who tried to overthrow him."

Amanda's on her feet in seconds. "You attacked my friend, you piece of shit!" She grabs her heavy bag of books like she's about to throw it at his head.

Anders's smirk falls off his face. My five-foot-nothing friend just put the fear of Odin into a Viking werewolf.

"Whoa, whoa, whoa!" Suddenly, Jamie is between Anders and us, smiling his easygoing smile. "I sincerely apologize for my new employee. He's *supposed* to be stocking the dark romance section. Aren't you, puppy dog?"

Puppy dog? Does Jamie know what Anders is? No, that can't be possible. Can it?

Red bursts in Anders's cheeks, his jaw tightening as he grinds his teeth. "I can't kill them?"

"No!" Jamie hisses, whirling toward him with his hands on his hips. He's a foot shorter than Anders.

A growl rumbles in Anders's chest. "Can I maim them? Just a little bit."

Jamie throws him a sunny smile and bats his eyelashes. "No."

To my amazement, Anders deflates, his scowl morphing into a pout. "Fine," he grumbles, turning away and hoisting a box of books off the floor. He goes to the back of the store behind a red curtain.

My jaw is on the floor. How has this guy managed to tame Anders?

Jamie flashes us a smile. "Sorry about him. He's all bark, but he's got the sweetest bite. Anything else I can get for you today?" he asks innocently, like I didn't just see him talk a hot-blooded Viking werewolf out of murder.

"Nope," I say, clearing my throat. "Think we'll leave now."

He grins. "No problem! Come back next week. We're hosting a special edition signing! Info's on our website." He holds the door for us.

I almost wish I could stay and figure out what's going on with him and Anders, but I'm itching to go back to Wulfric. Talking about him to Amanda only made me miss him more.

"I'm going back to Wulfric's time," I say.

Her lips tremble. "But you'll come back, right? I've got to meet this Viking guy of yours." She grasps my hands.

I squeeze tight. "Of course! We'll visit as often as we can. We should all have dinner together."

"That sounds amazing!" She pulls me into a hug. "As long as you don't cook."

I chuckle into her hair. "Hey, my burnt casserole is amazing."

I bet Wulfric would love a big feast and to meet Amanda.

Together, we ride the train to Central Park. We walk among autumn leaves and arrive at the lake shore where my boat is still overturned. Wading in up to our ankles, Amanda helps me turn the boat right side up. She gawks at the craftsmanship. "If I didn't believe you, I would now. Check it out! This looks as authentic as it gets."

I climb in, setting my suitcase on the wooden floor.

Up to her waist in the water, Amanda takes my hand. A frown creases her face but she wipes it away with a smile. "Dinner this next Saturday at six. Don't be late."

"I'll be there, Mandy. Promise."

Amanda pulls me down into a hug. "I'm so happy for you."

I hug her back, eyes stinging. I'll miss her, but I know that New York is no longer my home.

My home is wherever Wulfric is.

I unfurl my white furs over my shoulders. Instantly, my wolf stirs within me. I start to row. The runes etched into the wooden carving begin to glow and with a flash, a portal appears.

I think of him. His gray eyes. His rugged scent. The warmth of his arms and his deep, low voice. And from beyond the portal, a howl calls me home in a voice I would know anywhere. Faster I row, following my mate's melody through the portal and home where I belong.

I don't think I'll ever get used to the way my stomach turns upside down every time I travel.

The tide pulls me toward shore and as I get closer, figures spill onto the beach. Some are human while others run on four legs as wolves.

The moment my boat hits the wet sand, I'm on my feet and sprinting toward the shore. Cupping my hands to my mouth, I howl to my pack, and they howl back to welcome me home. Lyall greets me first as his huge white wolf, almost bowling me off my feet. He's like an overgrown puppy prancing around me, yelping his joy. Then Gunnar's there, an arm over my shoulder as he tousles my hair. Helga throws her arms around me and envelops me in a hug so full of warmth, it makes my heart ache.

And then I see him and everything else fades away. A black wolf larger than any other prowls from the crowd. His eyes are as bright as the moon above, and the moonlight glistens in his ebony coat. He runs toward me, paws thundering. Tears prick my eyes, and I rush to meet him. Halfway there, his body ripples, the fur pulling back from his body, his face warping from wolf to man.

I crash into his solid chest and then his arms are around me, his fingers in my hair. A sigh escapes him, full of the sweetest relief, like he's been holding his breath for the hours I've been gone. Squeezing my eyes shut, I breathe in the scent of my mate, my home, and a piece of me that was missing slots into place.

"You came back," he whispers, and his voice shakes with emotion, his arms gripping me tighter.

"Of course I did," I whisper back. Framing his face in my hands, I'm shocked to see tears in his beautiful silver eyes. "You're my anchor point. The place I'll always return to, time and again." Wulfric's lips tremble when he smiles, no doubt recognizing those very words he said to me when he taught me how to fight for myself, for a place here in this world with him. "I love you, Wulfric."

His lips find mine, and the ocean surges over our feet. "You honor me, my love. The gods chose well when they brought you to me."

"That wasn't what you said when we met," I tease.

"I was a fool," he concedes, taking my hand and walking farther up the shore with me. "In truth, I knew you were mine the moment I caught your scent. My wolf knew he'd found his match."

"Sure were a stubborn bastard about it."

He chuckles softly, a deep, rusty sound I want to hear more often.

"You were a jerk at first. Although if you wanna bring the cuffs back, I won't complain."

His eyes get comically wide. "Hush. Don't let the pack hear."

"Is that a no?"

His cheeks redden. "If that's something you'd be interested in..."

I bump his shoulder with mine. "Let's go back to the house and I'll show you how interested I am."

I'm scooped off my feet with a yelp and thrown like a sack of potatoes over his shoulder. I struggle at first and then I just laugh. Wulfric's shoulders shake with mirth, and he adjusts me, carrying me with his big arms beneath my thighs and my legs around his waist.

Our lips meet and the pack howls around us.

Wrapped in the arms of the man I love, I close my eyes and trust in the northern lights to guide us home.

Epilogue
Wulfric

After an amazing dinner with Kieran and his friend Amanda in the future, I'd thought my spirits would be lighter as I climb the familiar hill leading to my parents' barrow. Instead, my heart races. The scents of my brothers carry on the wind, and nervous sweat breaks out over my brow. I'm telling my brothers everything today. They deserve to know what really happened the day Father was killed. I need to know if they'll really blame me for his death. I can't bear the agony of guessing any longer.

Kieran convinced me this is the right thing to do. He also promised me a reward, something to look forward to when I finally get this weight off my chest. Of course, he was willing to give me this special gift even if I didn't tell them. But then what would be the point of the reward?

No, I'll tell my brothers everything, and then I'll go home and treat myself to my mate.

If I'm still in the mood, depending on how well things go.

Gods, I hope they won't hate me. The very idea of losing my brothers, my closest friends, eats away at me. If they do hate me, surely it can't be forever, can it?

Ahead of me two figures sit under the shadow of a standing stone: Gunnar and Lyall.

My stomach twists into knots and I wonder if I'll be sick. By the time I reach them, I'm out of breath, panting like I've been running. Gunnar acknowledges me with a tip of his head and a grunt. Lyall frowns, tilting his head. "Are you well, brother?"

"Aye," I lie, and they can tell from my scent and the way my heart trips.

When Lyall pats the grass, I go and sit between them. The wind blows, rippling the brown grass like waves. Curling my fingers, I take in a breath and let it out. I almost find my words but change the subject at the last second. "Did you hear? Kieran says he saw Anders in the future."

Lyall whips his head toward me at the mention of his twin, his blond hair blowing in the wind. "Really? Was he well?"

"Aye, seemed to be."

Gunnar narrows his eyes. "What was he doing, planning another attack against us?"

"No, no." A laugh escapes me. "He worked in a bookstore."

Lyall chuckles. "A... bookstore? I can't imagine that! Did Anders look well?"

"He looked different, Kieran said. He'd shaved, and his hair was short. Apparently, this book merchant managed to talk him out of starting a fight with Kieran and his companion."

Gunnar leans back against the tree. "Sounds like he's settling in. Mayhap this will be good for him."

Now's the time. The words try to stick in my throat. "I should have done better by Anders. He blamed me for so much of our childhood. I never knew how hurt he truly was. During our fight, he told me he blamed me for our mother's death and for stealing Father away from him." Balling my hands into fists, I ask, "Have either of you ever felt that way?"

Gunnar takes in a thoughtful breath. "It saddens me I never got to know Mother, not really. I was too young to remember her or even miss her when she passed. But I can't say I blamed you. Death is a part of life. It wasn't your fault."

Lyall smiles sadly. "She was beautiful and kind and strong. I'll always regret that our time with her was cut short. But Gunnar's right. And as for Da, well, he had to teach you how to become an alpha. You needed that time with him to grow into who you are now. It was necessary."

With a nod, Gunnar says, "True as well. Although I wish we could have helped you carry that burden."

There's a lump in my throat. They don't blame me for Mother, but they might change their mind. "Anders also believes that if he'd been on that beach, F-Father would still be alive." I swallow hard. I can no longer hold their gazes. My skin's buzzing. Sitting still is too hard. Rising, I walk away from them, far enough to have distance but close enough for them to hear me say, "And he's right."

Gunnar growls. "He's an ass for saying that to you. We were overwhelmed."

"You did everything you could to save Father," Lyall argues.

"I didn't." Closing my eyes tight, I force the words out. "It was my first real battle and it was... it was too much. I collapsed. Couldn't move or even breathe. I thought if I just lay down and stayed still, I would be able to go home alive." My eyes sting with shame. Grinding my teeth to hold back the flood of emotions, I drag the words out. "I did nothing but watch as our father was butchered in front of me."

There. I've said it, confessed my deepest, most shameful secret. I feel no better for it. My brothers are silent behind me. I can't bear to face them, to see the shame and fury in their eyes. Head bowed, I turn in their direction, then drop to my knees. "I'm so sorry. If I'd been stronger, braver, he would still be here." A gasp saws out of me, and tears spill down my cheeks, dampening my beard.

The grass rustles as one of them comes toward me. Lyall—I'd know his scent anywhere. He kneels beside me and leans in, grabbing the back of my neck. I flinch, expecting a blow. Then he touches his forehead to mine and exhales shakily against my skin. "Gods, little brother. How long has this tormented you?" The pain in his voice nearly tears me apart at the seams.

I can't speak, shaking against him.

Another hand grips the back of my head, ruffling my hair as Gunnar sits beside us. "It was not your fault." I've never heard Gunnar's voice so rough before. "Father would have wanted you to live. Your survival was not a mistake."

"If we'd lost you, too, it would have broken us. I'm glad you're here." Lyall tugs me into his arms and holds me fiercely.

"There's nothing to forgive," Gunnar says, and he puts his arm around my shoulder. "Not a thing."

And I break. Years of guilt and grief erupt from me like water from a dam. I can't stop it. All I can do is let my brothers hold me tight until I have room in my aching lungs to breathe and compose myself. I never imagined they could forgive me, but oh, how I've yearned for it. I don't know if I'll ever forgive myself, but with my brothers beside me, I won't ever be alone.

My heart is lighter on the walk back to the village but when I open the door to the longhouse and see Kieran playing the lyre with ease for an eager crowd, it all but bursts from joy in my chest.

Kieran smiles big and bright, his eyes closed as he strums. He's a natural, as comfortable with the instrument as I am with my axes. Since he started taking his medication again, he's been much happier and less anxious. It brings joy to my heart to see him so confident.

To think I once looked at him and scoffed, dismissed him as weak and soft. He is soft, but he doesn't chafe with my hardened edges. We fit perfectly. The gods chose the perfect man for me.

Kieran finishes playing and the crowd cheers. A few kids even beg him for another song, but when he meets my gaze, he politely excuses himself and comes toward me. His worry is apparent in his scent, but I smile at him and push waves of comfort and peace through our bond. Kieran's tense features relax into a smile, and he welcomes me into his arms.

"How'd it go?" he asks.

I kiss his hair, squeezing him close. "You were right."

He grins, pushing himself onto his toes to kiss me. "I usually am."

"Thank you."

"For?"

"Giving me strength."

Kieran nuzzles into my chest. "It's an honor."

"I think I've earned my reward, don't you?"

He chuckles, low and raspy. My cock takes interest. "Yes, you have."

"Tell everyone to leave. Can't have them hearing you when you get too loud."

Kieran shivers. Taking my hand, he says, "All right, everybody, time to clear out! Come back tomorrow!" The crowd disperses, and I lead him to our bedchamber. The moment the door has closed, my back is against it, and Kieran's mouth slams, eager and hungry, against mine.

"So... fucking... proud of you," he pants before his tongue is in my mouth, licking and stroking. I tangle my fingers in his hair, working open his pants with my other hand. He bats my hands away and focuses on getting my lower half undressed. "I'm going to suck the hell out of your cock." Kieran drops to his knees and throws my undergarments across the room, exposing my hard cock. "And then I'm going to sit on it."

"Gods, you're filthy."

He winks up at me. "Only for you."

"Damn right," I growl, fisting his hair and tugging him toward my cock.

He sucks me down, moaning around me. The wet suction of his lips is pure bliss, and I grip onto his hair so I don't thrust too deep and choke him. When Kieran's on his knees before me, I feel like Odin himself, worshipped and revered.

"Gods, you look so good on your knees." I give a tentative thrust, sinking deeper into his mouth, then pull out and slide right back in. We find a rhythm, him bobbing his head in time to my rocking hips. With every suck, he goes lower and lower down my length.

"You want it deeper, don't you? Want to choke on my cock, is that it?"

He moans around me, the sound traveling straight to my balls, making them ache. Gripping his hair, I yank, and he grunts in surprise before he gags on my cock. He grips my waist, nails biting in, but I know he isn't at his limit. He's told me before how he loves it when I'm rough with him. If it's too much, he'll let me know by pinching my waist, and he hasn't done it yet. I let go, pumping my cock into his mouth, using his lips like I'll use his hole later.

Fucking his mouth feels so damn good, I could do it forever, but I pull out and leave him gasping and coughing. His face is wet with tears, his lips glossy with drool. Gripping my cock, I slap it against his cheek. "Didn't tell you to stop," I growl, then grab his hair and shove my cock back down his throat where it belongs.

A raspy moan reverberates around my aching shaft. I could watch my cock disappear in and out of his beautiful swollen lips for hours. As he rolls my heavy balls, his tongue flicking the vein that runs the length of my shaft, my release barrels toward me. "Let go," I pant. "I want to see you swallow every drop."

He pulls off with a moan, eyes dark with lust. "Please, Alpha. Give it to me."

So fucking good.

I grasp myself and stroke fast, grinding my teeth as I start to spill. With a snarl, I stroke myself through my release, pumping rope after rope of seed over his tongue. Some of it streaks his cheek. He looks utterly debased. Claimed. Mine.

"Swallow," I command.

Kieran sticks his tongue back in, throat bobbing as he takes my load.

Gods. What a sight he is, on his knees, his lips swollen, covered in my cum. I swipe my thumb over his cheek and collect my seed, then rub it over the scar from my bite.

"Mine," I growl.

He shivers. "Yours, Alpha."

I smile, heart squeezing. "Now, get on our bed. It's time to reward you."

I meet him at our bed and layer by layer I undress him until he's bare before me. Shoving him down to the bed, I blanket his body with mine and kiss him, tasting myself on his tongue. His cock is a hard line against my stomach, sensitive to even the slightest touches as I stroke and squeeze him. "Put your knees up," I say and he obeys. "It's my turn to worship you now."

A gasp escapes him as I flick my tongue over his entrance. "Could do this all day," I tell him earnestly, then lick even deeper inside him. I suck at his rim, scrape my teeth over his plump ass cheek, then spear my tongue deep inside. Moaning, Kieran rubs my shoulders with his ankles, his hands fisting the bedsheets.

"Fuck, Wulfric... So good."

Hearing his little moans and praise sends blood rushing south again, and I harden inch by inch with every lick over his tight hole.

"Lube," I say.

Kieran opens the drawer by the bed, rifling through it. He brought quite a few toys back with him along with lube, which is even better than oil, and something he uses to make himself clean for me before we fuck. I can do without all the conveniences of modern living except for his sex toys. Those I'm very grateful for. Everything else is too complicated.

Slicking my fingers with lube, I sink them deep inside his tight, velvety heat. He gasps as I stretch him open, then rolls his hips to take me even deeper. My own cock twitches, remembering how he fucked me after that feast we had with his friend Amanda. Seeing Kieran's world for myself was amazing, though not as amazing as having his cock inside me or one of those vibrating toys he pleasured me with. Now that I know how good it feels to be filled by his cock, I can relate all too well to his pleasure.

Stretching him wide open for me, I lean down and flick my tongue between my fingers. He writhes above me, cursing me as I fuck him with my fingers and my tongue.

"Gonna come if you don't cut that out and fuck me already," Kieran pants.

Chuckling, I switch positions with him so that I'm on my back while he straddles my waist. He grips my cock, already hard and eager for the hot clutch of his body, then bends his knees. My eyes roll back as I sink inside his tight, perfect heat.

Biting his lip, Kieran bounces on me slowly, sinking down and then up, down and up. Stars burst behind my eyes as I roll my hips to help him along, and together we find a rhythm that takes us to a place that is ours alone.

"Feel like a god when I'm inside you." I groan, grabbing the perfect mounds of his ass and squeezing as he rides my cock faster. "Don't need Valhalla. Not when I have this tight, perfect hole clenching around my cock."

Kieran moans, sweaty and flushed. "Take me there. Take me to Valhalla."

Snarling, I buck my hips relentlessly, pounding up into his body.

"Oh fuck!" Kieran grabs onto my shoulders, holding on tight. His lips crash against mine, our tongues tangling, our fangs scraping. "Wulfric. God. Wulfric!"

The way we move together is indescribable. I never knew it was possible to love another not just with my heart but with my body, but that's just what we do. I move with him, and he moves with me, taking me to a place of pleasure beyond anything I've ever known.

"You own me, mate," I pant against his mouth. "This body, heart and soul, belongs to you. Move. Faster. Own me. Claim me."

Our lips collide, and his fingers curl in my hair as he rides my cock harder and faster. When my knot swells and catches on his rim, filling him to the brim, he breaks our kiss, groaning against my shoulder as he shudders and clenches around me. His seed paints my stomach as I fuck into his rippling channel. A roar escapes me and I find my own release, filling him with my seed.

We gasp together, arms locked around one another.

Kieran brushes my hair away from my face, a satisfied grin tilting his lips. "Did you really mean that? My ass is better than Valhalla?"

A bark of laughter escapes me, and I kiss him. "May the gods forgive me, but yes."

Kieran chuckles, and the sound makes me warm inside. "Tell me something else you mean."

Propping my chin on his shoulder, I kiss the bite scar I left upon his skin many moons ago when I bound his heart to mine. "Wherever we go, no matter where we are, in your time or mine, you are my home. My pack. My heart and my mate. I love you, little rabbit."

Kieran touches his forehead to mine, his sky-blue eyes dancing with tenderness and warmth. "And I love you. My warrior. My mate. My Alpha."

Once, I felt so undeserving of that title. A shadow of the man my father was. Now, when the man I love calls me Alpha, I feel as if I could conquer the world and lay it all at his feet.

In Kieran's arms, our hearts and bodies made one, the pain of my past at rest, there is truly nowhere else in all the nine realms I would rather be.

Thank you for reading! I hope you enjoyed Wulfric and Kieran's story.

Want to see Wulfric and Kieran's dinner with Amanda (and Kieran topping Wulfric)? Sign up for my newsletter for access to exclusive bonus epilogues for all my books! Scan the code now to sign up!

About CJ

CJ Ravenna loves to tell stories where the ordinary meets the extraordinary. Her books often feature an explosion or two, possessive and protective werewolves who adore their mates, steamy and swoony romance, and of course a happy ending.

Scan the code to connect with me on my socials, read my books, and more!

Also By CJ Ravenna

The Lycanthrope Protection Agency Series
To Hunt A Moonborn Beast (Gabe & Max)
Child Of The Moon (Gabe & Max)
The Moon Aways Rises (Gabe & Max)
The Moon Over The Oak (Zach & Ryan)
Redemption Under The Moon (Ben & Isaac)
Fire and Moonlight (Eddie & Vico)
A Paranormal Yakuza Duet
Secrets & Sake (A Paranormal Yakuza Duet Book 1)
Curses & Kitsune (A Paranormal Yakuza Duet Book 2)
Viking Wolves
Heart of a Wolf (Kieran & Wulfric)